ALSO BY

DEBORAH EISENBERG

Pastorale

Transactions in a Foreign Currency

Under the 82nd Airborne

Air: 24 Hours: Jennifer Bartlett

The Stories (So Far) of Deborah Eisenberg

All Around Atlantis

ALL AROUND
ATLANTIS

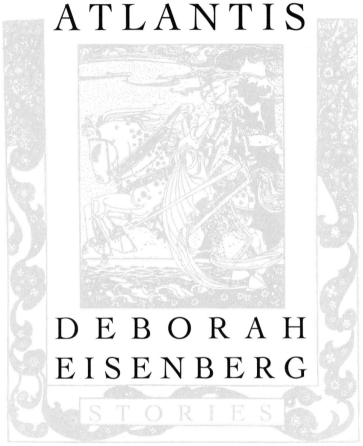

DEBORAH
EISENBERG

STORIES

FARRAR STRAUS GIROUX

NEW YORK

Farrar, Straus and Giroux
19 Union Square West, New York 10003

Copyright © 1997 by Deborah Eisenberg
All rights reserved
Distributed in Canada by Douglas & McIntyre Ltd.
Printed in the United States of America
Designed by Cynthia Krupat
First edition, 1997

Library of Congress Cataloging-in-Publication Data
Eisenberg, Deborah.
    All around Atlantis / Deborah Eisenberg.
        p.   cm.
    Contents: Across the lake—Tlaloc's paradise—Someone to talk
to—Rosie gets a soul—The girl who left her sock on the floor—
Mermaids—All around Atlantis.
    ISBN 0-374-27087-2 (cloth : alk. paper)
    I. Title.
PS3555.I793A79   1997
813'.54—dc21   97-7534

"Across the Lake" and "Tlaloc's Paradise" first appeared in
the Voice Literary Supplement. "Someone to Talk To,"
"Rosie Gets a Soul," and "The Girl Who Left Her Sock on
the Floor" originally appeared in The New Yorker.
"Mermaids" first appeared in The Yale Review.

profound thanks and a big hug from me, too, to the D.A.A.D.,
Berlin, and Joachim Sartorius,
profound thanks and respectful salutes to both the Ingram
Merrill Foundation and the American Academy of
Arts and Letters,
and thanks, hugs, and salutes to Amy Hotch, András Nagy,
and Libby Titus

For my brother, David

and our father, George

and in memory of our mother, Ruth

CONTENTS

The Girl Who Left Her Sock on the Floor   3

Across the Lake   29

Someone to Talk To   61

Tlaloc's Paradise   93

Rosie Gets a Soul   113

Mermaids   163

All Around Atlantis   203

The Girl Who Left
Her Sock on the Floor

JESSICA DANGLED A SOCK BETWEEN HER THUMB
and forefinger, studied it, and let it drop. "There are
times," she said, "one wearies of rooming with a pig."

Pig. Francie checked to see what page she was on and
slammed *World History* shut. "Why not go over to the nice,
clean library?" she said. "You could go to the nice, clean
library, and you could think nice, clean thoughts. I'll just
root around here in the homework." She pulled her blanket up and turned to the window, her eyes stinging.

Faint, constant crumblings and tricklings . . . Outside,
spring was sneaking up under the cradle of snow in the
valley, behind the lacy gray air that veiled everything except the girl, identifiable as hardly more than the red dot
of her jacket, who was winding up the hill toward the
dorm.

Jessica sighed noisily and dumped a stack of clothing
into a drawer. "I will get to that stuff, please, Jessica,"
Francie said, "if you'll just kindly leave it."

Jessica gazed sorrowfully at Francie's ear, then bent
down to retrieve a dust-festooned sweatshirt from beneath
Francie's bed.

"You know," Francie said, "there are people in the

world—not many, but a few—to whom the most important thing is not whether there happens to be a sock on the floor. There are people in the world who are not afraid to face reality, to face the fact that the floor is the natural place for a sock, that the floor is where a sock just naturally goes when it's off. But do we fearless few have a voice? No. No, these are words which must never be spoken—true, Jessica? This is a thought which must never be thought."

It was Cynthia in the red jacket, the secretary, Francie saw now—not one of the students. Cynthia wasn't much older than the seniors, but she lived in town and never came to meals. "Right, Jessica?" Francie said.

There was some little oddness about seeing Cynthia outside the office—as if something were leaking somewhere.

"Jessica?" Francie said. "Oh, well. *'But the poor, saintly girl had gone deaf as a post. The end.'*"

Jessica's voice sliced between Francie and the window. "Look, Francie, I don't want to trivialize your pain or anything, but I'm getting kind of bored over here. Besides which, I am not your personal maid."

"Oink oink," Francie said. "Grunt, grunt. *'Actually, not the end, really, at all, because God performed a miracle, and the beautiful deaf girl could hear again, though everything from that moment on sounded to her as the gruntings of pigs.'*"

"*As* the gruntings of pigs?" Jessica demanded. "Sounded *as* gruntings?"

"Oink oink," Francie said. She opened *World History* to page 359 again. "An Artist's Conception of the Storming of the Bastille." Well, and who were "Editors Clarke & Melton," for that matter, to be in charge of what was going on? To decide which, out of all the things that went on, were *things that had happened*? Yeah, "World History: The Journey of Two Editors and Their Jobs." Why not a picture of people trapped in their snooty boarding school with their snooty roommates? "Anyhow, guess what, next year we both get to pick new roommates."

"If we're both still here," Jessica said. "Besides, that's then—"

"What does *that* mean?" Francie said.

"You don't have to shout at me all the time," Jessica said. "Besides, as I was saying, that's then and this is now. And if I were you, I'd stop calling Mr. Klemper 'Sex Machine.' Sooner or later someone's going to—"

But just then the door opened, and the girl, Cynthia, was standing there in her red jacket. "Frances McIntyre?" Cynthia said. She stared at Francie and Jessica as though she had forgotten which one Francie was. And Francie and Jessica stared back as though they had forgotten, too. "Frances McIntyre, Mrs. Peck wants to see you in the Administration Building."

Jessica watched, flushed and round-eyed, as Francie put on her motorcycle jacket and work boots. "You're going to freeze like that, Francie," Jessica said, and then Cynthia held the door open.

"Francie—" Jessica said. "Francie, do you want me to go with you?"

Francie had paused on the threshold. She didn't turn around, and she couldn't speak. She shook her head.

What had she done? What had been seen or heard or said? Had someone already told Mr. Klemper? Was it cutting lacrosse? Had she been reported smoking again in back of the Science Building? Because if she had she was out. Out. Out. End. The end of her fancy scholarship, the end of her education, the end of her freedom, the end of her future. No, the beginning of a new future, her real future, the one that had been lying in wait for her all along, whose snuffly breathing she could hear in the dark. She'd live out her days as a checkout girl, choking on the toxic vapors of household cleaners and rotting baked goods, trudging home in the cold to rot, herself, in the scornful silence of her bulky, furious mother. Her mother, who had slaved to give ungrateful Francie this squandered opportunity. Her mother, who wouldn't tolerate a sock on the floor for as long as one instant.

Mrs. Peck's bleached blue eyes stared at Francie as Francie stood in front of her, shivering, each second becoming more vividly aware that her jacket, her little, filmy dress, her boots, her new nose ring all trod on the boundaries of the dress code. "Do sit down, please, Frances," Mrs. Peck said.

Mrs. Peck was wearing, of course, a well-made and proudly unflattering suit. On the walls around her were decorative, framed what-were-they-called, Francie thought—Wise Sayings. "I have something very, very sad, I'm afraid, to tell you, Frances," Mrs. Peck began.

Out, she was *out*. Francie's blood howled like a storm at sea; her heart pitched and tossed.

But Mrs. Peck's voice—what Mrs. Peck's voice seemed to be saying, was that Francie's mother was dead.

"What?" Francie said. The howling stopped abruptly, as though a door had been shut. "My mother's in the hospital. My mother broke her hip."

Mrs. Peck bowed her head slightly, over her folded hands. "EVERYTHING MUST BE TAKEN SERIOUSLY, NOTHING TRAGICALLY," the wall announced over her shoulder. "FORTUNE AND HUMOR GOVERN THE WORLD."

"My mother has a broken hip," Francie insisted. "Nobody dies from a broken fucking *hip*."

Mrs. Peck's eyes closed for a moment. "There was an embolism," she said. "Apparently, this is not unheard of. Patients who greatly exceed an ideal weight . . . That is, a Miss Healy called from the hospital. Do you remember Miss Healy? A student nurse, I believe. I understand you met each other when you went to visit your mother several weeks ago. Your mother must have tried to get up sometime during the night. And most probably—" Mrs. Peck frowned at a piece of paper and put on her glasses. "Yes. Most probably, according to Miss Healy, your mother wished to go to the toilet. Evidently, she would have fallen back against her pillow. The staff wouldn't have discovered her death until morning."

Bits of things were falling around Francie. " 'Wouldn't have'?" she plucked from the air.

"This is, of course, a reconstruction," Mrs. Peck said. "Miss Healy came on duty this afternoon. Your mother wasn't there, and Miss Healy became concerned that perhaps no one had thought to notify you. A thoughtful young woman. I had the impression she was acting outside official channels, but . . ."

"But *all's well that ends well*," Francie said.

Mrs. Peck's eyes rested distantly on Francie. "I wonder," she said. "It might be possible, under the terms of your scholarship, to arrange for some therapy when you return." Her gaze wandered up the chattering wall. "A hospital must be a terribly difficult thing to administer," she remarked to it graciously. "I have absolutely no one to bring you to Albany, Frances, I'm afraid. I'll have to call someone in your family to come for you."

Francie gasped. "You can't!" she said.

Mrs. Peck frowned. She appeared to be embarrassed. "Ah," she said, no doubt picturing, Francie thought, some abyss of mortifying circumstances. "In that case . . ." she said. "Yes. I'll have Mr. Klemper cancel French tomorrow, and he—"

"Why can't I take the morning bus?" Francie said. "I've taken that bus a thousand times." She was going red, she knew; one more second and she'd cry. "Don't cancel French," she said. "I always take that bus. *Please.*"

Mrs. Peck's glance strayed up the wall again, and hesitated. "HONI SOIT QUI MAL Y PENSE," Francie read.

Mrs. Peck took off her glasses and rubbed the bridge of her nose. "Miss Healy," she mused. "Such an unsuitable name for a nurse, isn't it. People must often make foolish remarks."

How could it be true? How could Francie be on the bus now, when she should be at school? The sky hadn't changed since yesterday, the trees and fields out the window hadn't changed; Francie could imagine her mother just as clearly as she'd ever been able to, so how could it be true?

And yet her mother would have been dead while she herself had been asleep, dreaming. Of what? Of what? Of Mr. Davis, probably. Not of her mother, not dreaming of a little wad of blood coalescing like a pearl in her mother's body, preparing to wedge itself into her mother's heart.

If you were to break, for example, your hip, there would be the pain, the proof, telling you all the time it was true: *that's then and this is now.* But this thing—each second it had to be true all over again; she was getting hurled against each second. *Now.* And *now again—thwack!* Maybe one of these seconds she'd smash right through and find herself in the clear place where her mother was alive, scowling, criticizing . . .

Out the window, snow was draining away from the patched fields of the small farms, the small, failing farms. Rusted machinery glowed against the sky in fragile tangles. Her mother would have been dead while Francie got up and took her shower and worried about being late to breakfast and was late to breakfast and went to biology and then to German and then dozed through English and then ate lunch and then hid in the dorm instead of playing lacrosse and then quarreled with Jessica about a sock. At some moment in the night her mother had gone from being completely alive to being completely dead.

The passengers were scraggy and exhausted-looking, like a committee assigned to the bus aeons earlier to puzzle out just this sort of thing—part of a rotating team whose members were picked up and dropped off at stations looping the planet. How different they were from the team of sleek girls at school, who already knew everything they needed to know. Which team was Francie on? Ha-ha. She glanced at the man across the aisle, who nodded commiseratingly between bites of the vile-smelling food he lifted from a plastic-foam container on his lap.

All those hours during which her life (along with her mother) had gone from being one thing to being another, it had held its shape, like a car window Francie once saw hit by a rock. The rock hit, a web of tiny, glittering lines fanned out, and only a minute or so later had the window tinkled to the street in splinters.

The dazzling, razor-edged splinters had tinkled around Francie yesterday afternoon in Mrs. Peck's voice. "Your family." "Have someone in your family come for you." Well, fine, but where on earth had Mrs. Peck got the idea there *was* anyone in Francie's family?

From Francie's mother, doubtless, the world's leading expert in giving people ideas without having to say a single word. "A proud woman" was an observation people tended to make, vague and flustered after encountering her. But what did that mean, "proud"? Proud of her poverty. Proud of her poor education. Proud of her unfashionable size. Proud of bringing up her Difficult Daughter, Without an Iota of Help. So what was the difference, when you got right down to it, between pride and shame?

Francie had a memory, one of her few from early childhood, that never altered or dimmed, however often it sprang out: herself in the building stairwell with Mrs. Dougherty, making Mrs. Dougherty laugh. She could still feel her feet fly up as her mother grabbed her and pulled her inside, still hear the door slam. She could still see (and yet this was something she could never have seen, really) skinny Mrs. Dougherty cackling alone in the hall. *"How could you embarrass me like that?"* her mother said. The wave of shock and outrage and humiliation engulfed Francie again with each remembering; she felt her mother's fierce grip on her arm. Francie was an embarrassment. What on earth could she have been doing in the hall? An *embarrassment*. Well, *so be it*.

On the day she had brought Francie all the way from Albany to be interviewed at school, Francie's mother—wearing gloves!—had a private conversation with Mrs. Peck. Francie sat in the outer office and waited. Cynthia had been typing demurely, and occasionally other girls would come through—perfect girls, beautiful and beautifully behaved and sly. Francie could just picture their mothers. When she eventually did see some—Jessica's tall, chestnut-haired mother among them—it turned out that her imagination had not exaggerated.

Waiting in the outer office, Francie feared (Francie hoped) she was to be turned ignominiously away. Instead, she was confronted by Mrs. Peck's withering smile of welcome; Mrs. Peck was gluttonous for Francie's test scores. That Francie and her mother looked, each in her own way, so entirely *unsuitable* appeared to increase, rather than diminish, their desirability.

When her mother and Mrs. Peck emerged from the office together that afternoon, a blaze of triumph and contempt crackled behind the veneer of patently suspect humility on her mother's face. Mrs. Peck, on the other hand, looked as if she'd been bonked on the head with a plank.

Surely it was during that conference that Francie's family had been born. Her mother's gift (the automatic nuancing of the unspoken) and Mrs. Peck's mandate (to heap distinction upon herself) had intertwined to generate little tendrils of plausible realities. Which were now generating tendrils of their own: an imaginary church with imaginary relatives—*suitable* relatives—wavering behind viscous organ music and bearing with simple dignity their imaginary grief. Oh, her poor mother! Her poor mother! What possible business was it of Mrs. Peck's *when* her mother had wanted to go to the toilet for the last time?

Several companionable tears made their way down

Francie's face, turning from hot to cold. The sensation consoled her as long as it lasted. When she opened her eyes, she saw the frayed outskirts of town.

Francie climbed the stairs cautiously, lest creakings draw the still gregarious Mrs. Dougherty to her peephole. She paused with her key in the lock before contaminating irreversibly the silence, her mother's special silence, which, she thought, a person had to shout to be heard over. Francie leaned her head against the door's cool plane, listening, then turned the key. The lock's tumbling sounded like a gunshot.

A little colorless sunlight had forced its way around the neighboring buildings and lay, exhausted, across the floor. A fine coating of city grime sealed the sills in front of the closed windows like insulation. Her mother's bed was tightly made; the bedspread was as mute as the surface of a lake into which a clue had been dropped long before.

The only disorder in the kitchen was a cup Francie had left in the sink when she'd come to see her mother in the hospital three weeks earlier, still full of dark liquid in which velvety spots had begun to blossom. Francie sat down at the table. The night she'd finally dared to ask her mother what had happened to her father they'd been in here, just finishing the dishes. Francie remembered: her mother was holding a white dish towel; she started to speak.

Too late, then, for Francie to retract the question—a question that had been clogging her mouth ever since the day, years before, when Corkie Patterson had pummeled into her the concept that every single person on earth had a father. As Francie clutched the wet counter her mother spoke of the sound—the terrible fused sound of brakes and the impact—the crowds out the window, which at first hid everything, the siren circling down on their block like a hawk. She did not use the word "blood," but when she finished her story and left the room without so much as a glance for Francie, Francie lifted her dripping fingers and stared at them.

After that, Francie's mother was even more unyielding, as though she were ashamed of her husband's death, or ashamed to have spoken of it. And Francie's father evaporated without a trace. Francie had only cryptic fragments from before that night in the kitchen with which to assemble the story: her parents married at eighteen, she'd figured out. Had they loved each other? The undiminishing vigor of her mother's resentment toward absolutely everything was warming, in its way—there must have been love to produce all that hatred.

The bathroom, too, was clean—spotless, actually, except for a tiny smudge on the mirror. A fingerprint. Hers? Her mother's? She peered past it, into her own face. Had he even known there was to be a baby? Just think—things that you did went on and on, turning into situations, for example. Into people . . .

As little as Francie knew about him, it would be infinitely more than he could have known about her. There were no pictures, but if she were to subtract her mother's eyes . . . In just a few years, she would see changes in her face that her father had not lived to see in his.

"In a few years!" Bad enough she had to deal with "in a few minutes." *When you return*, Mrs. Peck had said. Well, sure, a person couldn't just stay at school, probably, when her mother died. But what on earth was she supposed to do here?

Her mother would have told her. Francie snatched open a drawer and out flew the fact of her mother's slippery, pinkish heap of underwear. Her mother's toothbrush sat next to the mirror in a glass. In the mirror, past the fingerprint, her mother's eyes lay across her own reflection like a mask.

The hospital floated in the middle of a vast ocean of construction, or maybe it was demolition; a nation in itself,

of which all humans were, at every moment, potential cit-
izens. The inevitable false move, and it was wham, onto
the gurney, with workers grabbing smocks and gloves to
plunge into the cavity of you, and the lights that burned
all night. Outside this building you lived as though nothing
were happening to you that you didn't know about. But
here, there was simply no pretending.

Cynthia had come up the hill, Mrs. Peck had sent Francie home, and now here she was—completely lost; she'd
come in the wrong entrance. People passed, in small
groups, not touching or speaking. The proliferating corridors and rotundas bloomed with soft noises—chiming, and
disembodied announcements, and the muted tapping of
canes and rubber shoes and walkers. The ceilings and
floors were the same color and had the same brightness;
metal winked, signaling between wheelchairs and bedrails.
Francie tried to suppress the notion, which had popped up
from somewhere like a groundhog, that her mother was
still alive, lost here somewhere herself.

Two unfamiliar nurses sat at a desk at the mouth of the
wing where Section E, Room 418, was. In their crisp little
white hats they appeared to be exempt from error. They
looked up as Francie approached, and their faces were
blank and tired, as if they knew Francie through and
through—as if they knew everything there was to know
about this girl in the short, filmy dress and motorcycle
jacket and electric-green socks, who was coming toward
them with so much difficulty, as if the air were filled with
invisible restraints.

But, as it turned out, when Francie tried to explain herself, using (presumably) key, she thought, words, like
"Kathryn McIntyre," and "Room 418," and "dead," even
then neither of the nurses seemed to understand. "Did you
want to speak to a doctor?" one of them said.

A tiny, hot beading of sweat sprang out all over Francie.
From the moment she was born people had been happy to
tell her what to do, down to the most minute detail; Eds.

Clarke & Melton knew just what was happening; there were admonitions and exhortations plastered all over the walls—this is how to behave, this is what to think, this is how to think it, that's then, this is now, this is where to put your sock—but no one had ever said one little thing that would get her through any five given minutes of her life!

She stared at the nurse who had spoken: *Say it*, Francie willed her, but the nurse instead turned her attention to a form attached to a clipboard. "Is Miss Healy around?" Francie asked after a minute.

The fact was, Francie would not have recognized Miss Healy; she'd hardly noticed the broad-faced, slightly clumsy-looking girl who'd been changing the water in a vase of flowers as Francie had listened to her mother describe, with somber gloating, the damage to her body, the shock of finding herself on the ice with her pork chop and canned peaches and so forth strewn around her, the pitiable little trickle of milk she had watched flow from the ruined carton into the filthy slush before she understood that she couldn't move.

"She never complained," Miss Healy was saying, in a melancholy, slightly adenoidal voice. "She was such a pleasant person. You could tell the terrible pain she was in, but she never said a word." Miss Healy directed her mournful recital toward Francie's elbow, as if she were in danger of being derailed by Francie's face. "And when the people from her office brought candy and flowers? She was just so *polite*. Even though you could see those things were not what she wanted."

Oh, great. Who but her mother could get someone to say that her pain was obvious but that she never complained? Who but her mother could get someone to say she was polite even though everyone could tell she didn't want their gifts? No doubt about it, the body they'd carted off almost a day and a half ago from Room 418 had been her mother's—Miss Healy had just laid waste, in her squelchy voice, to *that* last wisp of hope.

"The thing is," Francie said, "what am I supposed to do?"

"To do?" Miss Healy said. Her look of suffering was momentarily whisked away. "I mean, unfortunately, your mother's dead."

"No, I know," Francie said. "I get that part. I just don't know what to *do*."

Miss Healy looked at her. Clearly Francie was turning out to be, unlike her mother, *not a pleasant person.* "Well, you'll want to grieve, of course," Miss Healy said, as if she were remembering a point from a legal document. "Everyone needs closure." She frowned, then unexpectedly addressed, after all, Francie's problem. "I'll call downstairs so you can see her."

Fading smells of bodies clung to the air like plaintive ghosts, their last friendly overtures vanquished by the stronger smells of disinfectants. An indecipherable muttering came from other ghosts, sequestered in a TV suspended from the ceiling. Outside the window huge, predatory machines prowled among mounds of trash.

Miss Healy returned. "Mrs. McIntyre isn't downstairs. I'm really sorry—I guess they've sent her on."

They? On? If only there were someone around to take over. Anyone. Jessica, even. At least Jessica would be able to ask some sensible question. "On . . ." Francie began uncertainly, and Jessica gave her a little shove. "On where?"

"Oh," Miss Healy said. "Well, I mean, does your family use any in particular?"

Francie stared: Where would Jessica even begin with that one?

"Does your family have a particular one they like," Miss Healy explained. "Mortuary."

"It's just me and mother," Francie said.

Miss Healy nodded, as if this confirmed her point. "Uh-huh. So they'd have sent her on to whatever place was specified by the next of kin."

Francie felt Jessica start to giggle. "It's just me and mother," Francie said again.

"Just whoever your mother put down on the AN37-53," Miss Healy said. "Not literally the next of kin necessarily —she couldn't have used you, for instance, because you're a minor. But just, if there's no spouse, people might put down someone at their office, say. Or she might have used that nice friend of hers who came to visit once, Mrs. Dougherty."

Yargh. It wasn't enough that her mother had died—no, they had to toss her out, into that huge, melted mob, *the dead*, who couldn't speak for themselves, who were too indistinguishable to be remembered, who could be used to prove anything, who could be represented any way at all! "My mother *hates* everyone at her office," Francie said. "My mother *hates* Mrs. Dougherty. Mother calls Mrs. Dougherty that buggy Irish slut."

Miss Healy drew back. "Well, I guess your mom wasn't expecting to *die*, exactly, when she filled out that form," she said, and then recovered herself. "There, now. I'll call down again. Even *this* crazy morgue has files, I guess."

Out the window a wrecking ball swung toward a solitary wall. Miss Healy hesitated. She seemed to be waiting for something. "I called that lady at the school," she said. She stood looking at Francie, and Francie realized that she and Miss Healy must be almost the same age. "I just didn't figure there'd be some other way you'd know."

"How did mother get all the way out here?" Francie asked the man who greeted her.

The man's little smile intensified the ruefulness of his expression. "We get a lot of folks out this way," he said. "You might be surprised."

"That's what I meant," Francie said. "I meant I was surprised."

The man jumped slightly, as if Francie had gummed him on the ankle, and then smiled ruefully again. "Serving all faiths," he explained, gesturing at a sign on the wall. *"Serving all faiths,"* Francie read. *"Owned and operated by Luther and Theodore T. Ade. When you're in need, call for Ade."* "Also," the man added, "competitive pricing. But mainly, first in the phone book."

He disappeared behind a door, and Francie jogged from foot to foot to warm herself—it had been a long walk from the last stop on the bus line. She looked around. Not much to see: a counter holding some file folders, a calendar and a mirror on the wall, several chairs, and a round table on which lay a dog-eared copy of *Consumer Reports*. So this was where her mother had got to—nowhere at all.

"Won't be another minute." The man was back in the room. "Teddy T.'s just doing the finishing touches."

Finishing touches? Francie blanched—she'd almost forgotten what this place was. "You're not using lipstick, are you?" she managed to say. "Mother hated it."

The man glanced rapidly at the mirror and then back at Francie.

"Lipstick," Francie said. "On her."

" 'On her . . .' " the man said. As he stared at Francie, the room lost its color and flattened; swarming black dots began to absorb the table and the counter and the mirror. "I'm very sorry if that's what you had in mind, Miss, ah . . ." dots streamed out of the dot man to say. The riffling of file folders amplified into a deafening splash of dots, and then Francie heard, "I'm very, very sorry, because those were definitely not the instructions. I've got the fax right here—from your dad, right? Yup, Mr. McIntyre."

Francie's vision and hearing cleared before her muscles got a grip on themselves. She was on the floor, splayed out, confusingly, as her mother must have been on the ice, and the man was kneeling next to her, holding a glass of water, although, also confusingly, her hair and clothing were drenched—sweat, she noted, amazed.

"O.K. now?" the man asked. Next to him was a cardboard box, about two feet square, tied up with twine.

Francie nodded.

"Happens," the man said, sympathetically.

Francie finished the water slowly and carefully while the man fetched a little wooden handle and affixed it to the twine around the box. Things had gone far beyond misrepresentation now.

"And here's the irony," the man said. "We deliver."

All night long, Francie fell, plummeting through the air. When she finally managed to pry herself awake with the help of the pale wands of light along the blinds, she found herself sprawled forcefully back on her mattress, aching, as if she'd been hurled from a great height. On the kitchen floor was the cardboard box. Francie hefted it experimentally—yesterday it had been intolerably heavy; this morning it was intolerably light.

O.K., first in the phone book, true enough. ("See display ad, page 182.") "Hi," Francie said when the man answered. "This is Francie McIntyre. The girl who fainted yesterday? Could you—" For an instant, Miss Healy stood in front of her again, looking helpless. "First of all," Francie said. "I mean, thanks for the water. But second of all, could you give me my father's address, please? And, I guess, his name."

Kevin McIntyre—not all that amazing, once you got your head around the notion that he happened to be alive. And he lived on a street called West Tenth, in New York City. Francie looked out the window to the place where there had been for some years now a silently shrieking crowd and a puddle of blood, into which long, splotty raindrops were now falling. Strange—it was raining into the puddle, but at the level of the window it was snowing.

In the closet she found an old plastic slicker. She took it from the hanger and wrapped it around the cardboard box, securing it roughly with tape. Yes, everything had to be *just right*. But the only thing she'd actually *said* to Francie in all these sixteen years was a lie.

Francie looked around at the bluish stillness. "Hello hello," she called. Was that her voice? Was that her mother's silence, fading? What had become of everything that had gone on here? "Hello hello," she said. "Hello hello hello hello . . ."

The bus ticket cost Francie eighteen dollars. Which left not all that much of the seventy-three and a bit that she'd saved up, fortunately, to get her back to school and, in fact, Francie thought, to last for the rest of her life. "But, hey," Jessica returned just long enough to point out, "you'll be getting free therapy."

Francie put her box on the overhead rack and scrambled to a window seat. *West Tenth Street*. West of what? The tenth of how many? How on earth was she going to find her way around? If only her mother had let her go last year when Jessica invited her to spend Thanksgiving in New York with her family. But Francie's mother had been able to picture Jessica's mother just as easily as Francie had been able to. "Out of the question," she'd said.

". . . if *there's no spouse* . . ." So, her mother must have used his name on that form! They must never have got a divorce. Could he be a bigamist? Some people were. And he might think Francie was coming to blackmail him. He might decide to kill her right then and there—just reach over and grab a . . . a . . .

Well, one thing—he wasn't living on the street; she had his address. And he wasn't totally feebleminded; he'd sent a fax. Whatever he was, at least what he wasn't was everything except that. And the main thing he wasn't, for absolute certain, was a guy who'd been mashed by a bus.

"Would you like a hankie?" the lady in the seat next

to Francie's asked, and Francie realized that she had wiped her eyes and nose on her sleeve. "I have one right here."

"Oh, wow," Francie said gratefully, and blew her nose on the handkerchief the lady produced from a large, shabby cloth sack on her lap.

Despite the shabbiness of the sack, Francie noticed, the lady was tidy. And pretty. Not pretty, really, but exact—with exact little hands and an exact little face. "Do you live in New York?" she asked Francie.

"I've never even been there," Francie said. "My roommate from school invited me to visit once, but my mother wouldn't let me go." Jessica's family had a whole apartment building to themselves, Jessica had told her; she'd called it a "brownstone." It was when Francie had foolishly reported this interesting fact that her mother put her foot down. "Actually," Francie added, "I think my mother was afraid. We had a giant fight about it."

"A mother worries, of course," the lady said. "But it's a lovely city. People tend to have exaggerated fears about New York."

"Yeah," Francie said. "Well, I guess maybe my mother had exaggerated fears about a lot of things. She—" The box! Where was the box? Oh, there—on the rack. Francie's heart was beating rapidly; clashing in her brain were the desire to reveal and the desire to conceal what had become, in the short course of the conversation, a secret. "Do you live in New York?" she asked.

"Technically, no," the lady said. "But I've spent a great deal of happy time there. I know the city very well."

Francie's jumping heart flipped over. "Have you ever been to West Tenth Street?" she asked.

"I have," the lady said.

Francie didn't dare look at the lady. "Is it a nice street?" she asked carefully.

"Very nice," the lady said. "All the streets are very nice. But it seems a strange day to be going there."

"It's strange for me," Francie said loudly. "My mother died."

"I'm terribly sorry," the lady said. "My mother died as well. But evidently no one was hurt in the accident."

"Huh?" Francie said.

"Amazing as it seems," the lady said, "I believe no one was hurt. Although you'd think, wouldn't you, that an accident of that sort—a blimp, simply sailing into a building . . ."

Francie felt slightly sickened—she wasn't going to have another opportunity to tell someone for the first time that her mother had died, to learn what that meant by hearing the words as she said them for the first time. "How could a blimp just go crashing into a building?" she said crossly.

"These are things we can't understand," the lady said with dignity.

Oops, Francie thought—she was really going to have to watch it; she kept being mean to people, and just completely by mistake.

" 'How could such-and-such a thing happen?' we say," the lady said. "As if this moment or that moment were fitted together, from . . . bits, and one bit or another bit might be some type of mistake. 'There's the building,' people say. 'It's a building. There's the blimp. It's a blimp.' That's the way people think."

Francie peered at the lady. "Wow . . ." she said, considering.

"You see, people tend to settle for the first explanation. People tend to take things at face value."

"Oh, definitely," Francie said. "I mean, absolutely."

"But a blimp or a building cannot be a mistake," the lady said. "Obviously. A blimp or a building are evidence. Oh, goodness—" she said as the bus slowed down. She stood up and gave her sack a little shake. "Here I am."

"Evidence . . ." Francie frowned; Cynthia's red jacket flashed against the snow. "Evidence, of, like . . . the future?"

"Well, more or less," the lady said, a bit impatiently, as the bus stopped in front of a small building. "Evidence of the present, really, I suppose. You know what I mean." She reached into her sack and drew out some papers. "You seem like a very sensitive person—I wonder if you'd be interested in learning about my situation. This is my stop, but you're welcome to the document. It's extra."

"Thank you," Francie said, although the situation she'd really like to learn about, she thought, was her own. "Wait—" The lady was halfway down the aisle. "I've still got your handkerchief—"

"Just hold on to it, dear," the lady called back. "I think it's got your name on it."

The manuscript had a title, *The Triumph of Untruth: A Society That Denies the Workings of the World Puts Us at Ever Greater Risk.* "I'd like to introduce myself," it began. "My name is Iris Ackerman."

Hmm, Francie thought: Two people with situations, sitting right next to each other. Coincidence? She glanced up. The sickening thing was, there were a lot of people on this bus.

"My name is Iris Ackerman," Francie read again. "And my belief is that one must try to keep an open mind in the face of puzzling experiences, no matter how laughable this approach may subsequently appear. For many years I maintained the attitude that I was merely a victim of circumstance, or chance, and perhaps now my reluctance to accept the ugliness of certain realities will be considered (with hindsight!) willful obtuseness."

Francie's attention sharpened—she read on. "Certainly my persecution (by literally thousands of men, on the street, in public buildings, and even, before I was forced to flee it, in my own apartment) is a known fact. (One, or several, of these ruffians went so far as to hide himself in my closet, and even under my bed, when least expected.)

"Why, you ask, should so large and powerful an organization concentrate its efforts on tormenting a single individual? This I do not know. It is not (please believe me) false humility that causes me to say I do not consider myself to be in any way 'special.' "

Francie sighed. She rested her eyes for a moment on the weedy lot moving by out the window. Not much point, probably, trying to figure out what Iris had been talking about. Yup, she should have known the minute Iris said the word "blimp."

"I know only," the manuscript continued, "that there was a moment when I fell into the channel, so to speak, of what was ultimately to be revealed as 'my life': In the fall of 1965, when I was twenty years old, I encountered a mathematics professor, an older man, whom I respected deeply. I became increasingly fascinated by certain theories he held regarding the nature of numbers, but he, alas, misunderstood my youthful enthusiasm, and although he had a wife and several children, I was soon forced to rebuff him.

"I continued to feel nothing but the purest and most intense admiration for him, and would gladly have continued our acquaintance. Nevertheless, this professor (Doctor N.) terminated all contact with me (or affected to do so), going so far as to change his telephone number to an unlisted one. Yet, at the same time, he began to pursue me in secret.

"For a period of many months I could detect only the suggestion of his presence—a sort of emanation. Do you know the sensation of a whisper? Or there would sometimes be a telltale hardening, a *crunchiness*, near me. Often, however, I could detect nothing other than a slight discoloration of the atmosphere . . . And then, one day, as I was walking to the library, he was there.

"It was a day of violent heat. People were milling on the sidewalks, waiting. One felt one was penetrating again and again a poisonous, yellow-gray screen that clung to the mouth and the nostrils. I had almost reached the library when I understood that he was behind me. So close, in fact, that he could fit his body to mine. I had never imagined how hard a man's arms could feel! His legs, too, which were pressed up against mine, were like iron, or lead, and he dug his chin into my temple as he clamped himself around me like a butcher about to slash the throat of a calf. I cried out; the bloated sky split, and out poured a filthy rain. The faces of all the people around me began to wash away in inky streaks. A terrible thing had happened to me—A terrible thing had happened—*it was like water gushing out of my body.*

"Since then, my life has not belonged to me. Why do I not go to the authorities? Of course, I have done so. And they have added their mockery to the mockery of my tormentors: *Psychological help!* Tell me: Will 'psychological help' alter my history? Will 'psychological help' locate Dr. N.? Any information regarding my case will be fervently appreciated. Please contact: Iris Ackerman, P.O. Box 139775, Rochester, N.Y. Yours sincerely, Iris Ackerman."

Enclaves of people wrapped in ragged blankets huddled against the walls of the glaring station. Policemen sauntered past in pairs, fingering their truncheons. Danger at every turn, Francie thought. Poor Iris—it was horrible to contemplate. And obviously love didn't exactly clarify the mind, either.

You had to give her credit, though—she was brave. At least she tried to figure things out, instead of just consulting, for example, the wall. To *really* figure things out. Francie blew her nose again. For all the good that did.

Any information regarding my case will be fervently appreciated. But this was not the moment, Francie thought, to lose her nerve. The huge city was just outside the door, and there was no one else to go to West Tenth Street. There was no one else to hear what she had to hear. There was no one else to remember her mother with accuracy. There was no one else to not get the story wrong. There was no one else to reserve judgment. Francie closed one hand tightly around her new handkerchief, and with the other she gripped the handle on her box. The city rose up around her through a peach-colored sunset; now there was no more time.

The man who stood at the door of the apartment (K. McIntyre, #4B) was nice-looking. Nice-looking, and weirdly unfamiliar, as if the whole thing, maybe, were a complete mistake, Francie thought over and over in the striated extrusion of eternity (that was then and this is then; that was now and this is now) it had taken the door to open.

She was filthy, she thought. She smelled. She'd been wearing the same dress, the same socks, for days.

"Can I help you?" he said.

He had no idea why she was there! "Kevin McIntyre?" she said.

"Not back yet," he said. His gaze was pleasant—serene and searching. "Any minute."

He brought her into a big room and sat her down near a fireplace, in a squashy chair. He reached for the chain of a lamp, but Francie shook her head.

"No?" He looked at her. "I'm having coffee," he said. "Want a cup? Or something else—water? Wine? Soda?"

Francie shook her head again.

"Anyhow," he said. "I'm Alex. I'll be in back if you want me."

Francie nodded.

"Can I put your package somewhere for you, at least?" he asked, but Francie folded her arms around the box and rested her cheek against its plastic wrapping.

"Suit yourself," the man said. He paused at the entrance to the room. "You're not a very demanding guest, you know."

Francie felt his attention hesitate and then withdraw. After a moment, she raised her head—yes, he was gone. But then there he was again in the entranceway. "Strange day, huh?" he paused there to say. "Starting with the blimp."

The night before Francie left school, when she'd known so much more about her mother and her father than she knew now, she and Jessica had lain in their beds, talking feverishly. "Anything can happen at any moment," Jessica kept exclaiming. "Anything can just *happen*."

"It's worse than that," Francie had said (and she could still close her eyes and see Cynthia coming up that hill). "It's much, much worse." And Jessica had burst into noisy sobs, as if she knew exactly what Francie meant, as if it were she who had brushed against the burning cable of her life.

Her body, Francie noticed, felt as if it had been crumpled up in a ball—she should stretch. *Strange day.* Well, true enough. That was something they could all be sure of. This room was really nice, though. Pretty and pleasantly messy, with interesting stuff all over the place. Interesting, nice stuff . . .

Twilight was thickening like a dark garden, and paintings and drawings glimmered behind it on the walls. As scary as it was to be waiting for him, it was nice to be having this quiet time. This quiet time together, in a way.

Peach, rose, pale green—yes, poor guy; it might be a moment he'd look back on—last panels of tinted light were falling through the window. He might be walking up the street this very second. Stopping to buy a newspaper.

She closed her eyes. He fished in his pocket for change, and then glanced up sharply. Holding her breath, Francie drew herself back into the darkness. *It's your imagination,* she promised; he was going to have to deal with her soon enough—no sense making him see her until he actually had to.

Across the Lake

AT FIRST, WHAT ROB SAW FROM THE BACK SEAT appeared to be projections of stone on the bluff just above—columns of lava, or basalt. Then the smoky morning split into gold rays, the black forms flickered human/mineral, human/mineral, and a shift of sun flashed against machetes, lighting up for one dazzling instant the kerchiefs tied over faces as masks, and the clothing—the wide, embroidered Indian trousers that Mick and Suky were headed toward the village to buy.

"Hoo hoo!" Mick said. "Worth the trip?" But his hand, extended for Suky's cigarette, was unsteady. How long, Rob wondered; how much longer until they reached the village?

When they arrived, he would eat something with Mick and Suky, maybe even check into the hotel, but he would look around for some way to get back to town immediately. There would be other tourists with cars, and there was supposed to be a boat, a little boat that carried mail across the lake, between town and the village to which they were going on the far side. In any case, he could hardly say it was Mick and Suky's fault that he had come; the fact was, he had knowingly—no, eagerly—given himself over to them, to these people he never would have dreamed of getting into a car with at home. And if something happened—if the guerrillas reappeared, or if there were robbers, or if he got sick, or if, most terrifying of all, they were stopped by the army—he would have only himself to blame.

Suky's small, tanned arm, draped across the seat, sparkled faintly. Her shoulder, the back of her neck . . . The car fishtailed and Rob turned his gaze to the steaming lake. Himself, himself to blame, himself, only himself. Perspiration—forming below the surface, squeezing its way up to collect in basins around each gold stalklet of a hair, in tiny, septic, bejeweling drops.

According to Mick, the crumbly, bunkerlike building they checked into was the village's premier hotel, the dirty pavilion where they sat now under a swarming thatch was the village's premier restaurant. "Only restaurant," Suky amended lazily. "Well, yeah, there's one other, but Mick got a wicked parasite there last year."

What difference did it make? Rob would be back on his way to town soon enough.

"Chicken everyone?" Mick said. "Always tasty, always safe." He put down the sticky menu and turned with a little bow to the child who was swinging idly against a chair, waiting to take their orders. *"Tres pollos."*

The child considered Mick before responding. *"Pollo no hay,"* he said impassively.

"Pués," Mick said, *"pescado. Bien fresco."*

"Pescado no hay," the child said.

"Bueno"—Mick folded his arms and leveled a ferocious grin at the child—*"Carne."*

The child stared back.

Suky yawned. *"Qué hay?"* she said.

"Frijoles," the child said, already wandering off. Pleased, Rob wondered, because he could offer them beans, or because he could offer them nothing else?

The pavilion sat on a rise overlooking the muddy road,

and beyond that, the lake. In front, just next to each of
the poles that supported the thatch, a soldier stood, aiming
a rifle at the shabby ladinos walking below, and the sound-
less Indians, in their elaborate, graceful, filthy textiles.
From town, the lake had seemed blue, and the air over it
tonic, a pure ether in which the volcanoes and the hills
presided, serene and picturesque. But on this side the air
was green, heavy with a vegetal shedding, sliding, with a
dull glint, like scales. The water, the volcano, the dense
growth, and the crust of tin-roofed shacks that covered the
hills all appeared to be discharging skeins of mist that
made everything waver, as though Rob were under the
lake, here, looking up.

"A gourmet paradise it may not be," Mick said. "But
you've got to admit it's beautiful."

In*cred*ible. Was Mick aware of his callousness? Even if
you were to succumb to some claim of the dark and pro-
tean landscape, you could hardly ignore those soldiers.
Their faces were smeared with anarchic black markings,
and their eyes glittered red with exhaustion or hatred, or
illness.

Of course, Rob was not unprepared for some kind of
unpleasantness. The other day in town, when Mick had
pointed across the lake to the village, Rob's insides had
registered a violent but incoherent response. He'd heard
vague but alluring mention of the area—its unparalleled
weaving and embroidery, its ancient indigenous religions.
He had the impression of an iridescence. But someone had
referred to guerrillas, and someone else had told him about
the people, Indian peasants, who had been untouched by
centuries of change but who now, during planting and
harvest seasons, were taken off to labor on the eastern
plantations under military guard. "It sounds really interesting," Rob had said politely to Mick.

"Interesting," Mick said. "It's sensational. Very dark,
very magical."

Suky sighed then, Rob remembered. And he had said

something about how he'd like to get there one day, and then Suky had said, "So why not come with us? We're going Wednesday."

Wednesday. Rob stared at her while she rooted around the bottom of her drink with her straw. "Why not?" she said. She looked up at him and pushed her drink aside. "This is a great time to go. Some general's up in the States, lobbying Congress for more aid, so the army's making kind of a point these days of not killing gringo tourist college boys." She had smiled then briefly, showing her funny little sharp, uneven teeth.

Shame (as though Rob were on the brink of doing or thinking something unworthy) abruptly presented him with another memory: his parents, with boxes of slides, resulting from various travels, which they showed on a screen in the living room to himself and his sister, and sometimes to others in the community who were considering similar adventures. His parents were vigorous and inquiring—much more energetic, physically and intellectually, than he was. There had never been any place, as far as Rob knew, they hadn't wanted to go. And although they had made a show of disapproval about the casualness of Rob's plans this summer, Rob could feel their pride, their eagerness to see new places through his eyes. If only he had their stamina. Bad weather seemed only to intensify their interest in the way other people lived. And bad food, and bugs. Only two or three times, as Rob remembered, had their trips worked out badly. Their sunny temperaments seemed damaged on those occasions, when they had come home plaintive and baffled. Which trips had those been? Haiti? The Philippines? Rob was no longer sure—the slides had stayed in their boxes.

The infant waiter reappeared, shoving three plates of rice and beans onto the table and dropping a plate of tortillas into the center so that it buzzed. *"Dos más, Pablo,"* said a voice from over Rob's shoulder. Then, *"Welcome, welcome."*

The owner of the voice was probably no more than thirty, just a few years older than Mick and Suky, but his weighty graciousness insisted on a wide margin of seniority. He held one hand out to Mick, and with the other he decorously reached a chair for the sphinxlike Indian girl who accompanied him. *"Y, Pablito,"* he called to the child, *"dos cervezas."*

Drugs, most likely, Rob thought. Rob had seen men like this in towns en route. But usually they kept to themselves, hanging around in clumps, or with various counterparts— burly, scarred Latins, or older good-for-nothings from the U.S., '60s casualties with greasy, faded ponytails, whose clattery frames and potbellies would have devolved from bodies as supple and powerful as this man's.

Rob started with dismay—his plate had been washed! A universe of disease trembled in a droplet of water on the rim. Think sick, get sick, was what Mick said, and that was probably true in some way, although the corollary— think healthy, stay healthy—seemed less of a sure thing.

"Rob, Suky, hey—" Mick was poking Rob on the arm, pointing to the beers Pablo was setting down in front of the newcomers. "Now this is smart. See what Kimball is doing?"

Kimball who? Who Kimball? Bad, Rob thought, not good—he had failed to control his attention. He channeled it now, with effort.

Despite the impression he made of size, this Kimball person was not tall, Rob saw—just rather broad, and well put together. Although his features were somewhat sharp and his dark blue eyes small, there was a suggestion of largesse, or costliness, possibly, about his creamy skin and loose black curls. And Mick had certainly fallen in behind him with disgusting alacrity. Astonishing, really. Lofty Mick, dignified Mick—but sensitivity to rank, evidently, was fundamental to this aristocracy of wanderers.

"People don't realize how easy it is to get dehydrated," Mick was saying showily to Rob. "Listen. The juice here is great. If you don't want to drink beer, you should have some juice, at least." But Kimball could obviously care less, Rob thought, who was a beer drinker and who was not; even though all the other tables were empty, he kept craning around as though he were expecting someone.

"I'm not thirsty," Rob said.

Suky's eyes were closed, though Rob thought he saw a mocking little smile flicker across her mouth. So what? He wasn't thirsty; he could wait—he had three safe bottles of water back at the hotel, in his pack, the weight of which had given Mick occasion to marvel, satirically, as they'd climbed into the car.

"Suky?" Mick said.

"Beer," she said.

"Well, I'mna have beer, and I'mna have juice," Mick said with infuriating cheer. "Pablo—" he called.

Was that really the child's name? Rob wondered. Or some demeaning generic business. And what was this Indian girl's name? Had she even been introduced? Her expression hadn't altered by a blink so far as Rob had observed, since she'd sat down. *"Señorita,"* he said, *"vive usted aquí?"*

Kimball turned to contemplate Rob. "She don't speak Spanish," he said. He put his arm around the girl and said something into her ear in a language full of *sh* and *z* sounds. The girl laughed—a tiny, harsh glitter. "But, yeah—" Kimball turned back to gaze at Rob. "She wants you to know. She does live here."

The girl's eyes passed over Rob with a smoldering chill, like dry ice. She was even more terrifying, Rob thought, than Kimball. What was it about her? If only he'd asked Meredith along. She'd had the summer free; she'd hinted. And if she were here, she'd know what was upsetting him—she always did. Sometimes, as Meredith pointed out, it was nothing more than beauty. "Rob, that's *beautiful*, don't you see?" she would say. Or: "That woman's not

weird-looking, she's *beautiful*." Then Meredith would
laugh and rub her head against his, and he would see:
whatever it was, was only beautiful.

He sighed and put down his fork—he had tried to eat
something, but both the rice and the beans had a scorched,
compost taste. Suky glanced at his plate, at him. She took
a sip of her beer, and stretched her arms high over her
head. It was appalling, the way so many girls traveling
around here dressed. With grimy bits of underwear showing, or worse, like Suky, with none, Rob observed as she
adjusted the strap of her sluttish camisole, to show. What
did people think about their country being turned into a
private beach? What could the Indian girl, for example, be
thinking? When Meredith traveled (Rob knew, though they
had never yet traveled together) she took particular care
to dress respectfully. Especially if she were going to some
Third World country, where, as she'd said to Rob, the inhabitants had little to offer one another aside from
courtesy.

Rob brought his mind to the table again, and found
Mick entrenched in a boast-fest—the places he and Suky
had gone hunting textiles to sell in the States, the foods
they'd survived, the dangers they'd faced . . . Still, if he
were to be honest with himself, Rob thought, he would
have to admit that Mick and Suky had an effect on him
even now. From the moment he'd met them, he'd con-
torted himself into all sorts of ridiculous postures—mis-
representing and stifling reactions, even exaggerating. And
even now, when Mick was evidencing wormlike, sycophan-
tic tendencies of his own, Rob couldn't control a desperation for their good opinion. Pathetic, but true.

He'd seen them as soon as he disembarked in town from
the bus. There they were, at a food stand, joking with the
proprietor in Spanish far too advanced for Rob. They were
clearly Americans, and he was pining for the sounds of
American English, but really, it was something about their

appearance that had stopped him—the way they looked together; their slightly feral, miniaturized quality, fastidious and carnal at once.

Although he'd been able to see from where he was standing the hotel recommended by his student guide book, he lingered near them, waiting to ask for their advice. When they finished their conversation, they directed him, without interest, to a hotel in the opposite direction from the one he was facing.

Their indifference had been disorienting. His sincerity, his good nature (and his looks, he conceded uncomfortably) generally made people attentive. But these two! It was hard to tell if they were even listening. *Most* people made an effort to show by their faces that they understood, were interested in, what one was saying. An unwelcome indignation branched quickly through Rob as he remembered this first encounter, clearing a path through which embarrassment then shot treacherously; he'd just been tricked by his *own brain* into thinking something distasteful—that the facial expressions displayed by most people, by himself, were social signals, like clothing.

The town was small, and over the next several days, Rob had seen Suky and Mick a number of times. They would nod from the sanctum of their unwashed majesty, and Rob was reminded, each time more keenly, that although they were the largest and most vivid figures in his small universe here, he was no more than a mote, for them, in a vast swarm of tourists.

But Sunday, they'd appeared at an overcrowded restaurant where Rob was sitting, and stood for a moment in the doorway. Rob gestured, more out of civility than hope, to the empty chairs next to him, but they made their way over and sat down without surprise or thanks. And when Mick put a leaf of lettuce and a slice of tomato—both virtually leaping with microbes—right onto his hamburger, Rob, giddy with happiness, had thrown caution to the winds and followed suit. How pure the lake had looked from that side, Rob thought again. He had a perfect view of it from their table, and had noted, he remembered, the way its surface reflected with such certainty the volcano and the little hills—the hills where he sat sweating, now.

Bali, blah blah blah—Mick was still going *on*; hill tribes, Panama, opium, blah blah—Rob had heard this all not three days before. Though no question Mick was a better performer for a worthier audience.

Worthier, but possibly less impressionable. Kimball merely rubbed his chin, frowning distantly. Only at one moment did his expression change. One of the soldiers had turned slightly; he seemed to be glancing up at Kimball. Did Kimball nod? It seemed to Rob he'd lowered his eyes a fraction of a second. Had something happened? No, there was only a young Indian walking quietly along the road below. Suky was squirming restlessly, her peculiar yellow eyes fixed on the lake, as she twisted a strand of her springy hair. Jealous, probably, Rob thought, for Mick's attention, and he was taken unawares by a harsh little clout of sympathy.

"We've come across a couple of times now," Mick was saying. "But we haven't had a whole lot of luck. Hard to find quality these days. Old stuff's in shit condition, new stuff's just plain shit . . ."

Kimball rested his fingertips together, indicating the Indian girl with a movement of his head, and Rob became fully aware of the fine, even stripe running through her clothing, the softness of the fabric, the yoke of her blouse, where flowers and jungle animals—jaguars, monkeys, snakes—bloomed and sported in a heavy embroidered wreath.

"I was noticing," Mick said.

"Made it herself," Kimball said.

Mick eyed the blouse sideways, then reached out and rubbed an edge of the fabric between his thumb and forefinger.

"Family does great work," Kimball said.

"Great piece," Mick said. "Yeah." He stared at the girl smokily.

Kimball leaned over to the girl and they spoke in low voices, as if, Rob thought, anyone else could possibly understand the preposterously arcane language they were speaking. "Listen," Kimball said. He pushed his empty plate aside. "She says when are you leaving? Because this is it—we could go check out her family's stuff, and then she and I could catch a ride with you back into town."

"Ideal," Mick said.

"Except we're sort of tight," Suky said.

"We can fit them," Mick objected. "No problem." He glanced at Rob.

"Sure," Rob said. "Of course."

"We've got a lot of luggage," Suky said, looking at Rob evenly. "Why don't you take the mail boat?" she said to Kimball. "It would probably be a lot more comfortable."

Rob felt himself flush. However comical Suky and Mick had found his pack, it would hardly prevent Kimball and the girl from sitting in the back seat with him.

Kimball was emitting a fog of absentmindedness. "Problem is," he said, "we got a business appointment—we got to get all the way to the capital by morning."

"See, so we couldn't help you out in that case," Suky said. "We're not going back to town until tomorrow."

"Huh," Kimball said. He reached over to the Indian girl's plate and wrapped a spoonful of her beans in one of the sour, hay-flavored tortillas. "Well, no sense our taking the boat anyhow," he said. "We'd get to town too late to go straight on. So we might as well spend one more night here, then squeeze in with you tomorrow."

"What about your appointment?" Suky said.

Kimball scooped up the remainder of the girl's meal. "Appointment'll just have to wait one day, because we're sure as shit not going to do the road from town to the capital after dark."

"After dark!" Mick said. "Hey, guess who we saw this morning. On *this* road. In broad daylight."

Kimball put his beer bottle down on the table and looked at Mick. "Who?" he said.

"The muchachos," Mick announced.

"You know this?" Kimball said, and only then did Mick appear to notice his unwavering stare.

"What he means," Mick said, turning to Rob as though it were Rob who'd committed some kind of faux pas, "is that around here you're never sure. Army dresses up like the guerrillas, guerrillas dress up like the army . . ."

Kimball was looking from one of them to another. "They didn't stop you?" he said.

"They were gone," Mick said. "They were there, and then they were gone, *vanished*."

Really, Rob thought, there really couldn't be any question of who it had been, standing mere yards from them this morning. Oh, anyone could put kerchiefs over their faces, but who could learn to become invisible? Only people who had lived in the mountains. Only people who had been hunted in the mountains like animals. "See, look at Rob," Mick said. "He still looks like he saw a ghost."

Rob turned to Kimball, disregarding Mick's witticism. "Are they stopping people? You know, I heard they were, some places. I met a kid in San Cristobal who told me they stopped him, I don't know if it was here, really, and took his last fifty dollars. He said it was the worst experience he ever had. Not the money, obviously, but when he felt the gun, sort of rubbing against his hair, he said it was like a switch on his head, and everything lit up with this strange, glowy light and became completely lucid, like one of those little glass things." Rob remembered the kid's voice, his white, wondering face. "He said his life had always been all dark and confused, but right then he could see how it all fit together, and his whole life made perfect sense. And the sense it made—the sense it *made*—was that it was completely, totally pointless."

The others looked at him. Then Suky smiled and slid a cigarette out of her pack.

"Of course," Rob said, "he was glad it wasn't the army."

"Excuse me, dear," Kimball said to Suky. "You got extra?"

She inhaled luxuriantly, then handed Kimball her cigarette. "By the way," she said to him. "How did you happen to know we came by car?"

Kimball gazed at her in sorrow. "How else could you have gotten here before the mail boat came in?" he asked reasonably. "Besides," he added. "I saw you drive up."

"Hey, lookit," Mick said. "No soldiers." And in fact they had disappeared from in front of the restaurant.

Kimball squinted down at the lake. "Yup, and the mail boat's coming in," he said. He glanced at his watch—an incongruously expensive one, Rob saw. "On the dot, give or take."

"Fabulous," Suky said. "Hours of Pantsuits before we've got the place to ourselves again."

Kimball twisted around in his chair to look full at her. "You know what?" he mused. "You kids are nice kids. You got a sense of propriety, and that's something that appeals to me. So what I'm saying is, if you've *got* to stay over tonight, I want you to do me this favor. I want you to take care of yourselves, and stay inside."

"Can't," Suky said. "Rob and I have tickets for the opera."

Mick looked annoyed. "Very funny," he said.

Kimball smiled indulgently. "Now, *her* family"—he pointed at the Indian girl—"barricades themselves in."

"No shit," Mick said. He pursed his lips and examined his juice glass. " 'Barricades.' "

"Hey, now," Kimball protested, as though Mick had maligned the girl's family. "These are good people."

Mick nodded gallantly at the immobile girl. "I don't doubt that for a second," he said. "But, what you're . . .

I mean, if there's actual . . . *con*flict." He turned the glass in his hands. "What do you say, Suke?"

"Besides." Suky smiled sweetly. "Rob wants to stay, obviously. Rob wants to see conflict."

"No conflict," Kimball said. "Oh, sure, the odd incident, naturally, now and again, but the real problem around here"—he lowered his voice—"is *brujos*. There was one recently, changed himself into a wild boar nights. Rampaged, was tearing up everyone's little plots of corn and beans, went after people whenever he got the chance." He studied Mick for a moment. "Now, Micky. We know that anybody who's out at night is up to mischief. I know that as well as you do. A person who's out at night is not a reliable human being. But things happen, and you got to take that into consideration. Someone's old lady gets sick, they have to get water from somewhere. A kid wanders out. You know how it is. And this *brujo* chewed up some folks something awful, they say, before they shot it one night in a cornfield. And in the morning? When the sun came up? The body turned into the sweetest old man you'd ever want to meet. One of our next-door neighbors." He sighed and shook his head. "But you know what?" He looked up as though surprised. "Rob—Suky—Are you listening? Because this is the interesting part, now. *Afterwards*, there were a lot of people who said that sweet old man and his wife were *guerrillas*."

Suky was looking at him thoughtfully. "No shit," she said, after a moment.

"No shit," he said. He stood, studying the empty spots where the soldiers had been, and hitched up his jeans. "Hey—" He whistled. "Pablito—"

"A buck fifty apiece," Mick said, when the bill was analyzed. "Can't beat that." He drained his juice, set the glass purposefully on the table, and stood. "Sure. We'll try to give you guys a hand, go back today if we do good business early—no real need to stay over, then. So, ready?"

"I think I'll just hang around," Rob said. "Explore."

Mick and Suky looked at him blankly.

"Okay, professor," Kimball said. "Explore away."

Now that Rob had succeeded in obtaining solitude, he found he had no idea what to do with it. The prospect of finding a ride back, which in the car had seemed so reasonable, was obviously absurd; he had noticed no other cars in the village. And who could he even ask? Pablo was at his elbow, staring at the little pile of money on the table. "*Sí.*" Rob nodded. "*Gracias.*" Pablo's eyes glinted as he seized it.

He could consult the man who had checked them in at the hotel, Rob thought. Though that didn't seem too promising. For a hotel keeper in a village to which few surely traveled, the man had been remarkably—not actually rude, Rob thought, but, well, . . . *preoccupied.*

There was one other party of guests at the hotel, Rob remembered. Three unsmiling button-faced blonds, of which one or two seemed to be boys. He could ask them. A good idea.

But when he imagined himself strolling back and finding them, a feeling of weakness overtook him. Their presence in the hotel's sunless courtyard earlier had been ghostly and forbidding. The hotel keeper had gestured to an enclosure beyond them—the shower, he explained. A shower! But Mick had been jittery and discouraging. "It'll be freezing, man. Let's go get some lunch—it'll warm up later." But Rob stood his ground—he'd earned the right, he felt, in the car. So Mick and Suky waited while he fetched the stiff little towel from his room—his cubicle—and disappeared into the shower stall. Instantly he was back in the courtyard, humiliated; the shower was *literally* unbearable. Mick had doubled up, and the blonds looked at him out of their button faces. But perhaps the blonds simply hadn't understood—they were foreigners. Well, foreigners, of course, but what he meant, he corrected himself, was, not American.

Rob gazed out at the watery sky, the cloudy lake. At the very worst, he'd only have to wait until late afternoon. Either Kimball would have succeeded in convincing Mick and Suky to return to town today, or he could take the mail boat by himself. Which was by far the more appealing alternative, actually—he was certainly in no hurry to be out on that road again. Anyhow, the urgency to leave had passed. There was something—well, something *correct* about being where he was. After all—the thought rose up dripping—it *was* where he was . . .

He had wanted to go, while he had the chance this summer before starting grad school, someplace very far away. Whenever his parents came home from their trips, they sparkled with things it was impossible to say. In fancy books of photographs you could see clues, hints, in the glossy pages, where boats rocked in the harbors of seaside towns, streetlamps spread a soft glamour through the rain of antique cities, where men and women of distant nationalities hunkered in the circle of the lens, enticing and resistant.

Since the beginning of summer he'd wound his way down and down and down, in buses throbbing with peasants and chickens. His heart had pounded at each blue and gold drop to the valley floors, at the crude white crosses marking death along the roads, at the shining, disinterested God-filled air, through which he had expected, at every moment, to plummet, along with his fellow passengers, bouncing in their tinny container from peak to peak. And he had felt, all the time, that he was following a trail of instructions that would lead him as far as it was possible to go.

Now here he was. As far as it was possible to go. The end of the trail, where the world trickled out into mud.

If Meredith were here, she would show him how to find

the beauty of this place as though it were a photograph. Through her eyes, it would acquire coherence, meaning, intelligibility. The lake with its sudsy rolls of fog—Meredith would know facts about it: its size, its depth, its geological origin. She would have researched the social organization, the language, the economy of these silent, unreadable villagers. She would smile, now, and coax him to his feet.

Oh, if only he could just go back to the hotel and have his shower! But he imagined Meredith's bewilderment: *You got all the way there and didn't even see the market? Or the church?* She shook her thick gold-brown hair and laughed. *You just took a shower and went back?* No, she didn't laugh—her white smile dimmed when she saw his face.

All right. So, market, church, *then* shower and return. A few tourists were struggling up the hill—evidently Suky had overestimated the impending plague. They would be headed for the market themselves, Rob reasoned, as he lost sight of them in the thicket of tin roofs and little hills.

But despite the intricacy of paths and turnings, the market turned out to be no more than two minutes' walk from the restaurant. Indian clothing hung from stalls, and careful heaps of dwarfed and fly-specked mangoes were displayed on crates.

Pale, smiling people, determined, apologetic, wearing squashy hats to protect them from the sun, aimed cameras at undersize children and their glowering mothers. Even worse was the dickering at the stalls. The scene had a sickening familiarity. It was like seeing as an adult one of those frenetic, mean-spirited, sentimental TV shows Rob had watched as a child. "They want you to bargain, they expect you to. It's insulting if you don't," one woman was informing her shame-faced husband. "Twenty dollar," she said to the shop owner, believing herself, apparently, to be speaking a foreign language.

The shop owner was a large woman. Some automatic

function was releasing rage evenly into her face. She held out for inspection a pair of trousers, embroidered with rich tiers of parrots and ice-cream cones, while the customer deliberated—with shrewdness and forced gaiety—as though she were trying on hats in Paris.

It was a large, rusty stain on the side of the trousers that decided the matter. The shop owner was adamant. The stain would wash out, she insisted without a trace of credibility. The customer was knowing, regretful. As she walked away, strength of character lighting up her face, the shop owner hissed after her. The retreating customer's step did not quicken, though her expression toughened slightly. Rob, rooted to the spot, waited for her skin to blossom with hemorrhages, her flesh to turn to pulp, her hair and teeth to spring out onto the mud.

Why did he feel he must redress the imbalance between buyer and seller? It was a stupid and superstitious impulse, he told himself. Humanity everywhere was at ease with the barbarism of his countryfellows. And how not? It was simple—one had power and money on one's side; inevitably every act one committed was predicated on that fact. If he were to give in and buy something now, his transaction would be predicated on that fact as well.

It was true, he thought. He could buy or not buy; he could exercise his power and money or refrain from doing so, and that was the extent of his choice. But the notion only fanned the agitation threatening to rattle him like a dried gourd should he leave the market with nothing.

At the nearest stall he gathered up, roughly, like a criminal, several sashes and a pair of trousers, the inferior workmanship of which suggested a low price. He paid what was asked and left before the incredulous saleswoman could determine whether he ought to be addressed with mockery or with pity. Had his gesture alleviated in the least degree the disarray of his pulse, his breathing, his glands? No.

Mick had been right, he thought; he should have ordered

some juice. His lightheadedness might well be dehydration, in part. But at least he'd managed to see the market already, and the church could not be far. He would take his dutiful glimpse, return to the hotel to drink some water and take his shower, and by that time Mick and Suky might be ready to leave. He tucked his purchases under his arm, noting that these new trousers of his were marred, too, by rusty stains. Should he deposit them by the side of the road? No point in that; whatever was on them was on him now, as well.

The church was not around the first turn he took, nor the second, nor the third. Around the fourth, little huts petered out into a foggy scrub. Figures were moving in the mist—women with water jugs on their heads and babies, wrapped in shawls, on their backs. Below, the gray lake and gray sky exchanged their vapors.

Something bulged from the scrub! No, only an old man, coming toward him. Sometimes these Indians looked a little pathetic, Rob thought, in their wide trousers, in all their loose, swaddling clothing. Clownish, almost, like patients. *"Señor,"* Rob called. *"Iglesia? Dónde está, por favor?"*

The old man approached Rob teeteringly. He held an old straw hat by the brim, and his expression was quizzical and humorous. Again, Rob asked where the church was, but the old man gave no sign of understanding, even of hearing, the question.

Moisture made his large black eyes radiant, his gaze penetrating but unspecific. His face was a patchwork with deep seams. His mouth had simply been left open, like a doorway, and inside, stumpy teeth tilted at random intervals. Yet the effect was pleasant, even soothing. Rob felt as though a thrumming sleep were beginning to enfold him as he watched the man approach. *"Iglesia,"* Rob said again. The word was a wooden ball, rolling on a wooden floor. It rolled toward the old man, who reached out, and Rob remembered, just in time, to retract his hand.

The old man paused in front of him, swaying. Drunk,

Rob decided. In several places along the road this morning, they had seen figures sprawled out in the mud. "Drunk," Mick pronounced at the first. And at the third, "Shit, all of these drunks."

The man's face crinkled up, as though he and Rob were the oldest of friends. It wouldn't hurt to let him hang on to my sleeve, Rob chided himself. He couldn't stop looking at the man—it was as though he really had fallen asleep.

But the man had lost interest in the arm Rob now offered. His mouth moved, and the silky sounds of the language of the village were slipping around Rob. Yes, like patients, wandering in the mist. "*No entiendo,*" Rob said, remembering that he was supposed to understand. The man smiled in agreement and nodded. They were both smiling, Rob observed with a mild, puzzled interest.

The old man pointed to a hovering strip of fog. "No," Rob said, smiling still, as the word breathed in and out— no, no—a sail, or wing, in front of him. But the old man beckoned, and retreated a few steps, looking at Rob.

Several yards off the path a cluster of freshly painted wooden crosses rose up from the mud. The man watched Rob, feeding out the silken cord of his language. "*No entiendo,*" Rob said again, smiling just the way the man was smiling. "*No entiendo . . .*"

Each declaration of Rob's ignorance seemed only to amuse the old man more. He nodded, held up a finger, then stood very still and bowed his head, as though he were preparing a recitation, or prayer. He looked up roguishly to check on Rob's attention, then bent over and picked up an imaginary bundle. Watching Rob playfully, he rocked the bundle in his arms, then replaced it on the ground.

He held his finger up again, waited for Rob to nod, then drew himself erect and saluted at someone beyond Rob. As Rob struggled with the thick air for breath, the old man aimed an imaginary gun at the spot where he had laid the bundle, and pulled its imaginary trigger. "*No entiendo,*" Rob said, as the performance began all over. "I don't—"

But the old man persevered in his nightmarish repetitions. Behind him the crosses gleamed like bone, new and white, as Rob scrabbled in his pocket for small bills; when he thrust some at the old man, a handful of change fell twinkling in the mud.

One more turn and Rob was at the church. It was enormous, ludicrous. Inside, the streaked blue-green paint and distant ceiling made it seem the size of a stadium. Rob's empty gut kept turning slowly inside out, like a sock. He was covered with a chilling sweat.

Aromatic grasses and flowers were scattered on the vast, cracked concrete floor. Here and there groups of Indians squatted, chanting over smoking vessels. A child skittered by him, cawing and waving his arms in play flight, or mental illness. The chanting spiraled high, modal, nasal— looping back, around the new Spanish god who starved on the altar, looping forward into the dark future . . . Rob wiped the sweat that was leaking into his eyes. Good heavens—the three button-faced blonds from the hotel were parading far down the nave, one of them holding, in both arms, a monstrous pineapple. A *pineapple*! Saints, dressed in embroidered trousers and battered straw hats, looked lustfully down at it from their niches, the hunger in their plaster eyes exaggerated, Rob saw as he felt about for something to lean on, by the kerchiefs—the guerrilla masks—the worshippers had tied across their saintly plaster noses and mouths.

His room faced the lake. The glass in the window was broken and filthy, but that hardly mattered since the window could not be closed, and from where Rob lay he could see clearly. Perhaps the old man had only . . . There were a few shacks scattered along the marshy strip between the hotel and the lake, and children played near the docked mail boat. Rob closed his eyes, and the children's voices floated up to him, intimate and allusive, like dreamed whispers in his ears. He had been lying there for some time. Two hours? Three? It was impossible to guess; the children's voices rose and fell, measuring nothing.

When Rob came in, he had slowly, carefully drained one of his three bottles of water. Then he'd gone back downstairs to the shower stall, where no trickle, of any temperature, was to be coaxed from the faucet. The hotel keeper was outside, at the door, staring up into the hills. He waited courteously for Rob to struggle through his question in Spanish. "Generator," the hotel keeper answered in English, and made an unmistakable gesture of termination before he returned to squinting up at the hills.

Graffiti were scratched into the dirt and old paint on Rob's wall. *Hi,* one said. *My name is Bob I like this place I am American so all here stinks The toilet doesn't work Too All here is disgusting I like Indians I like* ☺ *I like most one good dead Indian The food here in this place is disgusting All here is dirty dirty dirty Bye bye* ☺ *Your Bob.*

Rob stared at it stunned, then laughed. An American named Bob! Oh, sure. Some German, more likely. And they had nerve to talk. A *lot* of nerve. Besides, Rob thought, the toilet worked perfectly. Or at least, he pointed out to himself, it had while the generator was functioning.

His flat little pillow smelled of mildew. So did the shelf of uncompromising lumps that was his bed. He tried to isolate the strains of the odor, the ornate tangling of growth and decay; he concentrated as his body dripped from the heat into the mattress and plumes of gray light spread, confusing the water, the sky, the volcano. Where were Suky and Mick? If only Suky and Mick would walk in now, and they could all go back to town!

He closed his eyes and the village lay before him. For a moment the market stalls, the tin-roofed huts, the children looked pretty, and exotic—*beautiful*. But smells, rising up from the scanty heaps of rotting food set out for sale and from the tottering, fly-plagued animals, were saturating the glossy surface, causing it to decompose into a deep welter. The smells were making Rob soft, seeping into his body, allowing the chanting from the church to permeate him, too, and alter the codes of his cells with every tiny, insistent modulation.

He was now not merely dirty, he was contaminated. No, he was a crucible, originating poisons, spreading contaminants backward through his life. His parents appeared in their sunny kitchen. Rob drew himself in, but he could feel filth bleeding through his skin where his body pressed against the mattress.

Down below, a few tourists were drifting toward the dock. The children who had been playing were now harnessing themselves into work, begging caressingly for pencils. Rob could hear them: *Lápiz, lápiz*, in their sing-song Spanish, see them advance, surround, pull at sleeves, undeflected by the stony embarrassment of their prey. Obviously Mick had abandoned his prudent thought of attempting to return to town today, and Rob was actually going to have to get himself onto his feet, and go down to the boat.

In the kitchen, Meredith joined his mother and father. The sink was full of water. A pan bobbed up from under a merry mound of suds, and flashed. At home they hadn't yet noticed how the walls were beginning to stain, and buckle.

He turned over and curled himself around his pillow. Soap bubbles winked, breaking. He located one, and with great caution, introduced the tiny figures of his parents and Meredith into it—the soap vessel yielded and resealed around them. Then the bubble lifted and floated through the kitchen window. A little spasm jerked in his chest; he put his fingers to his eyes; his fingers came away wet and hot. "Knock knock," someone said.

"Who's there?" he said, sitting abruptly.

"Banana." Suky hovered in the doorway. "Listen—" She glanced away diplomatically. "—Two things. Number

one: the generator's out. Number two: Mick's sick." Rob
stared at her, waiting for the bits of speech to organize
themselves into information. For a moment it seemed that
she was going to come sit next to him on the bed.

A little bug was clambering insecurely over the strap of
her camisole, making its way to the cupid's bow peak of
her collarbone. She located it and let it board her finger,
with which she conveyed it to the window. Her hands were
fine and pliant, Rob noticed, her nails bitten savagely. A
protracted shudder rose the length of his spine. "Sick,
how?" he asked.

"Sick, plain old," Suky said. "I guess they put water in
that juice this morning, huh." That was all she seemed to
have to say. She stood aimlessly in the doorway.

Rob leaned over to sling his pack up on the bed. "I
brought some clean water," he said.

"Clever," Suky said, unenthusiastically.

So, what more could he possibly do? "Did you have a
good day?" he said.

"Yeah," Suky said. "Really great. And who knows—
maybe Mick will stop throwing up eventually and we'll be
able to go back tomorrow. I really look forward to the
drive, don't you? Through guerrilla country with an informer in the car?"

"Army informer?" Rob stared at Suky. "Kimball?"

"Consultant, if you prefer," she said. "What did you
think, he's an anthropologist?" She hugged herself despite
the heat. "You and Mick, Jesus." Her hair curled like
steam around her neck and temples, her camisole was
spotted with damp. From the window past her, Rob saw
the tourists assembling at the boat below. *Time to get up,
time to get up—* He remembered his parents' cheerful
morning voices; the way he had floated, waking from his
night voyages, back into his own bed.

"But what we have to do now," Suky said, "is get some
candles. The sun's going to set any minute."

"Candles," Rob said. "Candles . . . Oh, listen—better give these to Mick." He held out his two remaining bottles of water. "Before he gets dehydrated."

Suky watched him. "What about you?"

One of the dark blotches on her camisole seemed to be spreading slightly. Or possibly not. "The thing is," he said, "I've got to get down to the boat."

She took one of the bottles of water from him. "Great," she said. Her skin gave off its faint sparkle, her face was expressionless, "So. Well. Bon voyage."

"Wait—" Rob said. "Is there—is there some way I could help?" But she was gone, and the stiffness and insincerity of his voice stopped him from calling after her.

Down at the dock the children clung to him, their eyes huge, their tiny hands searching for his pockets. A skinny monkey of a boatman with bare feet and torn, rolled-up pants was collecting the last fares. Rob squinted back at the village: green, fog, glints of tin. But he! Yes, they were all exposed down here at the dock, pinned behind the hidden crosshairs.

Across the lake a cluster of boxy buildings, all no bigger than his fingernail, floated in a disk of harsh blue. Hard to believe town was so close, that he and Suky and Mick had been there only this morning. Hard to believe that he was simply going back there now, to the loud, junky restaurants; to the strained, moribund, fever-pitch cheer of ladinos and gringos vacationing . . . *Time to get up, time to get up* . . .

He found Suky at the pavilion, sitting over another meal of rice and beans. "I brought a flashlight," he said. He took it from his pack, and held it out as an offering. "I thought you might need it."

She glanced up at him, then held out a sheaf of candles in answer.

A little girl, no more than six, arrived with a Coke for

Suky. *"Dónde está Pablo?"* Rob asked. The girl stared at him.

"Reinforcements for the night crowd," Suky explained. "Pablo's in the kitchen, cooking."

Rob looked around; the restaurant was empty except for himself and Suky. "Mind if I sit with you?" Rob said, and waited until Suky shrugged.

Dusk was collecting rapidly, settling in heavy folds around the hills and shacks. All along the road, up and down the paths through the village, points of candles began to move at the stately pace of Indians. The volcano and the low vegetation appeared as a furze against the darkness; the sky and lake blended in a colorless sheen.

The little girl brought rice and beans for Rob. He ate a few bites—it was possible to eat, now that he was no longer hungry. Suky lit one of her candles and stuck it onto the table. The little girl drew close and gazed into the flame; she ran her finger sensuously along one of the other candles and looked at Suky, who shook her head no. The little girl leaned against Suky with a loud sigh, which turned into a yawn. *"Tienes hambre?"* Suky said.

"Hambre," the child agreed, and Suky picked her up. Settled in Suky's lap, the child finished Suky's meal, then Rob's, eating delicately with tortillas. When Suky stroked her glorious, filthy black hair, she responded with a snuffly little intake of breath, and they snuggled against each other, sated and filmy-eyed.

Pablo called from the kitchen; the little girl wriggled off Suky's lap. She picked up one of the candles and looked challengingly at Suky. "All right." Suky sighed. *"Sí."*

"Y para Pablo?" the little girl said.

Suky rubbed her forehead. Was she crying? No, just fatigued, apparently. "Okay," she said, and the child scampered off to the kitchen with her trophies.

The sky at the other side of the lake was still faintly blue; it had been clear the whole of the four, vanished days

Rob had spent there; clear, he thought with tunneled reverberations of grief.

"I didn't take the boat," he said.

"Is that so," Suky said. She rubbed her forehead again.

"I didn't think I should leave you alone when Mick wasn't well," Rob said.

"Rob," she said, and he floundered in her amber stare. "Rob, let me clarify something, please: Fuck you."

Rob sighed. He passed his finger idly through the candle flame. It had fascinated him as a child—that you could do it and not feel heat; that any household object might disclose inexplicable gaps within a supposed sequence of events. *Was everything he said some sort of lie?*

A dog barked, began to bay. "Shit," Suky said. Candles blinked out one after the other, and night gushed over the village as two dogs, three dogs, joined in until a claxon sprang up in a ring around Rob and Suky. "Let me guess," Rob said. *"Brujos."*

Suky pinched out their candle, making the sky huge with moonlight, and Rob saw what she and the dogs had seen already: a line of black dots, small black shapes moving down the hills closer and closer, winding off a silent cog—a dark chain of soldiers, holding their rifles, descending into the village.

"It's okay—" Suky's quiet voice hovered within the wheeling frenzy of the dogs. "It happens every night. Someone we bought from let it slip to me and Mick today. Remember the guys we saw out front this morning? Every night they all come down. The whole unit. And they stay in the village all night and into the day. But while the tourists are here they have to evaporate, right? So when the mail boat arrives they go back up to their barracks to sleep and the tourists stumble happily around."

On the road below, a few late stragglers hurried past with candles, their faces stark with purpose in the circle of illumination.

"The boat," Rob said. "The mail boat . . ."

"Uh huh," Suky said. "And now the tourists are gone."

The hotel keeper was still at the door. What was he always watching for, Rob wondered. Could he and Kimball discern one another through the blackness, across the hills, as clearly as if they were facing each other, inches apart? *I saw the village, I saw the market, I saw the church,* Rob insisted to himself, but all he could see now was a limitless dark, screened by the reflection of his own face, its expression of untested integrity, of convenient innocence.

Inside the courtyard the three blonds were feasting, fierce and ceremonial, on their pineapple. One of them hacked off a chunk of it with a long, shining knife, and held it out toward Suky. She paused. A troubling warmth floated off her. She shook her head, as though something had been denied, rather than offered to her. "Suky—" Rob said. She glanced at him, then turned away.

Tatters of shine lay on the center of the lake; the boat would have passed through them long before, and in the electric glare that was town, the tourists would just be tucking into steaks, ordering fancy mixed drinks, turning on the televisions in their hotel rooms . . . But from town, this hotel, the whole village, in fact, would be invisible. Even from Rob's window, the shacks scattered just outside showed only as indeterminate patches of depthless black. Were soldiers, their rifles cocked, squatting there against barricaded doors? *Hi, my name is Bob,* Rob saw. He blew out his candle, but night covered the story that was unfolding below for no other witnesses.

He stretched out on his bed. The darkness around him rustled and whispered, and a satiny gleam from the moon and stars began to collect on his body. In country like this there were probably animals, all kinds of animals, jungly things. Not lions or elephants, of course, but snakes, certainly, and even monkeys, perhaps—the kind that screamed at night—and small nocturnal creatures that looked like big cats or rats and frolicked through ruins of huts where people had recently lived. Just born, they would sleep for a few days in shaded hollows, and then one night unlid their jewel-like eyes.

And when they opened their tiny new mouths, when their new little natures ordained that this one or that one stretch the hinges of its sleek new jaws, what pleasures of discovery there would be! The flickering tongue, the high-pitched howl, the needle-pointed teeth, whatever marvelous instrument it was, discovered anew by each new being, that was the special gift of its species. Yes. Rob's heart pounded as though he'd run to keep an appointment.

When the knock came, he waited for one luxurious moment; the gleam slid off him as he stood.

"Mick wants water," Suky said from the doorway.

Rob cleared his throat. "How is Mick?" he asked. "Puking," she said. "As usual."

"Sit down," he said, breathless. "I've got that other bottle around here somewhere." Again, a long shudder ascended his spine.

Suky rested, propped up on one elbow, while Rob pretended to search. When he could stand it no longer, he retrieved the bottle and a stack of styrofoam cups from their corner. "Here," he said.

Suky reached for the bottle, but he held it back. "Careful, careful," he said, experimentally. "It's all I've got left."

She looked at him sharply, before her face became opaque.

When she held out her hand again slowly, he relinquished the bottle.

Trembling, he disengaged two cups from the stack. Suky poured some water into each; the sound was deafening. "Cheers," he thought he heard her say, and their cups scraped together.

He struggled to restrain his uncoiling mind as he traced Suky's collarbone with his finger and blinked back the veil of terror that kept gathering across his eyes. Darkness was reaching out like creepers, unfolding into thick, oily petals, and distant sounds were becoming audible; Rob's thoughts were pattering here and there in darkness. "What's going on?" he whispered against Suky's throat, but her eyes narrowed, gleamed, dilated—already she was gliding off. Those distant cries—something waking now to the fragrance of blood? Levering the straps down from Suky's shoulders, Rob strained to hear, and waited.

Someone to Talk To

"ARE YOU GOING TO BE ALL RIGHT, AARON?"
Caroline said.

Shapiro saw himself, as if in a dream, standing on a dark shore. "Yes," he heard himself say.

"Are you sure?" Caroline said.

Lady Chatterley leaned herself thuggishly against Shapiro's shin and began to purr. "Hello, there," he said. He reached down and patted her gingerly.

Caroline hesitated at the door, then took a few steps back toward Shapiro, and her delicious, clean fragrance spilled over him. "Your big concert's in less than a month now . . ." She tilted her head and managed a little smile.

Was she going to touch him? Shapiro went rigid with alarm, but she just looked vaguely around the room. "You know, it's supposed to be a beautiful country . . ." She scooped up Lady Chatterley and nuzzled the orange fur. "Chat. Dear little Chat. Are you going to take care of Aaron?" She took a paw in her hand. "Are you?"

Lady Chatterley wrenched herself free and bounded back to the floor. Caroline's eyes—like Lady Chatterley's—were large and light and spoked with black. Her small face was pale, always, as though with shock.

"Shall I help you with your things?" Shapiro said.

There was really only one suitcase, a good one—leather, old, genteel—which had probably accompanied Caroline to college; the rest had gone on before. "No need," she said. Tears wavered momentarily in her eyes. "Jim's picking me up."

The suitcase appeared to be heavy. Shapiro watched Caroline's thin legs as she struggled slightly with it. At the door she turned back. "Aaron?" she said.

He waited to hear himself answer, but this time no words came.

"Aaron, I know this is probably not what you want to hear right now, but I think it's important for me to say it —I'll always care about you, you know. I hope you know that."

Shapiro awoke suddenly and unpleasantly, as though a crateful of fruits had been emptied out on him. There was an unfamiliar wall next to him, and the window was all wrong. He heard footsteps, a snicker. A hotel room wobbled into place around him—yes, Richard Penwad would be coming to pick him up, and Caroline wasn't even in this country.

The night had been crowded with Caroline and endless versions of her departure—dreamed, reversed in dreams, modified, amended, transfigured, made tender and transcendently beautiful as though it had been an act of sacral purification. For a week or so he had been free of her, or at least anesthetized. But this morning he was battered by her absence; in this distant place his body and mind didn't know how to protect themselves.

As soon as she'd left that day, he'd closed his eyes. An afterimage of the door glowed. When he'd opened his eyes again, the room seemed strange in an undetectable way, as though he were seeing it after a hiatus of years. Hesitantly, he brushed cat fur from the armchair and sat down.

Six years. Six years of life that belonged to them both,

out the door in the form of Caroline's fragile person. If only there'd been less . . . tension about money. Caroline, from many generations of a background she referred to as "comfortable," was deeply sympathetic with, and at the same time deeply insensitive to, the distress of others. "Why not, Aaron?" she would say. "Why don't I just take care of the rent from now on?" Or, when she felt like going to some morbidly expensive restaurant, "I could treat. Wouldn't it be fun, for a change? Of course"—she would gaze at him with concern—"if you're not going to enjoy it . . ." Sometimes, when she noticed him grimly going through the mail or eying the telephone, she would say gently, "Something will turn up."

Though not quite a prodigy, Shapiro had been received with great enthusiasm at the youthful start of his career. He'd been shy and luminously pale, with dark curls and almost freakish technical abilities that delighted audiences. But the qualities he greatly admired and envied in other pianists—varieties of a profound musicianship which focussed the attention on the ear, hearing, rather than on the hand, executing—were ones he lacked. He practiced, he struggled, he cultivated patience, and he was rewarded—minimally. By just the faintest flicker of heat in his crystalline touch.

His curls, pallor, and technique lost some of their brilliance; his audience was distracted by newcomers and dispersed, and a sudden increase in the velocity of the earth's spin dumped Shapiro into his thirty-eighth year. *Aaron Shapiro.* Caroline had been starry-eyed when they'd met, although by that time he'd already moved out to the margin of the city and was beginning to take on private students, startlingly untalented children who at best thought of the piano as a defective substitute for something electronic. Gradually he ceased to be the sort of pianist who might expect to make recordings, give important concerts, be interviewed, hold posts at conservatories. His name, once received like a slab of precious metal, was now received like a slip of blank paper.

"Things will work out," Caroline said, although "things," in Shapiro's estimation, were deteriorating. She touched him less often. Her smiles became increasingly lambent and forbearing. Sometimes she called in the afternoon to say she'd be held up at work. Her voice would be hesitant, apprehensive; her words floated in the air like dying petals while he listened, reluctant to hang up but unable to think of anything to say.

Recently, he'd been silent for whole evenings, reading, or simply sitting. Rent, plus utilities, plus insurance, minus lessons, plus food—columns of figures went marching through his head, knocking everything else out of it. Once, after he'd had a day of particularly demoralizing students, Caroline perched on the arm of his chair. "Things will work out," she said, and touched his cheek.

She might just as well have socked him. "Things will work out?" he said. He was ready to weep with desire that this be true, yet it was manifestly not. "You mean—Ah. Perhaps what you mean is that things will work out for some other species. Or on some other planet. In which case, Caroline, you and I are in complete accord. After all, life moves on."

She was staring at him, her hand drawn back as though she'd inadvertently touched a hot stove. Was that his voice? Were those his words? He could hardly believe it himself. Those stiff words, like stiff little soldiers, stiff with shame at the atrocities they were committing.

"Life moves on," he continued, ruthless and miserable, "but not necessarily to the benefit of the individual, does it? Yes, things will work out eventually, I suppose. But do you think they'll work out for the guy who sleeps in front of our building? Do you think—" The danger and excitement of probing his terror narrowed his vision into a throbbing circle, from which Caroline, imprisoned, stared back. "Do you think they'll work out for me?"

She'd retreated to the other room, and he sat with his head in his hands. Evidently, Caroline herself did not understand or accept the very thing she had just forced him to understand and accept—that he, like most humans, was an experiment that had never been expected to succeed, a little padding around some evolutionary thrust, a scatter-shot nubbin of DNA. It was a matter of huge biological importance, for some reason, that he be desperate to meet the demands of his life, but it was a matter of no biological importance whatever that he be *able* to meet them.

But that week—that very week—an airmail letter arrived from a Richard Penwad inviting Shapiro to play Umberto García-Gutiérrez's Second Piano Concerto at a Pan-American music festival.

An amazing occurrence. Though one that, having occurred, was—like every other occurrence—plausible. The terrible feeling hanging over the apartment began to evaporate. Shapiro was embarrassed by his recent behavior and feelings, which now seemed absurdly theatrical, absurdly childish. Of course things would work out. Why wouldn't things work out? Why shouldn't he and Caroline go to whatever restaurant she pleased? And enjoy it. Order some decent wine, attend concerts, travel . . . Check in hand, he would lead Caroline into the bower of celebrity and international conviviality from which he'd been exiled. However gradually, in due course things would work out.

In the days that followed, Shapiro felt by turns precariously elated and violently dejected, as though he were emerging from the chaos of an accident that had left him impaired in as yet undisclosed ways. He would catch Caroline gazing at him soberly with her great, light-filled eyes. She mentioned the invitation frequently. "Isn't it terrific?" she said. "Aaron. How terrific." Her voice was tender and lingering—remote, the voice in which, when they'd first met, she'd recounted to Shapiro tales of her idyllic childhood. Then, one evening, when he came home with a guidebook, she said, "Listen, Aaron." And her voice had been especially gentle. "We have to talk."

Shapiro checked the clock by his uncomfortable bed; it would be a relief to go downstairs and meet Penwad. His brain felt unbalanced by Caroline's precipitous entrances and exits; anything to block them. He shut the door of his dark, cramped room behind him, and descended to the restaurant; yes, unbalanced! The corridors themselves seemed to buckle underfoot.

The festival would have been an attractive proposition even at the best of times. Shapiro had played once before in Latin America—a concert in Mexico City many years earlier. The air in the hall had been velvety with receptivity, the audience ideal, and although his piece had been first on the program, they had demanded an encore from him right then and there.

The García-Gutiérrez concerto had furnished other happy occasions in his career. He'd performed its United States première some seventeen years earlier. The piano part was splashy and difficult, perhaps not terribly substantial, but an excellent vehicle for Shapiro; it glittered in his hands. García-Gutiérrez had been there to congratulate him with a quiet intensity. What would he look like now, Shapiro wondered. At that time he'd been handsome—silvery hair, tall, hooded eyes. How young Shapiro must have seemed, with his abashed, eager gratitude!

Penwad was already downstairs at the restaurant drinking a coffee. He extended, with official enthusiasm, a carefully manicured but stubby hand, and grimaced as Shapiro shook it. "We're pleased we could get you down," he said, and glanced at his palm. "This is our first go at the festival, I think I must have written you, but we're hoping to bring people such as yourself annually, from all over the Americas—especially the States. We're starting out with García-Gutiérrez as our star attraction, you see, because he's a local boy."

On the walls were posters of palm-fringed lakes, frosted volcanoes, and Indians smiling regal, slightly haughty smiles. Interspersed with the posters were magnificent examples of Indian textiles.

"Charming, isn't it?" Penwad said. "Not a—an *ostentatious* place, but we felt you'd find it charming."

Charming, Shapiro thought. Well, probably the other hotels were even worse. He glanced at the walls again. Charming! It was well known, what was happening in this country to the descendants of its earliest inhabitants—massacres, internment, debt slavery, torture—and, *naturally*, the waiters who scurried around beneath the smiling posters, looking raddled and grief-stricken, were Indians, ceremonial costumes draping their skinny bodies.

"People don't tend to be aware how vigorous our sponsorship of the arts is," Penwad was saying. "We're hoping the festival will help to . . . rectify the, ah, perception that we're identified with the military here."

Shapiro's attention was wrenched from the waiters. "The perception that . . ."

"Rectify that perception," Penwad said.

Fee, Shapiro reminded himself. Fee plus lessons, minus rent, minus utilities . . . Well, and besides, there would be the credit. In a program note, even the most dubious event acquired grandeur. And why not? Concerts and exhibitions from the beginning of time had been funded by villains in search of endorsement, apologists, a place in history, or simple self-esteem. "Incidentally," Shapiro said, "who is 'we'?"

Penwad raised his eyebrows. "Who is we?" he said.

"That is, when you say 'we'—"

"Ah," Penwad said. "Well, I'm not including myself, actually. I'm just a liaison, really, between the Embassy and various local committees and groups concerned with the arts."

"I see," Shapiro said, with no attempt at tact.

"So," Penwad said. "We'll get you a bit of breakfast,

then go on over to the Arts Center, take a little look around— Rehearsal all day, rather strenuous, I'm afraid. After that we've fixed up a little interview for you—I trust that's all right—around dinnertime. Friday's free until the concert. Joan and I will pick you up first thing in the morning to show you around." He smiled. "Joan has her own ideas, but you must say what interests *you*. Then, after the concert, there's to be a party, a reception for you, essentially, at the home of some friends of ours, very fine people here. Then plane, yes? Very next morning." He already, Shapiro noticed, looked relieved. "Quite a whirlwind."

"Wonderful," Shapiro said. "But no need, you know, to take me over to the . . . Arts Center. Why don't I just grab a taxi?"

Penwad waved his hand. "I'm afraid the Center is difficult to find. Most of the drivers are unfamiliar with it. Besides," he added, "enjoy your company." He narrowed his eyes at his coffee cup, and raised it to his mouth.

There was something anatomical about the Center's great concrete sweeps and protuberances. Like all Arts Centers and Performing Arts Complexes and National Centers for the Performing Arts, though futuristic in design, it had a look of ancient decay, being left over from a period when leisure time and economic abundance were considered an imminent menace. How quaint a notion that now seemed! Shapiro almost laughed to think there had been a period, the period in which he'd grown up, no less, when it had been feared that wealth would soon cause humanity to devolve into a grunting mass sprawled in front of blood-drenched TV screens. But, no—*Art* (whatever that was), encouraged to flourish in its Centers, would prevent people from becoming intractable, illiterate, fat! And all the while poverty was accomplishing the devolution by itself.

"I see you're enjoying the, ah, prospect," Penwad said. Shapiro became aware that he was staring down over toothy crenellations into a city cleaved by deep ravines and encircled by mountains.

"Those tall buildings are the downtown area, of course," Penwad said. "And to the right and left, obviously, are residential sectors. Our place is over there—that's pretty much where the whole English-speaking community has . . . put down its little roots. And up there on the slopes is what we call the Gold Zone."

Shapiro, shading his eyes, noticed that the ravines below were encrusted with fuming slums. "My God," he said.

"Incredible, isn't it," Penwad said, "what an earthquake can do? You can really see the damage from up here. You probably noticed the floor of your hotel. The Center survived intact, though. We're very proud of the Center. The architect was truly successful, we feel, the way he . . . Yes, actually. You might be interested. A fellow named Santiago Méndez. He's done most of the better hotels in town, and our museum. There was a lecture last year. One of our events. It was explained. The way Méndez— Well, this was some time ago, of course—Joan would be better able to . . . But . . . the . . . combined influences." He gestured toward several concrete mounds. "The modernistic, the indigenous . . . well, *motifs*. A cross-fertilization, as Joan says."

Shapiro hesitated. A bunting-like stupefaction had enveloped him. "Of . . . what?" he asked.

"Of . . . ? What of what?" Penwad asked.

"Of . . ." Shapiro had lost the thread of his own question. "Of what . . . does *Joan* . . . say 'cross-fertilization'?"

"Joan *says* it . . ." Penwad glared at him. "She says it of . . . mo*tifs*."

The orchestra was from a small, nearby dictatorship, and the musicians had a startled appearance, as though a huge claw had snatched them from their beds and plonked them into their chairs. The conductor, a delicate and intelligent-looking man, welcomed Shapiro with reassuring collegiality, but when he brought down his baton Shapiro almost cried out; the sound was so peculiar that he feared he was suffering from some neurological damage.

How had the conductor come to find himself in his profession, Shapiro wondered. The man's waving arms seemed to be signalling for help rather than leading an orchestra. The poor musicians clutched their instruments, staring wildly at their sheet music as they played. But then it was Shapiro's entrance; notes began to leap froggily from his own fingers, and he understood: clearly the hall was demonic.

How to outwit these acoustics? As if this concerto were not difficult enough under the best of circumstances, with all its flash and bombast! But, of course, there was always something. Even in the loftiest, the most competently administered concert, catastrophes invented themselves from the far reaches of possibility. The piano bench would fall into splinters at seven forty-five, or the other musicians turned out to have a new version of the score, three measures shorter than one's own, or there was a bank holiday and it was impossible to retrieve one's tuxedo from the cleaner's—catastrophes far beneath the considerations of music, and yet!

How synthetic the concerto sounded in this inhospitable hall! Shapiro was surprised to find himself disliking it so. He had never tremendously admired it, exactly, but he'd always enjoyed playing it: he'd enjoyed the athletic challenge of its surface complexities; he'd enjoyed the response of the audience. It was *affirming*, people said upon hearing it, and their faces had the shining, decisive expressions of people who feel their worth to be recognized. *Affirming*, Shapiro thought, as sound sloshed and bulged, gummed up in clumps, liquefied, as though the air were full of whirling blades.

The interview that had been arranged for Shapiro was with an English journalist named Beale. An interview: implied interest on the part of someone. There would be clippings, at least, and, perhaps, therefore some shadowy retention of his name in the minds of those people—"we"—who put these festivals together.

Shapiro located Beale in a restaurant of the hotel, much larger than his own, where they'd been scheduled to meet. "Are you tired of it?" Beale inquired anxiously. "I was hoping not. In my opinion it's the best food in town, and the station will reimburse if it's an interview."

Beale's head was an interesting space-ship shape. Colorless and sensitive-looking filaments sprouted from it, and his ears looked like receiving devices. Sensors, transmitters, Shapiro thought, noting Beale's other large, responsive-looking features and his nervous, hesitant fingers. Beale's suit was faintly mottled by traces of stains; his shirt, from the evidence of his wrists, was short-sleeved, and he wore, incredibly, a tie that appeared to be made of rope.

"I'm not tired of it yet," Shapiro said. "I've never been here."

Beale squinted distrustfully at Shapiro. "They didn't put you here? They put a lot of guests here . . ."

Shapiro glanced around. So this was where they'd put an *important* musician. It was ugly and grandiose, with slippery-looking walls—the very air seemed soaked with a venal, melting luxe. "Santiago Méndez?" he said.

"Oh, you're good," Beale said with delight. "Seriously. If they bring you down again, insist. Nice, isn't it? They all speak English, and the furniture doesn't just"—he lunged toward Shapiro in illustration—"loom up at you. Now, will you drink something?"

Shapiro saw that two glasses already sat in front of Beale, one emptied and the other containing hardly more than a gold film. "Just water, thanks," Shapiro said.

"Oh, you can, here," Beale said. "Rest assured. Ice and all. I, on the other hand," he informed a waiter, "will have a whiskey, why not."

"And perhaps we could order," Shapiro added. Well, at least someone had seen fit to arrange a party for him.

Beale studied the menu worriedly, running his finger along the print. He had quantities of advice for Shapiro about it but seemed unable to make up his own mind. "A nice chop, perhaps," Beale said. "You know, this is the one place where it's perfectly safe to eat pork. That is if you—" His eyes blinked and reset themselves furiously, like lights on an overtaxed instrument panel.

While Beale entrusted his order to the waiter, Shapiro's attention wandered to posters on the wall. Plenty of charm here, too: more lakes, more volcanoes, more smiling Indians . . . Beale dove abruptly beneath the table, resurfacing with a tape recorder as primitive-looking as a trilobite. "I hope you don't mind if I . . . There are several publications that are reasonably, well . . . friendly to me, but mostly I do radio."

"Radio," Shapiro agreed politely. "And this would be for . . . the English-speaking community, I presume."

Beale looked at him blankly. "Not really. There are telephones for that sort of thing. Oh! No." His voice became gluey with attempted modesty. "No, this is a show back home in England, you see. They often ask me for a little story."

England. So, this was a bit more promising. "A show . . . about the arts," Shapiro suggested.

"The arts?" Beale said. "Well, there's not really too much scope for that sort of thing here. This country isn't just churning out the artists, you know. Not a very . . . well, 'favorable climate' I suppose is the expression. Actually, it's a show about just whatever happens to come up. I was glad when your Embassy called and put me on to this one, because there's not really a fantastic amount. You can file only just so often about dead students before people get sick of it. Still, don't think I'm complaining— I'm lucky to be here at all. When I was young, I was simply

frantic to get to this part of the world. Astonishing place.
Have you had much chance to get around? See the sights,
meet the people?"

"I got in last night," Shapiro said.

"Ah," Beale said. "Oh, yes. Well, it is truly staggering.
Very beautiful, as I'm sure you know. And the highlands
—when I first came it was like the dawn of the earth up
there, really. Oh, if I could only . . ." He sighed. "You
know, the Indians here had simply everything at one time.
A calendar. A written language—centuries, centuries, *centuries* before the Spanish came. And all sorts of other magnificent, um—appurtenances. While *we* were still running
around in—" He cast a veiled glance at Shapiro. "Yes.
Well, and the Spanish actually destroyed it all. But you
know that. Burned their books, herded them into villages
with Spanish overseers. Isn't it amazing? The written language was actually de*stroyed*, do you see. The calendar,
the architecture, the books . . . And so, I mean, we're
slaughtering these people and so forth, but we don't really
know anything about them. And if they know anything
about themselves they're not letting on. Who *are* they?
That is, who are *we*? I mean, *they're* here, *we're* here . . .
It's just terribly *strange*." He smiled a misty, wondering
smile, then frowned. "Oh dear. *Any*how, I tried and tried
to get people to send me here. They said, 'But *why*? Where
is it? Nothing *happens* there.' Then, fortunately, there
were all these insurrections and repressions and whatnot,
and that created demand, and so now I've been here over
fifteen years!"

Shapiro opened his mouth; a blob of sound came out.

"I tried to reach García-Gutiérrez yesterday," Beale
said. "But I gathered he hadn't arrived yet. He lives in
Europe a lot of the time now, you know. They told me
he'd be in today, but I thought I'd talk to you instead. I'm
sure he's a wonderful composer. They say he is. But, to
tell you the truth, the man gives me the shivers. I've seen

him around, at parties here, and I just don't like his sort. You know what I mean—well-fed, a bit of a dandy. *Suave.* Eye always on the main chance. A big smile for every colonel. Ladies all love him. Government always showing him off like a big, stuffed . . ." Beale brooded at his drink, then waved over a new one. "Anyhow," he said unhappily, "I've got you."

Shapiro took a sip of water. He would have liked a drink, too, but alcohol affected him unpredictably. Even Beale's alcohol seemed to be making Shapiro mentally peculiar. "Let me ask you," he said. "It isn't actually dangerous here, I suppose."

"Dangerous?" Beale said. "Why? What do you mean? Not for *you*, it isn't. You know"—he sat back and looked at Shapiro with drunken coldness—"I find it *most* comical. How Americans come down here, and they talk about danger. And they talk about *this*, and they talk about *that*. Well, I don't endorse slavery and torture myself, but who are you, may I ask, to talk? Dare I mention who kicked off all this ha-ha 'counterinsurgency' business here in the first place? Dare I mention whose country it was that killed *all* their Indians?"

"Now, look—" Shapiro began.

"A thousand apologies," Beale said. "How true. You're no more responsible for your country than I am for mine. But all this simply jerks my chain, I'm afraid. It simply does. And I mean *dangerous*! I mean this place is hardly in the league of—I mean, one's forever reading, isn't one? How some poor tourist? Who's saved his pennies for years and years and years. Who then *goes* to New York, to see a show on your great Broad*way*, and virtually the instant he arrives gets stabbed in the . . ." He took a violent gulp of his drink. "The—"

"Liver," Shapiro said.

"*Sub*way," Beale said. "Yes." He beamed at Shapiro in surprise. "I don't know why that's so difficult to . . . Oh, look," he exclaimed, as the waiter set down their plates. "Oh, my darling! That *is* nice." He extracted a pair of glasses from his pocket, put them on to peer at his plate, then removed them to clean them on his ropy tie.

Shapiro took a bite of his meal, but Beale's grubbiness had damaged his appetite.

"Of course the highlands are another story," Beale said. "The highlands, the whole countryside, really—still sheer carnage. But here in the city it's just sporadic violence. Of a whatsit sort. Really, about the worst that can happen to you here is Protestants. Random. Of a random sort."

"Protestants?" Shapiro said.

"Evangelicals," Beale said. "So bloody noisy. Haranguing in the streets, massive convocations every which place, speaking in tongues—YAGABAGABAGAGABAGAGA." He sighed. "Now, don't think I'm prejudiced, please. I'm Protestant myself. But that's the point, isn't it? That one can slag off one's own group, though one would never— That is, I, for instance, would never, oh, say, call . . . a Jew, for example, a '*kike*'—that's *your* prerogative. But all that shouting is simply not the point of speech. I mean, the point of speech is— Well, that is just very simply not the point. And it can be terribly, just terribly annoying when you're trying to conduct an interview or what have you, as you and I are here today."

"Perhaps . . ." Shapiro began with difficulty. "That is, perhaps, speaking of the interview, perhaps there's something you'd like to ask me."

"Ah," Beale said. "Right you are." He smiled, then frowned. "But the thing is, old man—I'm afraid I'm not all that familiar with . . . If you could help me out a bit. That is, perhaps we'd best stick to rather general concepts."

Shapiro nodded. "If you wish. What . . . for example, were you thinking we might—"

"Yes," Beale said. "Hmm. Well, I suppose we might talk

about your . . . oh, impressions, for example, of the country . . ."

Shapiro looked at him. "I only arrived last—"

"Last night," Beale said impatiently. He drummed his fingers on the tape recorder. "Well, but just generally, you know. Just something . . . spontaneous."

Shapiro pressed his fingers to the corners of his eyes.

"Not acceptable. I see, not acceptable," Beale said, bitterly. "Well, in that case . . . we could talk, for example, about what it feels like to come down here as an American."

"As an American?" Shapiro said. "I'm not *down* here as an American. I'm not down here *as* anything. I'm down here as a *pianist*."

"Yes," Beale said. "Quite."

Heat began to creep over Shapiro's skin as Beale stared at him.

"You know," Beale said, "I've always wondered. And this is something that I think would be very interesting to the radio audience. How do instrumentalists feel about their relationship—that is, via music, of course—to the composer?"

"What are you—" Shapiro began.

"Well, the very *word*—" Beale said. "That is, the word *literally*, well, it literally *means*—well, instru*men*talist. I mean, you're a—"

"Excuse me," Shapiro said. "I've got to . . . get to a phone."

Shapiro fled into a system of corridors and polyp-like lobbies or reception rooms. Oh, to be alone! The men's room? Maybe not. Well, actually, there was a phone booth. Shapiro sat down inside it, shutting himself into an oceanic silence. Beyond the glass wall people floated by—huge, serene, assured, like exhibits. Shapiro leaned against the wall. He rested his hand on the phone as though it were the hand of an old lover. Absently, he stroked the receiver, then lifted it, releasing a loud electronic jeer—the sound, as silence is not, of emptiness. He would tell Beale that he was unwell, that he had to go rest.

Shapiro paused at the entrance to the restaurant. Beale was sitting at the table alone, his narrow shoulders hunched and his spaceship head bent over the tape recorder as he spoke into it. There was urgency in Beale's posture, and his face was anguished. What could he be saying? Shapiro took a step closer.

"Ah!" Beale said, clicking off the machine with a bright smile, as though he'd been apprehended in some mild debauchery. "Get through?"

"Excuse me?" Shapiro said.

"Get your call through?"

"Oh," Shapiro said. He sat down and passed his hands across his face. "No."

"No," Beale agreed with unfocussed sympathy. "Oh, it's all so difficult. *So* difficult. Now—" He smiled sentimentally. Amazingly, he appeared to have completely forgotten he'd been in the process of attacking Shapiro. "Not to worry—we're going to get a very nice little segment about you. In fact"—he twinkled slyly—"I've already done something by way of an intro. Your name and so on, you're down here for the festival, you'll be playing the García-Gutiérrez . . . Hmm." He removed his glasses to study a crumpled piece of paper. "And, let's see." He turned on the machine and spoke into it again. "You've played the piece before with great success . . . Mr. Shapiro, I understand." He nodded encouragingly and indicated the machine.

Shapiro looked at it. "Yes," he said, wearily.

Beale gave him a wounded glance. "In fact, you premièred the piece in the U.S., I believe."

Shapiro closed his eyes.

"Yes," Beale said. He took a deep breath through his nose. "Well, *any*how, that was back in, let's see . . . nineteen . . . goodness me! You must be very fond of it."

"Well," Shapiro said, "I mean, it *is* in my repertory . . ."

Beale emitted a giggle, or hiccup. "I have a set of little spoons," he said. "Tiny little silver things. For olives or something of the sort, that someone gave a great-aunt of mine as a wedding present. And somehow *I've* ended up with them."

Shapiro opened his eyes and looked at Beale.

"Well, I don't throw them out, I mean, do I?" Beale said. "I say." He frowned. "Are you not going to . . . ?" He waved at Shapiro's plate.

"No, no," Shapiro said. "Go ahead. Please."

"Thank you." Beale switched off the tape recorder and placed Shapiro's full plate on top of his own empty one. "We'll go on in a minute. And I think we'll get something nice, don't you? Most people like doing radio. It's a lovely medium, lovely. Do you know what I especially like about it?" He interrupted himself to eat, then continued. "One meets people. Oh, I know one does in any profession—it can hardly be avoided. But I mean one *goes out* to meet people, on an equal basis. The voice—it's freeing, wouldn't you agree? Yet intimate. There one is, a great glob of . . . oh . . . pork pie!" His eyes gleamed briefly with lust. "But I mean all one's qualities and circumstances just . . . globbed together, if you see what I mean. The good, the bad, the . . . pointless . . ." He paused again, and rapidly forked food into his mouth. "But with radio, you see, there's a way to separate out the real bit. And all the rest of it—I mean one's body, one's face, one's age . . . even, even"— he glanced around as though bewildered—"even the place where one is sitting! Well, one is free of it, isn't one? One sees how free one really is.

"Great *leaps*. Teleportation. The world is so . . . *roomy*. So full of oddments. But there's that now-you-see-it, now-you-don't quality about life that makes one so very nervous. Danger, as you pointed out just now, yourself. Danger simply everywhere. Everything destroyed, lost, forgotten . . . Well, that's what they want, you know, most of them. *'There's nothing about it in the reports,'* they'll tell you. They'll say it straight to your face. Of course there are ghosts, people say. I suppose that's some help. But a ghost is simply not terribly . . . *communicative*. They haunt, they grieve, that sort of thing. But it's all rather general, you see. Because they don't much really talk.

"Oh, didn't you just love it when you were a boy? It's raining outside, your mum's still working in the shop, you haven't a friend in the world, then you turn on the radio, and someone's talking—to *you*. Oh, my darling! Someone is talking to you, and you don't know, before you turn that radio on, who will be there, or what thing they've found to tell you on that very day, at that very moment. Maybe someone will talk to you about cookery. Maybe someone will talk to you about a Cabinet minister. And then that particular thing is *yours*, do you see what I mean? Who *knows* whether it's something worth hearing? Who *knows* whether there's someone out there to hear it! It's a leap of faith, do you see? That both parties are making. Really the most enormous leap of faith." He paused to devour the food remaining on Shapiro's plate, and then looked helplessly into Shapiro's eyes. "I mean, I find that all enormously, just enormously . . ." He shook his head and turned away.

Shapiro set his alarm for 6 a.m., and slipped out of the hotel before Penwad could come for him, consequences be damned. *Ha-ha*—the day was his! Screechy traffic flew cheerfully through the streets, and toxins gave the air a silvery, fishlike flicker as the sun bobbed aloft on waves of industrial waste.

Shapiro walked and walked. He passed through grand neighborhoods, where armed guards lounged in front of high, white walls. And he passed through poor neighborhoods, where children, bloated with hunger, played in the gutters, their eyes dreamy and wild with drugs. Beyond the surrounding slopes lay the countryside—the gorgeous, blood-drenched countryside.

In some parts of the city Indians congregated on the sidewalk. Some sold chewing gum or trinkets on the corners, some seemed to be living the busy and inscrutable life of the homeless. Their clothing was filthy and tattered, but glorious nonetheless, Shapiro thought, glorious, noble, celebratory—like the banners of an army in rout.

Shapiro considered them with terror. The destitute. People who were almost invisible, almost inaudible. People to whom almost anything could be done: *other* people. At home, in the last five or ten years they had encamped in Shapiro's neighborhood. At first he thought of them as a small and temporary phenomenon. But now they were everywhere—sleeping in parks or on the pavement, ranging through the city night and day, hungry and diseased, in ragged suits and dresses acquired in some other life.

Everyone had become used to them; no one remembered how shocking it had been only a few years earlier to see someone curled up in a doorway, barefoot in freezing temperatures. Most of the time they were just a group at the periphery of Shapiro's vision. But when a student failed to show up for a lesson, or no concert work materialized, or the price of the newspaper went up, or some unexpected expense arose, Shapiro's precious hands would tingle. Injury? Arthritis? Even as it was, daily life was beginning to eat away at Shapiro's small savings. And at such times Shapiro would see those *other* people with an individualized and frigid clarity, would search their faces for proof that each was in some reliable way different from him, as though he were a dying man approaching the gauzy crowds waiting for judgment.

And they—what were they seeing? Perhaps he and his kind seemed a ghostly population to *them*—distant, fading . . . Perhaps at some terrible border you'd simply leave behind everything that you now considered life, forget about once precious concerns, as though they were worn-out shirts or last year's calendar or old lists of things that long ago it had seemed important to accomplish.

Oh, it was probably true, as Caroline had sometimes said, that his fears were irrational. That he'd always find some way to manage. But when the door closed behind her that day he ought to have understood—yes, he thought, that was the moment he ought to have understood—that success, the sort of success Penwad's letter seemed to promise for him again, was something he could just, finally, forget about.

But he had understood nothing; he'd simply sat there numb—for hours—until Lady Chatterley threw herself forward in a frenzy of carpet shredding. "Stop that," he'd said. "Stop, O.K., please?" He'd flicked a finger at her rear, and she'd leapt, snarling. The truth was he had always been a little afraid of the cat. She was Caroline's, but Jim, evidently, was allergic.

Shapiro supposed that, to whatever extent Caroline was thinking about *him*, she would be imagining him in debonair company here, taking part in animated and witty conversations of a sort no living person had ever experienced. Shapiro felt short of breath, as though Caroline were suffocating him with a pillow. "This is a wonderful opportunity for Aaron," she could be assuring Jim at this very instant. "Really it is." Oh, yes. *He*, Shapiro, must be happy so she could be.

An Indian child playing nearby in the street skinned a knee and howled for his mother. Shapiro felt an almost uncontainable sorrow, as though he were just about to cry himself. But to cry it's necessary to imagine the comforter.

Caroline had never cared what things were really like. He'd once overheard her saying thank you to a recorded message. Everything was nice, pleasant, good. If he spoke truthfully to her, she couldn't hear him. She despised no one. Those who were not nice, pleasant, happy simply ceased to exist.

Shapiro was ravenous. He entered an inviting little restaurant. Inside, it was very dark, but low-hanging, green-shaded lamps made a pool of light over each table.

The waiter spoke no English, but was agreeable when Shapiro pointed at a nearby diner's plate of soup. But there had been a time—truly there had—when Caroline actually loved him, had been fascinated by him, not just by his reputation. For a moment he saw her distinctly. She stood holding Lady Chatterley, gazing into space with a baffled sorrow. "Caroline—" he said.

Had he spoken aloud? Three men at a neighboring table were staring at him with a volatile blend of loathing and amusement. All three were mammoth. One appeared to be a North American; he and one of the others wore pistols, visible even in the restaurant's pleasant gloom, beneath their shirttails.

The waiter, bearing soup, interposed himself; Shapiro gestured fervent thanks. He took a spoonful of the soup. It was clear, and delicious. *Food,* he thought.

Plus rent. Plus utilities . . . Yes, tonight the stage of a concert hall, a tuxedo. A party, champagne, adulation. But tomorrow it was back to cat fur.

The waiter arrived with a second plate for him, huge and unexpected. A pretty selection of things that seemed to have been cooked in the broth. Mmm. Shapiro leaned into the light of his hanging lamp to poke around at it— carrots, onions, white beans, cabbage, celery, a small . . . haunch, something that looked . . . like . . . a snout . . .

One of the men at the next table chuckled softly. Shapiro glanced at them involuntarily again, and they stared back, their faces framing the teardrop of light from their hanging lamp. Then one of them, still staring, reached up and un-screwed the bulb.

The enfeebled musicians threw themselves on García-Gutiérrez's last, idiotic, triumphal chord. What had happened? Shapiro felt as though he'd awakened to find himself squatting naked in a glade, blinking up at a chort-ling TV crew that had just filmed him gnawing a huge bone. Had he played well or badly? He hardly knew. He'd played in a frenzy—the banal sonorities, the trivial purposes, the trashy approximations of treasures forged in the inferno of other composers' souls. Lacerating ribbons of notes streamed from his hands as he tried to flog something out of the piece, but it had simply sat there over them all —a great, indestructible, affirming block of suet.

The sparse audience stopped fanning themselves with their programs and made some little applause. Seething with confusion and misery, Shapiro stood to take his bow, and caught a glimpse of a man who could only be García-Gutiérrez, opaque and dignified in the face of tribute. At the sight, Shapiro reexperienced the frictional response of his skin, seventeen years earlier, to the man's blandishments, like an acquiescence to unwelcome sensual pleasure.

Outside, Penwad resumed his post at Shapiro's elbow. "We'll just stick around here for a few minutes," he said nervously, "then round everyone up and get going to the reception. Oh. I don't believe you've met. Joan."

"That was lovely," Joan said. "Just lovely. You know, we looked for you at your hotel today. We felt sure you'd want to see our Institute of Indigenous Textiles."

"Oh, Lord—" Shapiro floundered. "Yes! No, absolutely. I—"

"We left messages at the desk," Penwad said.

"Well," Joan said. "Those *people* at the desk . . ."

Night had ennobled the Center. Musicians and members of the audience milled about in the uncertain radiance of stars and klieg lights. A slow, continuous combustion of garbage sent up bulletins of ruin from the hut-blistered gorges, which were quickly snuffed out by the fragrance drifting down from the garlanded slopes of the Gold Zone.

Penwad pointed out various luminaries. There was a Cultural Attaché, a Something Attaché, several Somethings from the Department of Something—it was all a matter for experts.

"And do you see the lady over there?" Joan said, nodding discreetly in the direction of a stunning woman with arched eyebrows and a blood-red mouth. She was bending toward a boy who appeared to be about fifteen. "Our hostess. The reception for you is at her house. And her son. Well, as you see. They're identical. You'll enjoy talking to him. Perfect English—he's going to boarding school up in the States, and he just loves it. He loves to meet our visitors. The father's cattle, you know. Special, special people. Josefina's a marvel. You're not going to believe the house. She's a real force behind culture here. And, you can imagine, *some* of these wives . . ."

"Wonderful people," Penwad said. "And of course *you* two know each other from way back."

García-Gutiérrez had joined them, murmuring thanks to Shapiro. He was as handsome as before, though he'd be over sixty—a great tree of a man, at which age was hacking away fruitlessly. His loaflike body was still powerful; his long arms and legs, the musculature so emphatic one felt aware of its operations beneath the very correct clothing, the straining neck and jaws, the hooded eyes. "I feel that you brought something new to my music tonight," he was saying. "Something of a darkness, perhaps." In the man's lingering examination Shapiro felt the blind focussing, adversarial and comprehending, the arousal of the hunter. "Very interesting . . ."

Oh, that night seventeen years earlier! When it was reasonable for Shapiro to assume that he himself was going to be one of the favored. That he, too, would be respected, dignified, happy . . . The audience that night! How gratifying Shapiro had found their ardor then, how loathsome now, in memory. How thrilled they had been, seeing their own bright reflection in all the weightless glitter.

"We'll talk more, you and I, at the reception," García-Gutiérrez whispered, and glided off with Penwad and Joan to a huddle of musicians, who watched their approach with alarm.

Shapiro's heart jumped and blazed. People were beginning to float toward the parking lot. He played *better* now than he had then, but it made no difference—*no difference at all*. And those nights at the stage door; the faces, golden in the light, diamond earrings winking in the gold light . . . All the beautiful women. Gone now. No matter. What was it they'd adored? Those ardent glances, warm in the glow of his fame, the first shock, at the stage door, of Caroline's great, light eyes. Af*firm*ing, af*firm*ing—oh, what was he to *do*? They couldn't even put him in the decent hotel! Caroline was walking down the street. She wore a dainty little dress. The sun was on her hair, but black shadows swung overhead, and battling armies clanged behind her in the dust. Men and women lay on the sidewalk, their torn clothing exposing sticky lesions. One of them shifted painfully and held out a disintegrating paper cup. Caroline paused, opened her purse, and took out a quarter.

"Are you all right?" someone asked. Shapiro blinked, and saw the boy, the son of the woman who was having the reception. "You must be famished." He regarded Shapiro with the merry, complicitous look of a young person who anticipates approval. "What a workout for you, I think, that piece of G.-G.'s. But we'll have plenty of food back at home—the cooks have been racing around all day. Oh! Well, look at this. *He's* smart. He brought his own." The boy directed an amused glance toward Beale, who was ambling toward them, disemboweling an orange.

"Hello," Shapiro said. The boy's tone—despicable. He hoped Beale hadn't caught it.

"Would you care for any?" Beale said. "I'm afraid it's somewhat . . ." He nodded to the boy, who nodded distantly back. "You know," he said to Shapiro, "I'm sorry if I lost my bottle a bit last night. I tend to go on, from time to time, about one thing and another. Hope I said nothing to offend."

"Not at all," Shapiro said. *It made no difference at all.*

"Good good." A pink and rumpled smile wandered across Beale's face. "Goody goody."

Beale was making a complete mess of his orange. A small piece of peel had lodged in his webby tie. The boy was looking at it. "Oh," Beale said, glancing up. "Sorry. Difficult to handle. You know, it's strange about oranges, isn't it? They're so alluring. Irresistible, really. I mean, that color, for example—*orange*. And the *glossiness*. And that delicious smell they have. But it's all very strange. I mean, what good does it do them? They can't enjoy it. At least, so one supposes. All their deliciousness, do they get any fun out of it? No. It only gets them eaten. Isn't that strange? I mean, what is it for, from their point of view? I suppose you might ask the same of a flower. Flowers have sort of got it all, don't they. Looks, scent . . . But they have absolutely no way to appreciate that!" He giggled. "For all we know, they think of themselves as grotesque."

The boy was considering Beale with a dreamy, meditative look. His stare idled among the stains on Beale's suit. "Excuse me," he said. He smiled briefly at Shapiro. "I should go find some of our"—he glanced at Beale—"guests."

Beale gasped. "Did you hear that?" he said. "Little swine. Vicious little prick. As if I were going to crash the party! As if anyone *could* crash their fucking miserable party—they'll have half the fucking *army* at the gate."

"Mr. Shapiro, Mr. Shapiro," someone was calling.

"It's Joan," Shapiro said, hesitating. He heard his name again. "Just a moment!" he called out. "Just a moment," he said to Beale. "I've got to—"

"Little putrid viper," Beale was saying, as Shapiro hurried off.

"We're ready to leave now," Joan said cheerily as Shapiro approached. "Everyone's gone down to the parking lot."

"Just a moment," he said. "I'll be right—"

"Don't be long," she sang with warning gaiety, and tweaked the lapel of his tuxedo.

"I'll be right—" he said. A tuxedo! He might just as well be wearing grease-stained overalls with his name embroidered on the pocket. "One more minute." He hurried back to find Beale, but Beale had disappeared.

"Hello?" Shapiro said. "Hello? I just wanted to—" But where could Beale have gone to? How arrogant that young boy was! How— Well, and the fact was, Shapiro thought, a man in livery could hardly afford to turn up his nose at a sloppy suit. "Hello?" he said again.

For a moment there was just a gentle surf of night noises, but then Shapiro made out Beale's voice, faint, very faint. Following the sound, he saw Beale, a dark shape, crouched in the corner of a concrete trough that must have been intended as some sort of reflecting pool.

Beale was speaking into his tape recorder. His voice had a stealthy, incantatory tone. "And now . . ." But the little noises of the night were washing away his words. ". . . take you to the party I promised you. It's . . . prominent family here."

There was an oily stain, or fissure, Shapiro saw, at the bottom of the trough. "And any important artist from . . . And what a beautiful . . . high, white . . . and tasteful objets d'art. But tonight . . . to take you out into the . . ."

Shapiro stood as still as he could and strained to hear.

"How lovely it . . ." Beale crooned into the machine. "Fountains, flowers . . . And . . . of chirpings! Croakings! Can you hear, my darling?"

Beale held the tape recorder up in the lifeless trough. Shapiro shuddered—a slight chill was coming down from the mountains.

"And those other sounds—do you hear?" Beale said. His voice was growing louder or Shapiro's ears were adjusting, seeking out the words. "The little plashings?" Beale said. "The fountain, yes, but what else? Not Spanish. But a language, yes! Just so. A language that's much, much older.

"Yes, because we're right across from the servants' quarters. And right there, on the servants' portico, the children are playing. The Indian children. Their mothers are all inside, serving little goodies to the guests. Can you hear the chatter behind us, of the guests?" Shapiro closed his eyes. Yes, he could hear it, the chatter, the pointless chatter. And smell the orange-scented garden. Yes—and he could see the children, just beyond the fountain, with their black, black hair, and shrewd, ravishing little faces.

"Good," Beale said. "Yes. And one of the children has a piece of stone or crockery. The others whisper together. They're joining hands—they seem to be inventing a game, don't they? Or reinventing. Some sort of game. Maybe they remember . . ."

Shapiro's name floated up from the parking lot. They were beginning to shout for him. *Yes, yes,* he thought fiercely, and held up a hand as though both to forestall and to shush them. *In a moment . . .* He sat down, as quietly as he could manage, on the cool concrete. Another moment and he'd go.

"When I first came to this country," Beale was telling the tape recorder, "the sky was a blue dome over the highlands. People had more food then, and weren't so afraid. When you went hiking through the villages, suddenly there would be a waterfall, and fifty, a hundred, two hundred women, swaying along the mountain, coming to do their washing."

Ah! Along the mountain, coming closer. Their faces were in shadow still, and indistinct. But any minute, any minute now . . .

"I wanted to speak to them," Beale said. "But how could I? I was only an apparition! But—are you listening, my darling? I know they're still there—they'll always be there, beyond the curtain of blood." Beale stretched himself out in the trough, tucking the tape recorder under his head like a pillow, and a delicious sensation of rest poured into

Shapiro's body. "I'm tired now." Beale patted the tape recorder. "I think I'll sleep. But it's going to be all right. Because the first thing. In the morning. When the sun is up again and shining? I'll start back off to them. And finally we'll speak. Please be there with me. They'll be so happy. I know they will. Because everyone has something, some little thing, my darling, they've been waiting so long to tell you . . ."

Tlaloc's Paradise

THE YOUNG AMERICAN AT THE DOOR WAS LOOK-
ing for a place to rent; Jean knew that as soon as she saw
him. No, almost that soon, but in fact she was first seized,
facing him there, by the violent and irrational certainty
that he had come to tell her something—that he'd come
down from the States to tell her something about Leo.

It was a moment before she began to thaw out and catch
up with the boy's disorderly excuses. His name was Mark
something, he was telling her; he'd been talking to a man
in a café near the square. This man had said she and her
husband were likely to know if there were a place available. He was sorry to just show up at her home like this,
but he'd gone to the shop earlier and found it closed. He'd
tried to phone, of course, but the phones just didn't seem
to *work*, and since the man in the café had given him di-
rections to the house . . . How did people manage, by the
way, with these phones? Though that was part of the
charm of the country, wasn't it?

He looked at her, and immediately began to apologize
again: a cliché; it must be no end irritating to hear this
sort of thing constantly. And the fact was, he rarely found
himself anyplace where phones did work. But sometimes
one just opened one's mouth, and out came some—

"Of course," Jean said. "Well, and besides." He was large, and almost puffy, as though with fatigue, or some mild, chronic inflammation. "Anyhow, I don't think anyone would argue that malfunction and charm are related, at least here."

"Hmm." The boy frowned. " 'Related.' Right. *Complicated . . .*"

"I'm afraid I don't know of any places at the moment," she said. "Leo would, probably, but you'll have to come back. I'm sorry. I'm afraid he's up in the States right now."

"Ah," the boy said.

"I'm sorry," Jean said. "You just missed him. He only went up this morning."

"Well." The boy frowned again, nodding. "Thanks. Too bad. Oh— Should I come back sometime? Yes, you said that, didn't you."

"Some other time," Jean said. "Yes."

"So," he said. "I'll try again next week?"

"Fine," she said.

He was so big, just standing there.

He ducked his head. "Well," he said. "Thanks."

She sighed. "Would you like to come in?"

Inside, he seemed even larger, and more formless, as though her fatigue were allowing him to spread into the far reaches of the large room. "Did you take the bus?" she asked, attempting to anchor her attention to one spot.

He had. He was pleased to be asked, she saw; the ride was short—she and Leo were no more than twenty minutes from town—but it was confusing, and, for strangers, difficult to negotiate. Clearly the boy was a good traveler—he'd found her after only one day in town. Though he'd been in the country, he seemed to be saying now, for several weeks.

As he talked, his shadowy bulk moved here and there, beyond the soft canopy of lamp- and candlelight, vaguely inspecting her emissaries, as it amused Leo to call them— the tall figures she'd constructed over the years, of various materials. "The man in the café *mentioned* you were a sculptor," the boy said, as though it were astonishing that this should, in fact, be so. *Mark*, she reminded herself. They looked like they were loitering there, in the dim margins, or massing.

"Welded?" the boy said.

"That one, yes." Fine, something she could talk about almost automatically. "A number of the early ones are, but I haven't worked in metal for years."

He hovered near one of the figures, peering. "Interesting," he said.

His caution made Jean smile. "You don't have to . . . I have no great stake in their quality, as it turns out."

Each had represented—witnessed and represented—pressing matters; attitudes, preoccupations . . . Pressing at the time. But eventually each figure was merely subsumed into the slowly expanding crowd. "It's just something I enjoy."

"Mmm." Mark frowned. "Enjoy . . ."

It wasn't his size, exactly—it was his obstacle-like quality. Still, Jean reminded herself. New places. Things abruptly inflating with a puzzling significance, or, just as suddenly, draining of any significance at all. She remembered: Herself and Leo, sitting gingerly, like this boy, wary lest some chance phrase burst into flames . . . "There shouldn't be much of a problem with a house for you," she said. "You're off-season, and there are a few vacation places Leo's been looking after."

Actually, there were probably some things she should take care of herself—plants, lights to outwit the tireless thieves . . . Neither she nor Leo had given any of that a thought in all the chaos of booking his ticket, getting in touch with friends in San Antonio, getting him on the plane. "When Leo's back he'll . . ." She sighed.

"I'd hate to have . . . I mean, well—a *house*. I hadn't really been thinking of a whole— And I'd hate to have . . . your husband go to trouble if—"

"Leo likes it," Jean said. "Can you imagine? Well, who knows. Maybe that's the sort of thing you like, too. I can't stand it myself. Dealing with the propane, dealing with keys, dealing with cleaning girls. But I suppose it makes Leo feel . . ." She picked up a cushion near her on the sofa, looked at it, then let it drop. "Well, he likes it, that's all. That's all."

Mark took a deep breath. "Also, the price is something I'd . . . I mean, I don't have all that much—"

"Of course," Jean said. No, obviously this boy wouldn't have any money. "Well, that's something everyone down here . . . Anyhow, owners tend to want someone just to . . . Actually, you know, I've probably got all kinds of keys around here somewhere. Of course, even if I could find them I wouldn't know what key was what. Leo always says he's going to label, but you know how it is. *Years* go by . . ." Her head felt rubbery. She pushed her hair back; she'd forgotten to wash it in the morning.

The boy was watching her. "Oh, listen," she said. "Would you— How stupid I am tonight. Mark. Would you like something to drink?"

"Yes," he said. "Sure, great. Oh, but maybe you— God, it's late. I hadn't—"

"No," she said. "Believe me. I never sleep till two."

"Well, great, then," he said.

He kept his eyes lowered; he seemed almost afraid to look at her. But when he did, the intensity of his scrutiny was outrageous, practically comical. What did he suppose it was that licensed him to display such curiosity? The fact of his youth? His status as newcomer? There was nothing to prevent her from being annoyed, Jean thought, just as he blinked, and turned his gaze to the French doors.

She watched his large, moist eyes. "So," she said. "What's up?"

He shook his head and turned back to her, looking bewildered. "Lots of stars . . ."

"Oh, lots," Jean said. "Always. Very busy at night."

So busy. She'd never gotten over it—that sky, this room, dim and glossy with tiles and Mexican mirrors; all the faces amid the complex refractions—the faces of those figures of hers, of the pre-Columbian pieces and the masks she and Leo had scattered around; the brilliant Mexican night beyond the doors, with its festive, agitated stars and roses. Sometimes she and Leo stood here stricken, with all of that right around them, as though it were something that had eluded them . . . "Oh, heavens," she said. "Sorry. Usually I'm a bit more—Listen, all I can offer you is Canadian Club. Well, there's beer or tequila, but you'll get deeply sick of those if you're sticking around. We always used to have these great, sloshing reservoirs of alcohol, but I'm afraid we seem to be down to bedrock. The dreadful truth is, we're utterly at the mercy of whatever anyone grabs on the way through duty-free."

He'd picked up a small stone carving from the coffee table. "Actually, I don't really drink," he said, turning the figure over in his hand. "Do you have a Coke, or something like that? But really, I don't want to keep you up."

How often was she supposed to ask him to stay? "Pre-Columbian," she said. "Not a very good piece, and in terrible condition, but I like it."

"A big personality," he said.

"Oh, yes," she said. "That's Tlaloc. Very important—A harvest-cycle type. In charge of rain, also militia. He has this special little heaven you got to go to if you were a warrior, or died of drowning. A friend of ours brought it the last time he came through. He has great luck finding interesting ones. We have a little Olmec lady he brought us. And the one over there's Chac-Mool, the messenger. Who carried the sun around—Corrigan brought us that, too. And in fact he's responsible for most of our masks."

She reached over for the figure Mark was holding. It lay in her palm as she looked at it. "Good lord, you're dying of thirst, aren't you. You'll have to— I was up at the most horrible—"

"I'm sorry," Mark said. "You must be—"

"Mark, you know, people don't get *tired* when they get older, they get *impatient*. Oh, look—" Right, hardly his fault that she— "Is Sprite okay? Didn't even know we had it."

"Perfect," he said unhappily. "Sprite."

"Sprite it is." It had been a long time now since Corrigan had last been through. He hadn't even been living in his Mixtec village then, just out in the desert by himself. And he'd seemed to be floating, ever so slightly away from them. She'd thought perhaps she was imagining it, but looking back she was sure. Of course eccentricities often began as choices, or tools, or positions. But they could take you captive . . . "You're not going to have some sort of religious crisis, Mark, are you, if I have a drink?"

"No—" He cleared his throat. "Oh, not at all. I mean, I used to drink, myself."

"You used to?" she said. "My God. How old are you?"

"Twenty-eight." He looked at her. "Is that—"

"Reasonable," she said. "I suppose. And neutral. Insofar as I'm concerned, at least."

"Strange," he said. "Isn't it? Such a narrow range. I mean, I can't tell at all how old you are. And then it just closes up behind you again, doesn't it. I mean, I can't tell if someone's seventeen or twenty-two."

"Seventeen or twenty-two," Jean said. "Ha. I can't tell if someone's seventeen or fifty. Jesus, you know, if the truth be told, I *loathe* CC. And you know what else? I can't even remember who the cheapskate was who . . . You see, at one time we used to have all sorts of . . . Ah, well. The fact is, people simply don't come down here the way they used to."

"No." He frowned. "I suppose not."

Twenty-eight. Yes, she could see it. He was boyish-looking, and easily unbalanced, but a backlog of worry seemed to slow, or blur, his movements. Although his features were unremarkable and blunt, his expression reflected with great purity the finest modulations of his embarrassment and confusion. Her filthy hair! Her undisguised rancor! Well, all something for him to contemplate, wasn't it; Jean noted dispassionately the thorny little tendrils of amusement uncurling within her at the consternation she was causing her guest.

"When is—when is your husband expected back?" he asked.

"It shouldn't be long," she said. "He's just up for tests."

"I'm sorry," he said. "Is that bad?"

She rubbed the bridge of her nose. Amazing, the tiny, tiny things you could do to make yourself feel better. Rubbing the bridge of your nose, your temples . . . There was some spot on her palm where Leo could rest his thumb, and the muscles of her back and neck would relax . . .

"I'm sorry," the boy said again.

"It's just tests," Jean said.

She propped her feet—nice feet, small feet, even in their funny sneakers—against the coffee table and leaned back, looking at the ceiling. Mark had gotten his hands into the middle of some futile gesture; from the corner of her eye she watched him trying to resolve it.

"Anyway, though, it still is interesting," he said. "Isn't it."

"Yes?" She lifted an eyebrow. "What is?"

"This place." He squirmed, but persevered. "This country. Even though people don't come here as much. It's still interesting."

"Ah," Jean said.

"The man in the café was interesting," he offered after a moment.

Jean meted out a glance of enquiry.

"The man who told me about you and Mr. Soyer."

"Ah, yes."

"He was German, I think. Well, I mean, he was."

"Plenty of Germans around," Jean said.

"This one was old—"

"Plenty of old Germans."

"A real character. He kept making these sort of . . . dark allusions. You know, he'd say, 'The *coffee* at this place is better than the *coffee* next door. Have you *tried theirs*?' It was as though he was a spy, and I was a spy, too, only no one had bothered to let me know."

Jean laughed abruptly. Beyond the seismic dislocation of her body she saw the boy peering at her with hope.

"And then for hours afterwards," he said, "everything seemed like that. As though everyone was telling me something else."

"Sounds like Schacht," Jean said.

"Actually, though, you know what?" Mark said. "Everything *is* like that, sort of, isn't it? I mean everyone *is* telling you . . . *is* telling you— Oh, and he had a kind of funny eye, I think, too."

"Yup," Jean said. "Schacht." Schacht sat at the cafés all day, a hairy disk of a spider, hors de combat. His legs dangled from his chair and one eye would drift enigmatically in and out of alignment while he waited for Mexican boys. A sufficient number were on hand, always, desperate for a meal—the price was no greater than an hour or two of boredom and the humorous remarks of one's friends.

"He was sort of nice, though, I think," Mark said. Jean looked at him, but his face had gone deceptively blank. "He seemed lonely."

"Lonely," Jean said. "Well, if you can't really talk about your life—I mean, people manage to believe all sorts of things about themselves, don't they. And it's very isolating to have an official view of your life with something else locked up somewhere."

"Do you—" A slightly gluttonous shine appeared in Mark's stare. "God. I've never actually met anyone from that—"

"Well, who knows, really," Jean said. She and Leo always referred to Schacht as "the Nazi," but his hand, as it clung to hers in greeting, was the hand of any old man

—tremulous and age-spotted. "Actually, though, it's interesting—there's a place here, in town. Run by an Austrian family. And all the old Germans and Austrians in the area sit around shoveling down great slabs of swine and what-not, that's cooked and served by Mexicans. And they're all schmoozing away in German. Pretending, believe it or not, that they were born in Mexico, or that they were in this or that resistance. Oh, I mean there are bound to be a few old Jews, and a few old déclassé aristos from one side of the fence or the other, and maybe one or two of them really did hold a match to party headquarters at Berchtesgaden or whatever. But that was simply not the story with most of them, obviously—the place is swarming with fake passports and fake histories. But whoever those people were once, they're all sitting together now, missing the same real pastries, the same real streets . . ."

Mark nodded. "Oh, strangeness," he said. "Opacity."

As he and Jean raised their glasses to one another she saw a little heap—translucent, gelatinous, torn things. Memories, discarded by the barbed wire under a tiny, oil-colored sun. A little heap, growing on the icy soil as a shivering procession filed, naked and desperate as angels, past the guard post, where meaningless new memories were being issued. "Anyhow." Jean closed her eyes. "Pardon me, but another burning question—what's brought you down?"

"Oh, me." Mark shook his head. "Well, me. All right, let's —So who am I, what am I doing here, what—hmm. Okay, I was studying. Engineering, which is not such a ridiculous . . . But then I was finished, and I realized, my God, you know. This is my *life*, which I sort of hadn't grasped until then. And also at the same time, more or less, my father died. And I realized I hadn't known too much about him. And everything that I didn't know actually didn't *exist* any longer. And what did still exist was any little thing I did happen to know . . . And everything was just *flying* off the face of the earth, just flying *off* . . .

But I didn't know how to . . . But anything less just seemed pointless. So I began to just sort of rush around, I guess. For a while I was catching salmon. For big companies off the coast of Alaska." He looked at her. "It's amazingly hard."

She nodded.

"And then I was working in the oil fields. Along the Amazon. Which isn't so easy either, in fact." He stared at the little stone carving on the table. "Anyhow, my Spanish isn't that bad. So." He looked out the doors again, voyaging.

"Where did you stay last night?" Jean asked quietly.

He sighed hugely, coming to rest. "Oh, I've put myself at El Parque. It's kind of a splurge. I mean, the room is fairly primitive—except for the bugs. Those bugs—wow, *advanced*. But I've got a view. I look right out onto the square, you know? So this morning I ran out to the market for oranges and bread, and then I came back and had breakfast on my balcony."

Jean leaned back and smiled.

"That square," he said. "It's really . . ."

"Hypnotizing," she said. "I know. And the incredible thing is, it simply never changes. It's absolutely eternal. Every day, decade after decade. The children, the old people, the band in the bandshell, the flowers, the fountains . . . Except that the children are always new children and the old people are always new old people and the flowers are always new flowers . . . The sun comes up, the sun goes down—all these years, and we've never gotten tired of it . . ."

"How many years?" Mark leaned forward. "Incidentally."

Jean regarded her glass—the answer seemed to be sleeping, deliciously, at the bottom of her drink. "Well," she said, slowly, "the fact is. We came down in the fifties."

"Mm," he said, with tact so inept that she laughed out loud.

"Yes, hundreds of—"

"Not at—"

"Anyhow," she said, "a lot of us came down then. Terrible things were going on in the States. Comparatively subtle, but nonetheless . . ."

"Oh, right," he said. "My mom and dad used to tell me. How everyone had to look exactly alike, and everyone had to be completely happy . . ."

"Yes . . ." she said. "Well, listen, Mark. You probably don't know much about it, but there were these sort of mild purges . . . You know, nobody was going around killing anybody, so it was all very vague and insidious. It was sort of a warning, really. Later everyone laughed about how absurd it all was, but I tell you, Mark, people just kept on being very, very careful. In their actions and in their thoughts, without actually remembering, or even knowing, exactly why."

He squinted at her, as though he could extract her meaning by looking. "Yes," he said. "Oh, actually, you know, I had a cousin, or something. No. My mom's uncle, Frank, she told me. She was still absolutely furious. The FBI came to the house, and Frank lost his job. But"—Mark looked at Jean with surprise, as though it were he who was hearing the story for the first time—"he wasn't a *Communist*. He was an ichthyologist."

Jean looked at him. "Oh, yeah. Well. Anyhow, Mexico had a lot of glamour at that time. You know, that luster that moves around from place to place. Jesus, Mexico City— You can't— So jaunty. And pretty and chic. And the whole, strange, gorgeous country. The way those names sounded to us—Chiapas, Cuilapan, Pátzcuaro, Tepotzlan, Ixtlán del Rio . . . Imagine how that felt—going where words like that were still alive! And all these fresh memories of bandit-saints and campesino intellectuals and painter-revolutionaries. And wild people from simply everywhere, those people who always go places to start things new . . . There was this one woman—a sort of Russian Gypsy Jew, truly stunning. She'd arrive on horseback. All this *red* hair. Men were simply shooting each other by the score . . ."

Mark nodded respectfully.

"Boring, boring," Jean said. "I know. Jesus Christ, we don't even get *movies* anymore. The currency's so fucking rotten they can't even import movies." She rested her fingertips against her eyes; if she could only keep herself from *talking*, maybe he'd . . .

"Mexico City—" But there was his voice again. Soft, relentless. "Mexico City's gotten pretty difficult, I guess."

"The thing is—" Jean looked at him. "She *died* a week or so ago. Someone happened to tell us. We only heard by chance. She drank. I mean, she was old—considerably older than, than we are— But, I mean, she fell. She fell down the fucking *stairs*."

Mark reddened. "Wow, that's—"

"Isn't it just," Jean said. "Anyhow, difficult, difficult. Yes, difficult, now, Mexico City. We all started off there, of course. Then most of our friends just went back up, but some stayed, and we came down here. For a long time we lived right in town. Our friend Corrigan—the mask guy? —lived right next door to us. Then he moved out here, long before we did. Now he lives way off in hell-and-gone by himself. Well, not by himself in his opinion—he's got one of those hateful little, those dogs. An esquintle, it's called."

"Oh, yes," Mark said. "One of those—"

"It's Aztec, he says, so he speaks to it in Nahuatl."

"Oh." Mark frowned. "That's funny."

"Funny," Jean agreed. "So, Mark. I'm having another of those delicious— How about you? More yum-yum Sprite?"

"Well. Don't mind if I—" He handed her his glass and wiggled his eyebrows elaborately.

"Such talent," she said. "It's actually been a couple of years, now, since we've seen him. I mean, I'm sure he's

fine. Always up to his . . . In fact, we heard he was trying
to generate his own electricity. Out of old socks, you may
be sure, or something."

For a moment her voice split into harmonics, exposing
a chord of other voices, crowding the room. Then a blinding sheet of desert light fell, and against its silence the tiny,
distant figure of Corrigan was walking, walking . . . Jean
closed her eyes. "The last time we saw him, he was teaching it Mixtec, too."

"Pardon?" Mark said.

Jean shook her head.

"Those stars . . ." He stood and went to the French
doors.

There was no haze at all, Jean saw, or softness in the
air. The stars snapped brilliantly against flat black, as if
this were to be their final appearance.

"Strange," he said. "That people would get it into their
heads that those things determined what went on down
here."

"That anything determined what went on down here,"
Jean said.

He stood, looking out at the night. "Who are the women
in red?" he asked.

Jean stood in alarm. "The women—"

"No, sorry," he said. "Not—"

"Oh—" She flopped back down.

"Not here. I meant the women in the square who wear
those long red—"

"Yes, yes—" She'd known just who he meant. But for
an instant she'd thought he was *seeing* them; that they'd
come up here for some reason. For her.

"No, sorry, just—I watched them all day. The way they
glide. Up and down in the square. I couldn't imagine
who—"

"Yes," she said. "Indians. I mean, obviously."

"They look— They don't look—"

"No, not exactly real. A Tzotzil group, but I don't . . .

They're not really from this area; they seem to be . . . well, 'displaced' is how people . . . God, Leo did the most marvelous paintings of them in the square at one time. I wonder—"

"I'd love to see them." Mark squinted eagerly past the fuzzy goldish mass of light in the center of the room.

"Ah, well," Jean said. "There aren't any here, in any case."

All this talk of hers, this evening; all this noise. And now she seemed to have implied this boy should come back. For more talk, more noise. "Actually, I think Leo probably threw all that stuff out when he gave up painting."

Mark started to speak, then stopped.

Jean shrugged. "He didn't think he would ever be good enough," she said clearly.

After a minute Mark spoke. "That's very courageous."

"Is it?" Jean said. "Oh, listen. Courageous, cowardly, who knows. It actually wasn't very painful for Leo to give it up. He just stopped, the same way I just continued. People have different ways of holding on to things. Our friend Corrigan, for example. In a sense he's the most acquisitive person I've ever met. If he sees something that interests him, an unusual mask, for example, or one of those pieces like that little thing on the table, he'll go to any lengths to get ahold of it. But then he just gives it away again as soon as he possibly can. The fact is, it makes Leo happy to give things up. It's a kind of exercise, I suppose. He's never so happy as when he's giving something up, or leaving something behind." The phrase sounded flat to Jean, as she heard herself saying it now, or sententious. Was it true, she wondered— Had it been true at some point? Or was it just something rather like the truth that she and Leo had settled on?

Mark was watching her intently. "Tell me something," he said. "Do you ever think of going back?"

"Back," she said. "And what would that mean, 'back'?"

Every day, how many species was it that disappeared,

now, forever? There was some horrifying statistic—it used to be four hundred a year, she had read somewhere; now it was hundreds every day. And cadres of botanists, zoologists, anthropologists, God only knew what, swarming over the globe with instruments of every sort, praying to catch sight of one rare, precious organism or another as it died. "Oh, of course it's very nice to think—very seductive—that you have some sort of 'home' somewhere, that you could return to, that would make some kind of sense of your life. And Leo and I have always prided ourselves, I suppose, on resisting that. Because, a *place*—I mean, what is that? A place. What you leave, what you go to; here or there, 'home' or 'foreign'— Well, it's all based on, on the most fantastic misunderstanding, isn't it."

But was that true, either? Chiapas, Cuilapan, Pátzcuaro, Tepotzlan, Ixtlán del Rio—ancient fragments irradiated by an ancient light. Yes, what she and Leo had left behind vanished with their departure, and what they'd wanted here had vanished, too. Vanished, not into the past, nor into some relinquished area of fantasy, but into the future. Into the future. Evidence of a continuity, of a fugitive precision would appear without notice—a swift concentration of the afternoon into heavy, golden shapes; a face like a key, glimpsed in the market; a perfect, trembling balance in the square as seen for an instant from a balcony . . . promises.

The nights here still smelled like honey. Jean could still be made happy by the braying of a neighbor's burro. Back when Mexico City had faded and they'd come out here, the nights always smelled of honey and woodsmoke, the days of chocolate and earth and peppers—rich anchos and poblanos in sacks at the market. How clean everything had been! The revolution had left the campesinos as penniless as ever, as clean as bones. They'd worn white; the coarse-loomed cloth showed up in the fields miles away. Roosters woke you, cacti bloomed in the churchyards. Toxins from new industry and traffic seeped into the earth, corroded the organs of the children. One murderous poverty replaced another. Refugees appeared, Indians, fleeing internment and slaughter in Guatemala and the secret wars up here, out in the muffled desert. Corrigan used to bring word of skirmishes. From time to time rumors would flicker through town. Alicia, who cooked for them, might let something slip, or Ramón, who brought the great jars of water. Once in a while, someone was said to disappear —someone's cousin, someone's son . . . The Tzotzil women moved back and forth across the square, in constantly changing configurations of blood red against the white walkways. They approached as you sat by the fountains, under the elegant palms. They stretched out their arms. You could hardly hear their voices. They looked past you, at something that happened in the distance. The tourists, dazzled by the beauty of their clothing and unearthly, famished faces, dropped small sums into their hands. Who were the women in red, they asked.

One shrugged: They were widows.

Often now—whispers of special forces deployed in the desert. Sometimes one would hear faint, high tones in the night, like bullets striking rock— "Was that the phone?" Jean said.

"No," Mark said.

"Ah," Jean said.

"Yes." He stood. "It's late. I'll leave you." His soft voice floated next to her ear. "Thank you, Mrs. Soyer, you've been—"

"Jean," she said. "Hardly." She closed her eyes, and the room blazed again with desert light. Why hadn't she gone up this morning? So long ago, that bright sun. The Tzotzil women would be dozing now, wrapped in lengths of red. Schacht, having a final tequila while he gazed out at the dark square. And up there— The suffocating imminence of drugged sleep? Rapid footsteps down the corridor? Whatever was happening in that white bed, she would wake up here in the mornings, she would go to the shop.

She would come home and eat the food Alicia had pre-
pared, have a drink, look at the stars . . . It had seemed
ridiculous, in all that sunlight, to think of going along.
Ridiculous, and imprudent, as though panic itself were
malignant. All yesterday he had done his little tasks
around the house, around the yard. Even this morning—
He'd looked up at her from his gardening, shading his
eyes against the sun, with the trowel still wedged in the
earth—

"So then." That soft voice. "Next week."

"Next week . . ." Jean repeated, but for moments she
couldn't think what the boy was talking about.

Rosie Gets a Soul

ROSIE DIPS HER BRUSH INTO THE DARK-GREEN
paint and makes a careful little curve with it on the wall.
She does it again, and then she does it again. Jamie was
right—a monkey could do this.

When the green dries, Jamie will show her how to add
another color, and, when that dries, another. And pretty
soon, at the rate Jamie is painting, there will be three lush
tiers, high around the room, of curling vines and flowers.
Fruit, or some such shit, is going to go up there, too.

Morgan, the ridiculously handsome decorator, is out in
the living room, discussing this, *the concept*, with Jamie,
no doubt driving him nuts. Not for one second could
even the dimmest person alive mistake Jamie's attitude
about the whole thing for enthusiasm. Poor Morgan.

The blue sky and water lie seamlessly just outside the
window, across from Rosie's little scaffold. Sometimes Rosie takes a moment to rest her mind and her aching arm,
and lets herself float out there until the whir of time going
by in the room recalls her to her task. It's warm enough
now so that a few little sails and wisps of cloud glide over
the blue. When Rosie arrived in this city, it was winter,
and the water and the sky looked like liquid metal.

This whole apartment is gleaming and slidey. You could

be inside a bubble, here—a dark pearl, hanging in the middle of the sky. Monday, Tuesday, Thursday, Friday: four mornings a week Lupe comes to clean and launder and put things in order. The floors have been bleached almost translucent, and stained, and a crew of other painters has done something to the walls to make them dark and glassy, so that Jamie's leaves look like they're twining right in the air. Every afternoon when Rosie and Jamie open the door on their way out, Rosie is shocked to see that they're in an ordinary apartment building, where other people live—just ordinary people.

Almost thirty years old, Rosie thinks, and this is where she finds herself—on someone's bedroom ceiling. Can it be true? But here's the corroborating smell of the paints and mineral spirits, the feel of the brush against the hard surface, and, even more surprisingly, that little mark on the wall afterward: Rosie did this . . .

The people have moved in, although Jamie and Rosie still have the bedroom to do. The important thing was to have finished the smallish room—office, study, whatever —where the man frequently works, on a sleek assemblage of technology which Rosie watched arrive. The woman works in an office nearby, evidently, when she's not traveling.

"Not to worry," Morgan said to Rosie and Jamie. "They won't get in your way." He meant, obviously, that Rosie and Jamie had to figure out how not to get in *their* way. If he'd been talking to her, Rosie thinks, that's pretty much how he would have put it. But, hey—he wasn't talking to her.

Of course they'll be pleased to see the last of Rosie and Jamie, these people. These people, obviously, like to keep things moving along. Already, pretty little objects have been placed out on tables and shelves, and a shining silk slip has been slung over a French screen in the bathroom —things like that. But framed pictures still lean against walls, and so do mirrors, which ambush Rosie with her own pale, fugitive presence.

Really, it would be just about impossible for anyone to get seriously in anyone else's way here. The place is too large; the thick padding of money soaks up disturbance. The other day Rosie felt something behind her, and when she twirled around, Lupe was right there, working.

So Rosie has seen the maid, but she's never seen the man or the woman who actually live in this place. Maybe they can't be seen by ordinary eyes, is what Jamie says; maybe they're just too special.

In the broad marshes between waking and sleep, where Rosie used to watch pictures fold and unfold like flowers, she is now plagued by visitors. Here's a woman carrying a parcel from the German butcher shop around the corner. Blood has soaked through the waxed wrapping, staining the string that ties it. She models herself for Rosie: print dress; lumpy, shifting contours; resentful smile fading after some encounter. Several pretty hookers, one black, the others maybe Polish, totter about in platform shoes, on beautiful, spindly legs, laughing together, ruined, it looks like, every which way. A man in a hurry—good-looking, preoccupied, pleased with himself, *spoiled*, Rosie thinks— pulls up the collar of his expensive raincoat against the stinging drizzle.

The visitors assemble around Rosie and draw closer. When she sits up irritably, they scatter to the corners of the room, then draw back, flaunting themselves and their lives—their lives which are so particular and binding, as heavy as crowns and gold chains and royal robes. The weight falls across Rosie's mouth and nose as she lies back down to sleep. She can hardly breathe.

People always say, you can't run away. It's one of those things Rosie's heard a million times: Whatever it is you're running from, people say, you're sure to bring it with you. But that's not her problem, Rosie thinks—not at all. Unless what she always had was nothing.

When she came to this city and left what—at least, in her opinion—was quite a lot, back at Ian's, there must have been something in her mind which made it possible for her to leave: she must have thought that while she (as it had suddenly come to appear) was taking time out the shuttle kept on moving back and forth; she must have thought that she could weave herself back into the web whenever she was ready; she must have thought it would be obvious what she was supposed to do next; she must have thought she'd just find herself doing whatever it was people did. Who knows what she was thinking? Whatever it was, she was wrong.

Once in a while she resorts to the notion that Ian is back there wishing her well, in whatever manner he can. She *draws strength* from that, she thinks. Oh, well; shit.

No doubt he'd been incensed to find her gone. Still, she left all her effects—the pretty suède pouch containing her syringe, her silver spoon, her rubber tubing, everything—right there on the pillow, so he'd see right away, and he'd know, more or less, just what she'd be going through. Better than leaving a note, Rosie thought—she just didn't know what more to say.

From time to time she regrets not having told Ian she was leaving. But what was the point? She was leaving. And Ian would have said no, stay, he'd help her to stop; hadn't he always told her to stop? Just what she needed, Rosie thinks—Ian in charge of her free will.

It's not Ian's way to lie, but Rosie has to wonder what he really wanted from her. All that talk about his clients —their weakness, their needs, the things they pretended to themselves. But the whole point, Rosie thinks, is that, high, she was as strong as wire, she needed nothing, and she never had to pretend a thing. All that talk about Rosie abusing her body (with not a word, of course, about what her body was doing to her!), but how did Ian think he'd met her, if not selling her and Cathy what they'd started snorting during lunch hour, years ago? The truth is, Ian could afford to say anything at all that made him feel righteous: it seemed he could count on her not to stop.

Another one of those things that Rosie's heard for years and years is people asking other people, *Why did you start taking drugs?* You turn on the *tele*vision and you hear that. But this is not a real question; it's just a sticky, juicy treat. Pornography. The shining faces, the eager and self-congratulatory answers—everyone feels great, everyone's rubbing it in their hair. My mother, my father, whatever —not real answers, but the question's not a real question. *Why did you start taking drugs?* Not a real question. Here, the real question: *Why didn't you, dear?* No. The real question: *Why did you stop?*

Not long before Rosie left, Ian took her on a call to some clients. There was an architect, and a man who owned a restaurant that the architect had designed, and their wives. It was an occasion, a birthday party, of sorts. Ian, as usual, wore his English hat with his initials stamped in gold on the inside band, and he carried his good briefcase. Very impressive, no doubt, to the hopheads stumbling around River Street, but the architect and the restaurateur were wearing suits obviously woven of fibers plucked for them personally from some rare beast. One of the wives wore a suit as well, a tiny little black thing, and the other wife wore a tiny little black dress. The house, which the architect had designed, was glaringly white. Almost the only color in it, aside from the soft green of Rosie's longish, graceful dress, was a huge crystal vase of roses, dark, dark red, like a blackening heart.

Ian had been called in to supply the birthday present— for the architect, as Rosie remembers, though all four of those people were pretty jacked up, controlled and furtively absent, like kids who have planned to sneak out and have sex.

The whole thing is even worse to remember than it was when it was happening. Ian and his *database*; earlier that evening he'd called the architect and the restaurateur up on the screen to make Rosie look. Lists of accomplishments vibrated in the synthetic blue depths. "Prominent people," Ian had said.

The lowered eyes, the swinishly clean whiteness, the hair like sculpture—Rosie practically gags, thinking of it. Never has she heard the words "my wife" used so often in so short a time. At moments the two couples had behaved as though Ian and Rosie weren't there; at other moments they were terribly, terribly polite—as if Ian and Rosie were the stableboys, called away from rolling in manure to come into the house for, say, a Christmas eggnog. What a waste of good drugs.

Ian had hustled Rosie along. They were just going to drop by on this thing, he'd said; they'd be home in good time, he meant, before she got uncomfortable. But then he was talking and talking. He knew about everything, of course. He knew about the new restaurant and other buildings the architect had designed, the wine they were all drinking, the variety of rose in the big crystal vase. Naturally he knew about the house—building techniques, materials . . . pretty much whatever could be known.

Rosie could perfectly well have excused herself and emerged decorously from the bathroom in mere minutes, in a much more accommodating frame of mind—she'd tucked her pouch prudently in her purse—but Ian would have gone absolutely nuts.

The little thorns of his voice caught and caught at her. She made herself get up, cross the room, and examine the bookshelves. In all those shelves there were about ten books—the tall kind, with pictures. She opened one: photograph after photograph showed a nude girl strapped down, with medical equipment inserted into her. Rosie closed her eyes, as if to bring the ocean, and a whooshing sound came up around her. Cars, obviously, going and going outside on the highway. When she turned around again, Ian was nowhere to be seen.

She found him standing in the long sweep of the kitchen. His briefcase was open and his scales were out on the table. The wife in the suit was there, too, counting out money, slowly and carefully, her head tilted down as she watched the bills leave her hands. Her thick lashes were very dark against her skin, and her smooth hair was pouring slowly forward. Ian leaned against the refrigerator, not touching the money, of course, or even looking at it. "I have to get back," Rosie said. Ian glanced at her, and his glance held. "Right," he said. "With you in a sec."

The others seemed not to have moved while Rosie was out of the room. The air was fantastically still. "It's going to storm," she said, but none of the others responded. Perhaps she hadn't actually spoken.

"Where's Ashley?" one of the men said.

"Out in the kitchen," the other man said. "With the Connoisseur. Your competition." And they made that little pause that stands for a laugh.

On the way home, Ian was calm, and happy, telling Rosie about a building in Seattle that the architect had designed. Yes, Rosie kept saying; that's great, yes. It was like listening to the happy stories of a child who doesn't yet know his home has been destroyed in a fire.

How could he have been such an idiot? And those people! How pleased they were with themselves—with all their things, with all their accomplishments. *My wife, my wife* . . . So pleased to have used their time so well. Those people had treated their lives so well, tending them and worshipping them and *using* them (however moronically), and she had just tossed hers into the freezer, like some old chunk of something you didn't exactly know what to do with. But why should her life be more despised than theirs?

Yeah, you've got to *play your cards right* with time, Rosie thinks. It's not merely the thing that kills you; evidently it's also the thing that keeps you alive. You can inoculate yourself against it, you can rid yourself of it, but then where are you? Not dead, true, but not alive, either; you've got rid of the thing inside you that pulls you along toward the end of the line, but don't you want to go anywhere? Because if you want to go somewhere, the end of the line is the only available destination.

The trees by the side of the road had begun to rustle anxiously, and a peal of thunder tore open the sky, exposing a jagged edge of lightning. When the sky went black again, it was as if a fissure in the earth had been revealed.

On one side of the chasm was the house with the architect and the restaurateur and their wives, and Rosie's school friends, and the others in her office, and stadiums full of people, and the students traveling in packs through Europe—all the people in the world, in fact, studying and working and playing sports and having colds and running errands and doing whatever it is humans do. And on the other was Rosie, sitting in her little bathroom, cleaning her syringe. All those people rushing around, but they can't touch Rosie. Their awful thoughts and desires, their disdain, their demands—nothing coming from them can stain or damage Rosie; she never changes, never gets older, just dries out into nothing as she cleans her syringe in a glass of pure spring water.

Poor Ian—how could he ever have expected to protect her when he couldn't begin to protect even himself? In just one instant that evening Rosie had been shown both of them with perfect clarity.

"Look at that," he said, as water poured from the sky. "Just what we need."

If he'd actually cared about her he wouldn't have taken her along to meet those people. At least, not in the condition she happened to be in. Because by the time you see there's a decision to be made, you can be pretty sure it's a decision you already have made.

Rosie thinks so often these days of people, children, who have had to leave the country where they live. What it must be, that last morning, pressing every detail into your brain to preserve it on your long journey—the journey that's going to last for the rest of your life. The color of the light that day, or the feel of the air, a certain little shrub in the park you always pass on your way home from school, the tender little waves that reach out for the boat as you embark—all those precious things which once breathed and lived in your casual attention, no better than powdery old petals pressed in a book: you've left your country for good.

That last night, proceeding through her bedtime ritual as always, she thought at every step: *This.* And *this.* Her cup of good cappuccino sat in front of her, and the rubbing alcohol, and the glass of Evian water. Her hairbrush was waiting, and the clean, clean sheets.

Opening the white-paper bindle; pouring, more carefully than ever, the contents into her silver spoon; drawing the water all the way up into the syringe and discharging it gently over the pure white powder. The match bursting into flame, the softly boiling solution, the needle pointing heavenward to coax the air bubble up and out, the bubble moving higher, higher . . . the precious liquid glittering for a moment at the tip. The rubber around her arm, good and tight, the pumped vein rising, the seeking needle, the stunning penetration, the drop of hungry blood, released to commune in a faint whorl with the contents of the barrel and plunge back into her body, step by teasing step: the first floating radiance with its delicious burn, the second, and, finally, the third, lighting up the splendid corridors.

After swabbing the site of the injection and sluicing the pure water through the syringe, she put the cap on the bright point for good. She brushed her hair over and over, watching her reflection, went into the bedroom, and lay down to sleep, as if on a bier.

In the morning, Ian gave her a little kiss, checked his E-mail, and went out on rounds.

Rosie had planned well; she'd contacted Jamie, checked schedules, looked at maps, and so on, but it came on quickly, the outrage of her body. It was as if she'd swallowed in her sleep a sleeping bird that awoke, then panicked, and by the middle of the day all those plans of hers were rearing up in shivering columns, swaying and crashing back down. Could her hands actually have been shaking the way she saw them shake? And what on earth was happening with her legs!

How did she get out that afternoon? Practically crawling, through the air's hammer blows and sirens, her vision all fretted and dazzled, falling away in glaring planes, past the razor-sharp, poison-colored blades of grass growing by the house . . .

How far was her foot from the step, the step from the ground? How big was the doorknob? She'd had to jam her things into the duffel with her fist. In the cab to the station, for all she knows she was screaming.

She was a reverse pioneer. The train brought her in from the western edge, steaming east toward the plains. The settled territories flickered by the window like film, into oblivion, as the vacuum of Rosie's brain stripped off the names of the towns, and then the towns themselves.

She stopped for some days, as she'd planned, to let the worst of it come up and drain away before she presented herself to Jamie. Not much she remembers about *that*: a room up some stairs, stumbling down to get Cokes, or once in a while, when the nausea gave over a bit, a sandwich; cold sweats in sheets that absorbed nothing and slid around on the mattress.

The configuration of wrinkles on the sheet, the untied shoelace of the waiter downstairs in the coffee shop, the little stain on the plastic lid of her Coke, the sickle of dust on the bureau, echoing the curve of the ice bucket—details hung at the forefront of her attention, like inadequately assimilated commands. In the halls, the Asian maids congregated by their filthy canvas bins full of used linens, talking for hour after hour in a cool, rippling language that blended with the noise of machines working on the pavement outside and of the televisions in the nearby rooms. Sometimes it seemed to Rosie that she could almost understand, that if she could only assemble the elements of her brain properly . . . and then sometimes a slippery phosphorescence would irradiate the sounds, and she did understand: they were whispering stories, complicated, tiresome, and interminable, about talking animals, underground kingdoms . . .

One morning, she woke up to silence. The thrashing wings inside her had drawn back, folding into a painful little lump in the region of her lungs. She stood looking at the long mirror in the thin sunshine that came through the window. Well, well; so this is what the person who had risen from the bed looked like—skim-milk pale, much younger than she really is. The drug-becalmed marble glow of her skin has moderated into a petal-like softness, as if she'd just been born. Her body is thin, unmuscular, childish—unmarked except for the raised, red dots on her arm.

How had she ever had the nerve to call Jamie, she wonders. She wouldn't have it now. Fortunately, though, at the time she'd been desperate; fortunately, she hadn't been thinking clearly. And who else could she have called, anyway—Mona McCauley? With her house and her husband and her dog and her child? Lexi Feld?

Jamie was two years older, and he had been kind, all through school. It had been obvious that he'd be going on to college and obvious that Rosie wouldn't; God knows, her mother had never had that kind of money, and, assuming her father did, it would go, presumably, to his younger children, wherever. So there'd always been plenty of differences between her and Jamie, but there are differences which when you're young, she thinks, run all up and down your life that you still assume are just incidental.

After school, Jamie had gone on to college, and then to art school, and by then Rosie had pretty much lost track of him. Bits of news came back, through one person or another. Jamie was still painting. But not (people were quick to point out) making any money at it. And there was Vincent. Who moved in, and, fairly recently, had moved out.

With every phone call Rosie had made to trace Jamie, it became more of a certainty that she really was going to leave. But leaving was one thing, she realized when the taxi let her out at a real house, and she rang the real bell of Jamie's apartment, and she walked up the two flights of real steps, and arriving was another.

Of course you could forget about your past, but then— how funny—there's someone on your doorstep ten years later: *Hey, didn't you drop something?* She and Jamie looked at each other as if they were studying a map, an aerial map of all the years that the mirror Rosie had studied earlier was not able to see.

In the morning, Rosie awoke in a dark-blue room. She was in Jamie's apartment. Yes, and the room, obviously, must have been Vincent's. There was nothing in it except a bed, a light, and a painting. A door opened into a small closet with a few shelves and a place to hang some clothes. Rosie has since noted that the painting is the only one in the apartment. It's by Jamie; this she knows from the signature. Most likely, it was a gift to Vincent.

Rosie paused in the kitchen doorway. Jamie was sitting at the table, beyond a pillar of dusty light, drinking coffee, and just staring out. He was wearing a heavy kimono— faded red silk, covered with designs of clouds and birds.

Impossible: Her ten-years-later self, in underpants and a tank top, standing at the door of a place that's Jamie's kitchen. But maybe that's what life is always like. All the time, for everyone. Maybe any moment you could say, this is normal; it's just what's happening. And you could equally well say, this is the strangest thing that ever could be. Probably so—it'll just depend on where you start the story.

She stood for a moment, shivering, feeling her body taking up space, pushing the air around in ways that were unfamiliar to the room, sending off its tiny, continuous demands. Jamie's face had changed so much, really; by more than just time. Well, but what would that be—*just time*? "Morning," she said.

Jamie glanced up. "Morning," he said. He indicated her arm. "Very chic." Then he wandered out and returned with another kimono—also heavy old silk, but blue, with designs of waves and flowering trees. "Here. Say yes to shame."

He sat again, folded his arms, and rested his head on the table. It looked as though he were exhausted, too, although, throughout the long night, Rosie had pictured him luxuriously asleep in the next room—his silky hair, his comfortable, appealing body, which her body had had sex with a few times back in high school, before Mr. Tomlinson showed up and settled the matter for Jamie once and for all.

Jamie opened his eyes and considered Rosie in the kimono. "O.K.," he said, and sighed. "Well, that's all right."

He took her through the frozen city. The neighborhood, with its Polish, Greek, and Hungarian bakeries, the hardware store, the German butcher shop, the fish market, the bank, the stationery store. Then farther afield to bars with sad pianos, and coffee shops that stayed open all night, to a bookstore with its webs of old light, to several little neon-festooned night clubs in a jaunty row, and to the downtown, where he and Rosie are working now, with its gentlemanly old office buildings and shining towers. What has all this to do with her? Once, glimpsing a cluster of blue needle caps discarded in a gutter, she is blinded for a moment; she might as well have glimpsed a company of angels departing the earth forever. Yes, this was where she lived; this barren, icy planet was where she lived now.

She was still feeling far from recovered—though who was to say what "recovered" felt like? Her legs were still subject to involuntary actions; her body rebelled against its new unprivileged condition with small colds, infections, and rashes. Going to the corner for ice cream, washing a dish or two—for the first weeks anything might take her most of the day. She'd get lost no farther than a block from the apartment. Things slipped from her grasp, as if her hands had been confiscated and exchanged for paws. No amount of clothing was adequate to keep her warm or to locate her in space. She spent most of her time in Vincent's room, in bed, wearing Vincent's kimono. It was fantastically difficult to bathe; the prospect of water next to her skin brought her nerves right up to the surface, and Jamie's best towel could have been sandpaper. Her hair became stiff with grime. By way of encouragement, Jamie bought her a little rubber duck. She saw its sunny shadings and its calm, blue eyes, and she rocked unsteadily on her feet. "Jamie—?" she said.

"Drug-crazed twisto," he said, and put an arm around her.

They went on the little train, winding quietly among lines of laundry and fire stairs. They stared into back windows at people staring out at them just as they stare out from Jamie's kitchen window at the people going by on the train. Rosie leaned back and closed her eyes. A voice near her said to someone, "This is my stop."

"How does he know?" Rosie said.

"Well, I guess it's on his card," Jamie said.

Rosie opened her eyes.

"His card, the little card they give you that tells you

what your stop is." Jamie looked at her. "Oh, didn't you get one?"

The train is audible from Vincent's room, but the tracks run by the back of the apartment, just outside the window of the kitchen. The people on the train stare into the window as they go by, and Rosie and Jamie stare back. *Who are they? Who are they?*

Beyond the tracks are the backs of other houses, hung with a dirty lace of fire stairs. From Vincent's window and from Jamie's what you see are the fronts of the houses—turrets and complicated shingles—all dilapidated, with the oily gold light spreading out at night in the windows, and the grape-colored shadows.

Nights, Rosie fades in and out, echoing with footsteps and whispers, traces of invisible inhabitants. She lies awake in Vincent's room with its peeling, dark-blue paint, and the city breaks up into pieces, like a puzzle. All the various neighborhoods that Jamie showed her, the little train, the narrow tracks with street lights drooping over them tenderly, like dying flowers, this tiny, dark-blue room, the downtown—that shining wedge that pushes up from flatness and drops off in a sheer glass-and-steel cliff by the water. It floats through the darkness now in a bright sphere. The windows are cold and starry; green tendrils wind around the bed.

The pieces of the city stream off into the darkness, and even in her sleep, the watery, transparent kind of sleep she has these days, Rosie listens for the little train to start up in the morning, swinging through the city, fitting the pieces back together.

There are some things, Rosie thinks, that she ought to have dealt with long before she did. To be fair, of course, she's had her hands full just standing upright. Just trying to work up some traction. Just dealing with the fact of herself, which pops up in front of her every day when she awakes, like some doltish puppet. So certain other worrisome items have just slid right off the agenda.

Jamie didn't make a living from his paintings, it was true. He did other kinds of painting, Rosie learned, to make money. From time to time he'd spend a few days or a week on the job, getting up early in the morning and going off to work in some rich person's home. But when he wasn't making paintings in his studio, Rosie noticed, Jamie became very . . . distant. *Estranged* . . . How long would it be before he got sick of her and tossed her out? It was a miracle he'd taken her in in the first place.

What on earth was she going to do when he didn't feel like taking care of her any longer? She hadn't meant to just throw herself in a heap on his floor. On the other hand, she hadn't meant not to; she hadn't meant anything at all—she was just scrambling. And now she was going to have to get some money together, herself. And fast, too—she'd almost gone through her savings.

Maybe the best thing about drugs, Rosie thinks now (or, on the other hand, maybe it's the worst), is the way they unhook you from that stupid step-by-step business—first one moment, then the next, then the one after that. No skipping, no detours, no time off. Which is what she's had to live through for all these long, recent months, and what she'll have to live through, now, every day until she dies. No wonder she hadn't particularly minded working in an office before. Beginning of day, end of day; pure-white time in between. The hands of the clock might sleep or twirl—that was discretionary.

But the laws of human time must have registered on some template lying around in Rosie's brain, because, facing the prospect of going back, Rosie remembers herself as a miner, hacking her way through the stony mass, instant after intolerably boring instant.

And if only boringness were the whole problem! Again, Rosie's memory offers up things Rosie didn't even notice at the time: the sadness of herself, the sadness of all the others—the secretaries and clerks, working away like mice in their little cubicles, at their endless, miniature tasks, their careful clothes and clean hands, *Good morning, good morning, how was your weekend?* And Mr. Gage and Mr. Peralta in their horrible suits and ties, appearing at the doorways of their offices with sheaves of paper, the light from their windows flashing into the fluorescent light over Rosie's desk.

How polite everyone was, and how cheery! Their cheerfulness lay like boulders over geysers of misery. *Have a nice night. See you tomorrow.* By five in the evening you were abrim with filth.

Rosie asked Jamie: Did he know of any jobs? Any people who worked in an office?

"Are you out of your mind?" he said.

Fine, she thought; that was her opinion of the whole thing, too, obviously.

"You don't want to do that," he said. "You'd hate it."

"Really," Rosie said.

"Why are you pissed off at me?" he said.

"I'm not," she said. "Pissed off at anyone."

"Well, good, then. Hey, where are you going? Aren't you going to say good night, at least?"

"Good night," Rosie said. "So you think I should be a doctor, right? You think I should be a famous artist."

Jamie looked at her. "Wow, Rosie . . ."

Rosie put her hands over her ears. "Look, Jamie. Could we just not talk about this, please?"

The next day she apologized, of course.

"Hey, I was thinking last night," Jamie said. "Now please don't get pissed off again. But maybe you could be my assistant."

The room dimmed. "I know you're trying to help me," Rosie said laboriously, as if she were picking her way through the words in the dark. She was silting up, her blood was draining out. She should have stayed back there, she thought, where the spears just bounced right off. "I appreciate everything you've done to help me. But listen, Jamie . . ." She put her head in her hands.

". . . 'Listen, Jamie'?"

"Well, I *can't*. Obviously."

"Can't what? Let's see. Can you . . ." He plucked a paintbrush from a jar sitting beneath the kitchen table, and prodded her with the handle. "Perfect," he said, as her hand closed around it to push it away. "Great reflexes."

"Oh, Jesus," she said. "Should I show you how I draw a house? I never even learned to finger paint."

"Rosie, we are not talking Sistine Chapel, here. Do you know what these jobs are about? The whole thing is ridiculous. A lot of these people like to think that there are only a few special people—really *gifted* people—who can do this shit. They get So-and-So, you know? Or So-and-So. *Artists.* But anyone could do it, a monkey could do it. Plus, do you know what kind of stuff they want? Once, I was flown to the Cayman Islands to paint an extra inch of rug on some guy's floor. Once, I had to marbleize all of some lady's toilet-paper holders."

"You think anyone can do it because you can do it," Rosie said.

"Wrong," Jamie said. "I think anyone can do it because anyone can do it. Especially the easy parts, which I'm going to show you, foolproofily, how to do. Look, how do you think people get to be able to do a thing? First they pretend they can do it, and then they do it, and then they can do it."

Rosie stared; he wiggled the brush. "The main thing you've got to learn is to stay out of the medicine cabinet. Hey, lighten up—that was a joke."

The first job was an hour's drive distant, and there were four of them—Jamie and Rosie and Marina and Jean-

Michel, squashed into Marina's red pickup truck. Marina and Jean-Michel looked at Rosie. What had Jamie said to them? "Great," Marina said. "A new face. Someone to bore with our war stories."

The sun was round and yellow. The city melted away. Lawns and trees and driveways flowed by. Massive houses sat behind hedges. The houses looked like pictures from travel posters: Spanish, Rosie thought; Japanese; English, maybe from some other century. "Where are we?" she said.

"We're dead now," Marina said dreamily. "This is the land of the dead. Unfortunately, this civilization wasn't worth preserving, so all these people fell into their pools and died. Isn't that sad?"

"Darling—" Jean-Michel sighed. "It's not for us to judge these people. Scum though they be, it's just not our job to judge them."

"No?" Marina looked at him with enormous gray eyes. "So, what is our job?"

"Our job," Jean-Michel said. "Our job . . . Right. Well, our job is to make a mockery of our God-given talents."

"Oh, yeah . . ." Marina said. "Right . . ."

Rosie sighed; she was never going to be able to do this stuff . . .

The red truck rattled and screeched into a driveway; the house at the end of it looked shocked into its whiteness. With noisy rapidity, Jamie and Marina and Jean-Michel unloaded pails and jars and stained rags and cloths, wooden sticks and cans and huge, old sponges, heaping it all up in the driveway like booty. Rosie blinked. "Trash," Jamie said into her ear. She looked at him. "Trash," he said again, as if he were patiently teaching a parrot.

The lady of the house came out and greeted them nervously; her glance snagged on Jean-Michel, as if she'd been briefly hypnotized by his elaborate mass of little braids.

She probably didn't see too many black people out here, Rosie thought, who weren't in uniforms. "I'm so glad you could come," the lady said confusedly. Jean-Michel inclined his head, disengaging her stare with kingly ease.

Upstairs, the four inspected a room where they were to paint a border of stenciled sheep, and a blue ceiling with white clouds, and then another room, where they were to make a border of stenciled flowers.

"For this she needed *us?*" Marina said.

Jamie shrugged. "It's only our prices that can justify the misery of her husband's existence."

A carton stood in the corner of the room, containing a whole little life—a jumble of soft toys and dolls, and a small, fuzzy blanket. "Hey, wow—" Rosie said, and the three others wheeled around.

"I was just *looking*," she said.

"No, I know," Jamie said, as Marina and Jean-Michel returned to setting out their tools. "Just, it's . . ."

"Fine," Rosie said. "So I won't look."

Jamie gave her a stencil and a round brush, and showed her how to hold them both and to pat the paint onto the wall instead of stroking it on.

It was hard. You had to hold the brush just right and the stencil just right or you'd smear or drip. Rosie's heart pounded in her ears as she lifted the stencil from the wall. "Right," Jamie said. "Perfect."

Did children really like these little sheep? Or was it just the sort of thing adults insisted they like. Would Rosie have liked sheep on her wall when she was little? Sheep: She doubted they would have applied. She doubted these petrified-looking creatures would have improved her dreams any. She liked them now, though, poor things. Now it was easy enough to imagine them jumping over their fences, on their way off to slaughter . . .

Painted sheep, stuffed animals, ribbons, sweet little-girly things—it reminded Rosie of sitting in the pretty bathroom back at Ian's with her cappuccino and her bottle of rubbing alcohol and her needle and her hairbrush. "You're doing good," Jean-Michel said, and she jumped.

"Thanks," she said, flushing with rage and shame. Yeah, thanks. She knew perfectly well she was a charity case.

The others laughed and joked—they didn't even have to concentrate, though it was all Rosie could do to remember what, out of all the rags and brushes and stencils and containers she had to juggle, she was holding in what hand. "Oh, no!" she said; she'd blurred an edge. "No problem," Marina said, quickly dipping a rag into some thinner and dabbing it expertly against the wall. "See? All better now." Without looking at Rosie she returned to her own section of wall.

But, after the third time Rosie smeared, Marina sighed loudly. "Sorry, but stencils are not the easiest way to start," Marina said. She looked at Jamie. "You've got to be really, really careful with them."

"We've got too many people doing this anyhow," Jamie said. "What we really need are some clean brushes."

He showed Rosie how to clean the brushes and lay them neatly out on a rag to dry. Fuck you, she thought; fuck you, fuck you. But the fact was it wasn't all that easy to clean the brushes, either. You had to swish them around in a little jar of thinner, Jamie explained, and just keep changing to new thinner until it stayed clear. Changing it over and over, and over and over and over. And obviously, Rosie thought, the thinner was never going to stay clear.

Marina was applying two bands of blue tape to the wall, in order to paint a thin pink stripe between them; the space between the bands didn't vary by an iota, as far as Rosie could see. Marina and Jamie and Jean-Michel were working away, bending and reaching, with unhurried, engaged precision as the toxic incense of the paint rose up and swirled around them. Their hair was bound up in brilliant scarves, and their clothing and the exposed parts of their bodies were smeared with glistening colors.

There were times Rosie missed her needle so much she could have burst into tears. She'd done just that, in fact—over coffee at some counter, in line at the bank where she went to open a tiny checking account, and once simply walking down the street she'd sobbed loudly, as if she'd been flung at the wall of a prison.

For a few moments the tears would dissolve the distance between herself and her bartered immortality. When the tears were gone, the distance was back, as solid as before. But each time it happened, she felt a bit better—she'd had a little visit.

"How's it going?" Marina said brightly, not waiting for an answer. All friendly solicitude now that the walls were out of harm's way.

Rosie wandered into the bathroom they'd been instructed to use. Oily stains were ingrained all up her arms—phantom badges she had no right to wear. Her skin was already sore and stinging from the turpentine she'd rubbed on it, but she worked at the stains with soap, and then shook her hands to dry them. Were they allowed to use the towels? The lady hadn't said; best not to. Rosie checked the mirror again, and smiled at it falsely. There. All better now.

Stay out of the medicine cabinet. Some joke. Well, what did people like this keep in those things? Jamie had aspirin, and that was about it. These people were more serious, of course. Serious people: Rogaine, Aldomet, Propanolol, Zovorax, Imodium, and oh—there. Fiorinal. Marina with that blue tape! The patience of a robot.

The bottle of Fiorinal was in Rosie's hand, she noticed. She looked at it, and replaced it in the cabinet. She stared into the mirror, then smiled falsely at it once again. Ha— a person. But what a disappointment that *she* was the person she'd turned out to be. She reached for the bottle, opened it, and shook about half its contents out into a Kleenex.

She found Jamie and the other two in the second room

they were to paint. The lady of the house was with them. "Well," the lady said. "Now I want *her* opinion." She turned to Rosie. "He's almost got me convinced. And these people"—she indicated Jean-Michel and Marina—"agree with him." Jean-Michel, Marina, and Jamie stood by, splendid, like rabble in their raggy work clothes, their eyes gleaming and their faces streaked. "You've seen the samples, I'm sure. Let's hear what you think."

What samples? Rosie glanced at Jamie.

"You can be perfectly honest with Mrs. Howell, Rosie," Jamie said.

"I can't do any worse than I'm doing now," the lady said.

Rosie gasped, as though she'd been slapped. *Oh, no?*

"Well, Mrs. Howell," Rosie said slowly, "It's your house, after all, and no matter what *we* think it's you who—"

"I see," Mrs. Howell said. "So. Four against one."

Over Mrs. Howell's shoulder, the others smiled.

Rosie learned a lot there, she thinks. Well, at least she learned something. And though this place downtown is only her second job, she can clean the brushes without wrecking them or going insane, she can stir the paints and put them out and straighten up at the end of the day without making a mess, she can maneuver her scaffold around with a modicum of authority, she always remembers to lock the wheels on Jamie's so he won't go flying through the window, she can navigate the treacherous shoals of someone else's rooms without dripping, spilling, or breaking a thing, she can manage (once in a while) the huge, necessary array of implements and liquids simultaneously, she's learned to become invisible at will, and, best of all, she can actually do a bit of the painting, even though this job's so much fancier and more complicated than the one in Mrs. Howell's house.

It's beautiful, what Jamie's done, in Rosie's opinion—no matter what Jamie has to say about it himself. And it's all but finished. Even the garlands near the bedroom ceiling are all but finished now.

It was Jamie who painted the forms of the leaves and flowers and fruit, of course, and it was Jamie, of course, who drew them all on the wall in the first place. And Jamie did the complicated shadings and details. But Rosie actually painted a lot of the veining on the leaves and most of the stems, and today Jamie's going to show her how to make highlights. Without Marina and Jean-Michel around to make her feel terrible, Rosie can manage reasonably well.

A couple of days later Jamie asks Rosie to work the whole following week all alone. "There's really nothing left for me to do, now that you're so expert with the highlighting."

"But I can't," Rosie says. "I can't do it if you're not there. How am I supposed to know what to do?"

"I'll draw you a map," Jamie says. "Look. You know how to do the grapes, right? You know how to do the plums, you know how to do the pears . . . It's just a question of where."

"But that won't take much more than a day or two anyhow," Rosie says.

"And there are a few other things that have to be done," Jamie says. "Look, Rosie, there's some stuff of my own I really want to work on, and I'm going to go truly nuts if I don't get to it right away. And you know what'll happen if we both disappear. I mean, they'll absolutely send in the Marines."

"But—" Rosie says.

"You can," Jamie says. "I've seen you work. Rosie, you can do everything that's going to be required this week. You can do the highlights, you can stand around on the scaffold looking fabulous, and I know you'll treat all their tastefully priceless shit with the . . . the reverence it . . . Have I ever asked you for anything else? *Anything?* Please.

I'm under a lot of time pressure. And besides. Well, look. Actually, also, I've met someone."

Rosie stares, trying to let all the meanings of the words come to her, through a closing gate of panic. "Oh," she says. "Well. So, I mean, do you need Vincent's room back?"

Jamie stretches, and yawns. "Hey," he says in rebuke. "Besides. I doubt this thing with Trevor is going to work out."

By Monday afternoon she's already finished the highlights, and, as instructed by Jamie, she's working with the blue tape, making a thin gold line around the cornice.

According to Jamie, this bit is the easiest of all. Just a thin gold line! It hardly even requires a monkey—a one-celled organism with an opposable thumb would do. Right. Of course, it's all but impossible to get the tape on straight, to keep the interval between the strips even, to restrain yourself from diving down onto the bed to relieve your aching back and arm, to work the tape off at the necessary glacial speed rather than yanking down the whole damn wall . . . A thin gold line. The horizonless depth. Tiny little boats, bobbing . . . Rosie is gazing out the window when the door opens and a woman strides in. "Sorry," the woman says. "Have to get some things. Hope I won't be in your way."

How very tactful, Rosie thinks. But she stays put: do they want her to work or not?

What you can do if something belongs to you! The way you can behave! Rosie always slips into this room, taking care not to disrupt the serenity so carefully tended by Lupe, but this woman just plunges right through it, as though she'd arrived by diving board. Now she's tossed a suitcase right down on the bedcover—that fragile bedcover. But why not? The suitcase itself is clearly leather, probably as fine-grained as silk.

The woman goes back and forth between the suitcase and the closet. This is the first time Rosie has seen the closets open. The hangers are the puffy, satiny kind, and the suits and blouses on them are delicious colors: colors that could be worn only by someone who expects people to be glad to see her—coral, pale yellow, the most shamelessly pretty blues. There are plenty of built-in drawers in the closet, too, which must have taken someone a lot of time to make, and racks and racks for shoes.

The woman pauses to consider. Her eyes come to rest on a tiny lacquer box sitting on the table. She scrutinizes it for a moment, then reaches out and repositions it, almost imperceptibly.

As if Rosie would have gone near the thing! The woman's cream silk blouse is escaping from her skirt. She tucks it back in, and Rosie can't help noticing the little bulge of flesh over the waistband. She did not ask to be up here watching this!

Flop! Into the suitcase with a dark-blue suit. Now a yellow one. Rosie is surprised by something, she notices; what is it? Ah—it's the woman's appearance. Well, she does have good legs, this woman, that's for sure; anybody might be jealous. Anybody at all. And her hair—thick, glossy, dark gold, like something with a lot of calories. People must just plunge their hands in and grab fistfuls.

But she isn't actually beautiful. And, Rosie judges, she probably never really was. She must be around forty, and she looks like she's been used to getting her way every minute of those years. Well, of course. And maybe people say she's beautiful without actually looking. But if she were just a few pounds heavier, Rosie thinks, everyone would see how it worked: sheer brute force. No one would mistake it for charm or ability or intelligence, let alone beauty.

The woman rolls the two suits up into plastic bags—no question she knows what she's doing. She jostles everything about in the suitcase, roughly and expertly, snaps the bright clasps closed, and clicks on a little lock. She pulls her suit jacket from the closet and puts it on. Goodbye, little bulge! "Harris—" she calls. She stops to listen

and then sighs with exasperation, as though she were an
actress in a play. "Harris?" And Rosie's the audience. The
woman picks up the suitcase and hurries out of the room.

Well, she's gone.

But the sliding door of the closet is still open. It looks
as if someone had slashed the wall, and its insides are all
exposed, spilling out of the cavity. A scent, too sweet for
Rosie, swells out from it, as if it were warm.

The room vibrates with silence, as though the woman
had slammed the door on her way out. There are a few
slight dents in the bedcover, and on it is something green
—a cool green. Rosie wipes her hands with a thinner-
drenched rag and climbs down from the scaffold, her legs
shaking a little, to look.

It's a pair of gloves—palms up, wrists tilted away from
one another, fingers of one adjacent to the fingers of the
other, all slightly curled, as though the body they belonged
to were responding to someone's touch.

Rosie stands, looking; she glances at her own hand:
clean, to all appearances. She extends it and picks up one
of the gloves, holding it gingerly between her thumb and
index finger. It's amazingly pliant and soft—slightly adhe-
sive.

And so small! Is it possible that this woman's hand is
smaller than Rosie's? *Ladies* . . . used to use talc to get
those things on: Rosie observes this fact her memory offers
up as if it were a strange object for which she's just discovered a fascinating use. How tight those gloves must
have been—slick smooth, no bones, no veins . . .

The door opens; a man is standing in front of Rosie.
Saying something; saying, *Sorry*. Loops of silvery black
curls; expensive raincoat folded over one arm. "Sorry, my
wife says she forgot her gloves." The glove is dangling
from Rosie's hand. He sees it. He's looking at it. What if
he tells Jamie? What if he tells *Morgan*? "I was just—"
Rosie begins, and her throat shuts down.

"Ah," the man says. "Kind of you, but you wouldn't

have found us in any case. That parking lot's the size of France."

Without moving from the spot, he extends his hand. His eyes are almost black. Watching him, Rosie reaches the second glove from the bed and then steps forward to drop both into his outstretched palm.

"Thanks." His hand closes around the gloves, and he smiles. "Thanks very much."

On Tuesday the room seems different. To the eye, it's as usual: Lupe has been here, the closet door is closed, the bed is traceless. But something is altered.

Rosie reruns the scene that took place right here the day before, trying to slow it down so she can search into its folds and crevices. But with each repeated exposure the scene slips more out of control. Rosie knows very well, for instance, that she was not watching from far above as the man extended his hand. She could not have seen her hair escaping from the scarf it was bound up in. She could not have seen the glistening smear of fresh paint just under her own ear at her jawbone any more than she could have seen herself standing there, staring, dropping the green gloves into the outstretched palm. She could not have observed her T-shirt flutter slightly with her breathing.

There's only tinkering left—cleaning up her mistakes and blotches, and she might as well refine some of the highlights and some stems that now look amateurish to her. In the late afternoon, she organizes things for the following day, putting lids on cans and cleaning brushes, and goes to wash up and change out of her painting clothes. The splendid silk slip is still hanging over the screen in the bathroom. Rosie looks at it. She turns away, concentrating on cleaning off the paint she always ends up streaked with, even under her clothing, in the most improbable places, but the slip behind her seems to have some claim on her today; she'd just as soon she'd never seen inside that woman's closet.

When Rosie gives the slip just the gentlest tug, it tumbles down, twinkling, into her hands. The slip pours tremblingly around her body, transforming it into a thrilling landscape, all gleams and shadows. Her skin looks an edible white. And the way the thing feels! Rosie lifts her arms; it slides against her. Her painting clothing—shoes, T-shirt, jeans, underwear—lies in a heap at her feet.

How does that woman look in this? Easy to imagine. Rosie pictures that hair of hers, swooshing around, Harris's hands in it.

She closes her eyes to erase the scene. She takes the slip off, sniffs it to see whether her body has left any trace of paint or mineral spirits on it, replaces it carefully over the screen, and breathes in and out to calm her pounding heart. Then she puts on her clean clothes, and returns to the bedroom to collect her things. Out the window, the sails float, so far away. One detaches itself from the blue and flutters off—not a sail, a gull.

"Didn't mean to startle you—" a voice says behind her. "I thought you'd gone."

Rosie spins around. "Actually," she says, "I thought *you'd* gone."

Harris blinks, evidently searching his mind. "Oh, I see," he says. "Other day, yesterday, whatever it was? Just giving Elizabeth a lift to the airport."

Rosie stares. The way she just spoke to him!

He seems not to have noticed, though. "I usually do," he's saying, as if this would clear up some confusion. "She says it's the only time we see each other anymore. Not completely a joke . . ." He frowns. "Will it bother you if I grab a tie?"

Will it *bother* her? Rosie closes her eyes again for a moment.

Harris pulls a lustrous sheaf of ties from his closet and leafs through it, extracting several. He holds one up to himself, peering at the small mirror over the dressing table.

Sight, sound, smell, taste, touch, Rosie thinks. All of

that, and you don't have the faintest idea what's going on with another person. "This one, I think," he says. "Yes?"

She watches as he makes the knot, his collar up, concentrating—his eyes on her face, as if she were the mirror. It's impossible for her to turn away from the rapid, complicated performance.

"Really hate this," he says, turning down his collar and smiling quickly at her.

She feels slightly dizzy. "You hate . . ."

He gestures, as if the whole thing were simply too difficult to explain. "Oh, putting on a tie at this hour." He looks at her, apparently for sympathy. "A meeting. In a bar, if you please. Downsizing—this is what it comes to. Now that we're all laptops and cellulars, there's no place that isn't the office. Bar, apartment, plane, car, street . . . I liked it better when you went somewhere, didn't you? Well, you're too young to remember. But you used to *go* somewhere. There was your desk, there was your secretary. And then, the point is, you left."

Rosie looks at him uncertainly.

He smiles. Oh—this is his home! She picks up her backpack. "Well, goodbye," she says.

"Goodbye," he says. "By the way, why don't I know your name?"

"It's Rosie," Rosie says.

"Rosie," he says, and turns briefly back to the mirror. "Rosie. Well, good. Now we have a basis."

It's Lupe's day off. And Harris, evidently, is not by nature a housekeeper. The cover has been thrown sloppily over the bed, and a thick book is propped open, pages down, near a pillow. A tumbler containing what seems to be the watery remains of a whiskey sits on the floor by the bed next to a cup holding some boiled-smelling coffee. A robe lies open over the little chair.

Rosie squints at the book's cover. Some sort of fancy

thriller, it looks like. About high finance. No sign of Harris himself. Maybe he's in his study. Maybe he's out . . .

Does Rosie hear someone? Yes, someone's come in. But —oh, no!—it's *Morgan.* And of course Jamie's not around to deal with him. "Hello, there," Morgan says, inattentively, as he wanders into the bedroom. Does he happen to remember who she is? "How's it going? Everything fine?"

He glances around, and Rosie does, too. The glass, the bed, the robe . . .

"Looking good," Morgan comments, vaguely. He stands back from a wall, scrutinizing it, then approaches. He takes a fabric swatch from his briefcase, tacks it up by the window, stands back, and approaches again. "Very, very good. So. She'll be back Tuesday night, I understand— after the holiday. I'd assume she'll be pleased, but of course she'll have to look at it. And if there are no adjustments, perhaps James will want to go ahead and seal it on Wednesday? Do you think?"

"I guess . . ." Rosie says. "So, where did she go anyhow?"

"Sorry?" Morgan raises his eyebrows slightly.

Rosie looks at him.

"Oh," he says. "Business, I suppose."

"She travels a lot . . ." Rosie suggests.

Morgan is loftily forbearing, as though he were waiting for a child to conclude a tantrum, but after a moment he concedes. "Some high-end international-hotel concern, I believe. Well—" he looks at Rosie, then away. "And where might James be?"

Where indeed? Jamie didn't get around to mentioning what she was to do in this contingency. "Actually," Rosie says, "he's sick."

Terror ripples in the depths of Morgan's beautiful face, and tears spring, astonishingly, into Rosie's eyes; it's as if Jamie really were sick. "It's nothing much, I'm sure," she says. "We ate at the Golden Calf last night. Big mistake."

"I see," Morgan says.

Obviously he's realized she's lying. "That's too bad. Well, do ask him to give me a call if he has a moment. No, never mind, don't bother."

"Morgan asked if you want to seal it Wednesday," Rosie says that night.

"I know," Jamie says. "He called."

"Will that take long?" Rosie asks, though she pretty much knows how long it will take, since she and Jamie sealed the other rooms.

Jamie shakes his head. "A couple of hours, maybe. How's it been going, by the way? Any problems?"

"Problems?" Rosie says. "Painting a line?"

"Well . . ." Jamie says. "Listen, if you've finished, there really isn't any reason for you to go back tomorrow."

"I've got a bit more to do, anyhow," Rosie says.

"It's great you were there when Morgan came by. He won't show up again, probably."

A basis! Rosie is thinking—she'll probably never catch another glimpse of that person. And did he simply assume she'd know *his* name? Of course, the fact, ha-ha, is that she did happen to.

"And in case I haven't thanked you . . . This has really been great for me. I've gotten a lot done."

A lot of what? "I'm going to make some tea," Rosie says. "Want some?"

"No, thanks," he says. "I want to wash my hair. You got any immediate plans for the tub?"

Rosie wanders into the kitchen. She's got into the habit of thinking of this as her life, but what is it, really? An accident, a coincidence—nothing. And now Jamie's letting go.

Already, in fact, she's being completely colonized by the first person to happen by. Concentrate, she tells herself. Put the water in the kettle, put the kettle on the stove, turn the burner on, reach yourself a tea bag, and drop it in the cup.

This is one good reason why people take care to have a past, Rosie thinks. So their minds are full of stuff—big, heavy things. Anchors, buoys, urns, old statuary, armoires, lots of clutter, lots of buffers, so that some perfect stranger can't just wander in and use up all the space.

Take a seat, she'd like to say. There, over in the corner, in the shadows with all that old junk. I'm making tea just now; don't loaf around there in the middle of the room, please. Take a seat in the back, and I'll be with you when it's convenient.

Unfortunately, though, he's a spreading blob. She doesn't have any shapes to think of him in; she doesn't know anything about him. She can't make any observations about him, she can't have any opinions about him, and she certainly can't push him out of her mind—he just oozes back around the slammed door.

In fact, it seems to Rosie that all her resistance is just getting him more entrenched. Why not relax a bit? Why think every second about how much she's thinking about him? Maybe she should just give him full run. Let him lounge around and put his feet up—she's bound to get sick of it after a while, and throw him out.

"Hey, Rosie—" Jamie calls from the bathroom. "Can I borrow your duck?"

"Help yourself," Rosie calls back.

Or, one thing that Ian used to do when he got stuck on something was just sit himself down in front of his computer and sort things out. *It's right there*, he'd say, *in your mind. What's keeping you hung up? What do you know that you don't know you know?*

"Instrumental meditation," he'd called it. "A technique." Taught to him by some simpleton of a therapist he'd boasted about knowing. *Taught*, Rosie thinks. *Technique.* How's that for something to get taught—making a *list*?

Ludicrous. Still, what's there to lose? Rosie locates some lined yellow paper in the kitchen, and brings it into Vincent's room along with a cup of tea. She takes a sip of tea and stares at the piece of paper. Well, you can see why Ian likes that computer of his so much—it's a crystal ball. All that information swimming around in that blue cyberspace, ready to jump to the right bait and get reeled up to the surface of the screen. Whereas you can be sure nothing's going to just appear on this piece of paper.

Rosie sees Ian tapping the silent keys to make a list. He's replaced by Harris, at his screen, sending out the orders that raise up and demolish the invisible empire.

"Hey," Jamie says, pausing at Vincent's door, a towel around his neck and his hair dripping wet.

"Which of them makes more money, do you think?" Rosie says.

"Er . . ." Jamie says.

Oh, great, Rosie thinks. Why not just make a general announcement? That she's actively thinking about some people who are hardly aware of her existence. That before she'd even laid eyes on them, her mind had gone so far as to form expectations of them, without her permission, and even without her knowledge. "Those people we're working for. I was just wondering today—which one do you think makes more?"

Jamie shrugs. "You can't count that kind of money. It's indivisible. No metal coins, no flappy little bills. It's abstract. It's a construct. It's outer-space gunk. Their bank accounts are just big, mad-scientist thingies, with gunk gurgling around in the tubes. People like that can't even buy a hot dog on the street."

"She's not beautiful," Rosie says.

"Huh," Jamie says. "And so?" He sits down on the bed, next to Rosie, and she takes the towel from him to dry his silky hair. "Mmm," he says. "That feels good."

True: *And so?* She's going to miss Jamie one of these days. She misses him now.

"So, why do you think they got married?" Rosie says, stanching a little rivulet of water behind his ear.

"Rosie, I'm surprised at you. 'Why'—now, *that's* a question that won't take you there. Why did they get married? Why does anybody marry anybody instead of anybody else? Why does anybody anything?"

Rosie lowers the towel, thinking.

"Besides, judging by the archaeological evidence, they're perfect for each other. Don't stop, don't stop! The two least interesting people on the planet."

Also true: *Why*—a completely primitive concept. Still, why *does* anybody anything, Rosie thinks, looking around the next day at the pure, breathing silence of the bedroom. Why does this person want to be with that person rather than with any other? Why did Lexi Feld get together with Arnold Schaefer? Because he was blocking her path? To Rosie neither Lexi nor Arnold ever seemed to have much in the way of attributes, let alone allure. What is it about the mere sight of Jamie that does to Morgan the strange things it does? What could have been so special about Vincent that to this day Jamie never says a word about him? What on earth could it be about some stranger, who does not, in fact, seem particularly interesting, that keeps Rosie's attention nailed to him? And why *did* he marry that woman?

Lots of people want to have a dog around; others prefer cats. Once in a while, someone goes into the pet store and comes out with a mynah bird or a snake or a miniature African hedgehog. And even about this matter, which should be pretty simple to figure out, what do people say? They say, "It doesn't shed"; or, "You can walk it"; or, "You don't have to walk it"—whatever. In other words, no one has a clue why it's some particular creature rather than another that causes them to exclaim, "Oh, hey, now —that's for me!"

Rosie's hungry, she notices. This whole Thursday has

gone by as if it had been poured slowly into sand. It would be nice to have a bite with Jamie tonight, but he's sure to be at his studio, or with Trevor. No matter. She looks around—still a few smears left to clean up.

She'll do it tomorrow, though. It's taken her all day to do about fifteen minutes worth of work. Because when you're waiting, she thinks, waiting is all you can do.

So much for all the wasted head space. By afternoon of the following day, Rosie has pretty much resigned herself —*really*, she thinks—to the idea that she's not going to be running into Harris again. Obviously she's not going to run into him. She hadn't actually thought she was going to run into him anyway. And she just isn't.

How stupid this has all been. What had she actually hoped to gain by sacrificing the magic hum of her blood, anyway? Ordinary human experience? Ordinary human experience—something, obviously, only an elephant could survive.

Not a sound in the place other than the creakings of the scaffold as Rosie clambers up and down, the comforting little clicks of the paint-can lids as she removes and re-places them, and the handles of the brushes against the jars of paint and mineral spirits. Tarnished gold veils are beginning to drop through the blue at the window; soon, the planet will turn its back on the day.

In half an hour she'll be gone. Rosie finishes cleaning up slowly. She could just take the little train back to the apartment. Or she could walk around for a while, stalling in the grimy air, or hang out at a bar, watching the early-evening drunks ricochet between desperation and pointless hope . . .

The room glitters with cool shadows, like a garden on the last day of summer. She should have used her time here better—her time on this job. On Wednesday, she'll return with Jamie, and within a few hours everything she's been doing with her day will be sealed off from

her. And then what? In these weeks Jamie's done some
brand-new paintings; in these weeks Jamie's acquired a
brand-new lover.

Rosie goes to wash up and change out of her painting
clothes. The silk slip is hanging over the screen, of course,
glimmering, winking at her. She turns away, as if she'd
encountered in genteel company someone with whom she'd
once had a sordid affair.

Just one last look at the view that will cease to be hers,
today, the moment she shuts the door of the apartment
behind her. Bright days out on the water, indigo nights
. . . Oh, yeah—memory! *Now* Rosie gets it; *memory*—the
thing humans get to keep, a little travel kit to bring along
with you. A little substitute for eternity. Pathetic. Rosie
looks at her hands, her arms, every part of her body she
can see that isn't covered by her dress. No fresh paint, she's
certain. She sits down as gently as possible on the bed, and
after a minute or two leans back against the cloud of
pillows.

She can see only one sail now, in the darkening blue.
Someone out there, gliding farther into the darkness, a
hand trailing in the water, edged with light . . .

Later, Rosie once again finds it impossible to recapitu-
late in any way that seems trustworthy the thing that happened next—the last, unexpected entrance of Harris.

Unexpected? Of course not. Shocking, yes, but not unexpected. And there it all is, over and over—a wedge of
dark where the door is opening, herself against the pillows,
his hand resting on the doorframe, his watch flashing
against his wrist—as though it were all being reflected in
the falling pieces of a shattered mirror. Rosie sits herself
up fast, speechless.

They stare at one another. "Not feeling well?" he says.

"No, no—" she says, her heart pounding. "I'll be fine
in a moment—"

"Mmm," he says. He shakes his head, as if he'd fallen
asleep for an instant. "Probably best to be still." He runs

a hand through his black-and-silver hair. "Very pale. Migraine? Do you get migraines?"

"Not often," Rosie says, truthfully.

"Sometimes tea works," he says. "They say not, but what do they know? I say it does."

The kitchen is a million miles away. Of course Rosie can't even hear Harris there, clattering around, let alone see him. And yet this, too, is something that happens later: watching him search for the teakettle, the cup, the saucer, observing his intent expression as he fills the kettle at the tap, waits for it to boil . . .

And then he returns, with a pretty little tray. "There," he says, pleased.

The tray holds a tiny china teapot, the most beautiful cup and saucer Rosie's ever seen, a paper napkin, a silver spoon, a small silver bowl of sugar, and a little dish containing various sorts of tea bags. "This is not the way it's done," Harris says. "I do know that. And, to tell you the truth, there are boxes and boxes of the real thing out there—the stuff in shreds. But all that paraphernalia! The little mesh things . . ." He presents her with an expression of cheery bewilderment. "I don't know why we've got that stuff, anyhow. Neither of us drinks it. Just to persuade Lupe we're legit, I suppose. Oh, Christ—lemon."

"This is perfect," Rosie says.

"Just as well," Harris says, sitting down in the little chair. "Probably is no lemon."

Rosie selects a tea bag and puts it in the cup. She looks up at Harris; he's watching her. She pours the water out from the teapot, and nearly chokes from the stench of synthetic fruit. Harris frowns worriedly. "O.K.?" he says.

Rosie nods. "Perfect."

"Things really do fall apart back there when Elizabeth's away," he says. "Not that Elizabeth's all that domestic. But she is very . . ."

Rosie looks demurely at her teacup.

". . . well organized," he says. "Funny to remember, but there was a time, back in our very first place, when we used to cook a lot. Penthouse, *miles* of terrace. That was all back then, when people did that. You wouldn't remember, probably. Maybe your parents were into it."

Jesus fucking Christ, Rosie thinks. Who on earth might he imagine her parents to be?

"Little dinner parties," he says. "Sort of a blood sport. Everything just right. Very competitive. Stakes escalating . . ." He laughs. "Seriously, though, it was grim . . ."

And how on earth old does he imagine her to be?

He's got the facts all wrong. But, Rosie thinks, only the facts. This man has some quality that works like intuition. It's confidence. Or generosity of a sort. He seems to believe he has only to say something in order for her to understand it; that he'll understand whatever it is she might say . . .

He's tapped into some great, generous reserve—the ocean that flows around everyone, between everyone, rolling like a heartbeat, making big, comforting, heartbeat sounds, oceanic sounds . . . approbation, pleasure . . .

Mr. Gage and Mr. Peralta, the men she used to work for, were so nervous—as if they were afraid that she or one of the other secretaries would suddenly speak up. *Calm down, guys*, Rosie could have told them; *no fear of that. What do you think those suits of yours are for?* Those sad, furry suits . . . The shirt Harris is wearing right now probably cost what any of those suits did.

"I wonder where these things disappear to," Harris is saying. "These trends, or whatever you want to call them. You do something all the time, and then one day you're telling somebody about the things you used to do. It's peculiar, getting older." He smiles at Rosie. "I'd advise against it. Oh, well, who has time for those little dinners? Who can afford that sort of thing these days? More expensive than eating out every night. Which is pretty much what we do now. Well, or order in, actually. Elizabeth gets sick of it, but to tell you the truth I'd much rather have Chinese in those cardboard things than one of those grand—just something from the deli. A sandwich . . ."

"Pastrami sandwich," Rosie says.

"Pastrami sandwich," he agrees. "In bed. Hmm!" He stands up impatiently, and walks over to the window. "Light so late."

Rosie looks at him. "I should probably leave," she says.

"No, no," he says. "Not at all. Finish your tea."

For a moment there's disastrously nothing to say. It would be rude to just run now, Rosie thinks; it would make him feel that he'd been rude. "Aren't you going to have some, too?" Rosie manages. "Tea?"

"Hmm," Harris says. "Or something. Now, that's a thought."

Rosie swings her feet over the side of the bed.

"Easy does it," he says.

What he seems to want, it turns out, is not really to hustle her away but to resettle her in the living room. "More comfortable here, yes?" he says. "Less like death's door."

She's curled up on some divan-type thing, and he's given her an astonishingly soft little blanket—*cashmere*, she thinks—to tuck around her feet.

"So, tell me," he says, as he makes himself a drink. "Tell me something. Who are you? What are you?"

Rosie looks at him.

"Quite a sight, you realize. Strolling into your own room and there's a dying artist on the bed."

"I'm feeling better," Rosie says.

"Good," Harris says.

"Really much better."

"I notice," Harris says, "that you're evading my subtle but probing questions. No matter—I'll try another. Are you . . . let's see . . . in art school?"

Rosie hesitates. "Actually, I'm not in school at all anymore."

"Um-hmm," he says. He waits for a moment, taking a sip of his drink. "So, you are no longer in school, and now you are . . ."

Rosie shakes her head, and gestures helplessly.

"Biding your time," Harris says. "Just biding your time . . ."

"Yes . . ." Rosie says.

"And painting while you're doing it . . . That's a nice thing to be able to do—paint . . ."

Rosie looks down at the undrinkable reddish liquid in her teacup.

"But it must be very interesting, what you do," she says.

"Not really," he says. "It's really rather boring, most of the time over here on our side. Tense, but boring. Elizabeth gets some of the fun—travel, dinners, armies at her command . . . I just sit here." He smiles at Rosie. "Oh, not to complain. The *situations*, I suppose you'd call them, in my line can be quite . . . There are some real pirates out there, I'll tell you. Rascals. Real buccaneers. Of course, you don't know how some of those characters can live with themselves."

He doesn't *look* bored, Rosie notes; a little smile has crept over his face as he thinks about it all.

"Much better to be a painter," he says. "You've got to be able to look at yourself in the mirror. Well. And is that your beau?"

"My . . . ?" she begins.

"The other painter. Your beau?"

"Oh," she says. "Jamie?" Harris is holding his drink up so that the ice casts strange reflections on the wall. "No, Jamie's just a friend."

"Ah ha," Harris says.

The potent, otherworldly aroma of paint pervades even this room faintly. Rosie leans back, shutting her eyes, and breathes it in. Maybe it's coming from her.

"I understand, from the decorator, that he's very serious about his art."

"Very," Rosie says, happily; Harris doesn't even know Morgan's name! "But people don't buy his paintings much. It's discouraging . . ."

"Of course," Harris says. "It must be hard not to lose heart . . . but I suppose you all must really love what you do."

Rosie bows her head. Poor Jamie; lucky Jamie.

It's twilight, she notices—twilight has drifted into the room like a fragrance, entwining with the smell of the oils. "So. You're feeling better?" Harris says.

"Oh," Rosie says. "I should—"

"Because if you are, maybe you'd like a drink."

She looks at him. "Well, yes, actually. Actually, I would."

He pours another for himself and one of whatever it is for her. "I drink so rarely these days," he says. "Mostly when Elizabeth's away. The thing is, drinking makes me crazy for a cigarette."

Rosie smiles.

"Would you be horrified?" he says.

She shakes her head.

"Because I happen to know where Elizabeth hides them."

He leaves the room and comes back in a moment, flourishing one. "We quit together years ago, but I happen to know she still sneaks one from time to time." He wiggles an eyebrow at Rosie. "The sneak. Oh, damn—" he says, looking around.

"Matches?" Rosie says. "I've got matches—" She dives into her backpack. She's sure there are some in there, from the old days. She comes up with a matchbook, opens it, bends a match over, and strikes it, holding it out for Harris.

For an instant, his eyes flicker over the matches, half of them creased and blackened, then he inclines toward them and inhales, bringing the cigarette to life.

He leans back, eyes closed, and exhales a rich plume. "Fantastic," he says. He opens his eyes and smiles at her. "Back to the subject. So. Where were we? Artists: not losing heart. Other painter: not your boyfriend . . ."

"Well," Rosie says. "I was going out with someone, but we broke up this winter."

"Pity," Harris says.

Rosie shrugs. Another life. Had she even really cared about Ian? No—her magic blood saw to its own cravings.

Harris is looking at her. "Artist, too?"

"Oh, no," Rosie says. "Ian, never."

"And what was his field?"

Rosie frowns. "Well," she says. "Commodities, basically."

Harris inhales, and exhales luxuriously again. "Not for you, was it?" he says. "You found the life restricting?"

"Yes, I guess . . ." Rosie says. "I was . . . Actually, I felt as if I weren't even alive . . ."

"Ah," Harris says. "That's the choice, isn't it. That's the question. I'm sure it seems very hard to you, an artist's life. Restlessness, fear, discouragement . . . despair, yes? Even despair. While for people like me or your ex, it all seems to be under control. And in many ways, it all is under control. I'm sure you artistic types think we have it easy, and we do—aside from the normal quota of human misery, of course. But it's all *settled*—it's settled. We've answered the questions a certain way, we've made our choices. But then what? Not to say we aren't . . . Not to say . . . which is all very well, but come my age a lot of men look around and say, '*Wait*, this is my life, it's my only life, the only one I'm ever going to have.' I know men whose lives were just perfect. Men who had a perfect life and just threw it all over. Left perfect wives, perfect jobs, perfect families . . . Because they just couldn't resist some impulse. To spoil the perfect thing, is what some people say. But I think it's more the thought of . . . we're all going to *die*, do you see? Think of it, Rosie—the cold, the still-ness, the *finality* . . ." He stubs out his cigarette. "Well. But you must know men like that."

For a moment they sit in silence. "It's dark," Harris says, in surprise, and switches on a lamp. "There. *Let there be* . . . You know, I've got so much stuff here I bet you'd really appreciate. Elizabeth and I aren't collectors in any serious sense of the word, but we have picked up some awfully good things over the years, in my opinion. Should we see if you agree?"

He takes her through the apartment, turning on little lights over paintings and drawings, which are now hung on all but the bedroom walls, and speaks of each one knowledgeably and lovingly. His hand rests on her shoul-der, her wrist, the small of her back, as he shows her around, causing tears to come to her eyes and cruel little flames to flick at her bones, snapping around them like a lash. "What do you think of this?" he says, pausing in front of a painting.

Rosie's eyes clear, and the painting appears in front of her. "It's wonderful . . ." she says, surprised. The pain-ting's alight; the whole room is alight. "Really wonder-ful . . ."

"Yes, it's wonderful," he says. "That's right. This is the one." He gives her a pleased, brief little hug. "You're very easy to talk to," he says. "It's absolutely frightening. I wish you didn't have to go."

She stares at the painting in front of her. Its shapes leap and dance as Harris rests his hand on the back of her neck.

"I just can't tell what's in your mind," Harris says. "It's an attractive quality, you know; I'll bet you're very at-tractive to men."

She shakes her head, slowly. Hot shame creeps up her skin as she thinks back to the sort of men she used to be attractive to, in the days when it was easier just to fuck the guy instead of having the tedious discussion about why

you weren't going to and then doing it anyhow, to get him
to leave. "A long time ago," she says, "there were a lot of
men. But then, thank God, Ian came along."

"Hmm," Harris says. His hand drops away. "Well," he
says again. But this time clearly, it's an instruction: "I wish
you didn't have to go . . ."

Rosie's heart plunges. "I wish I didn't, too," she says,
and steps obediently to the door.

He holds it open and smiles, but when she looks up at
him to see what she's done wrong, his smile fades, and he
folds his arms around her. "Going to be here this weekend?" he says into her ear.

She rubs her cheek against his marvelous shirt; her heart
is beating so furiously that for a moment she can't speak.
"Do you want my number at Jamie's?" she says.

"I do," he says, and releases her. "I certainly do. Maybe
we can . . . grab a pastrami sandwich—I'll be at loose ends
here till Tuesday evening."

Paper is waiting at a little maple desk. Rosie writes out
her number, and when she hands it to him he puts his
arms around her again, adjusts her slightly, and gives her
a kiss more debilitating than whole encounters she's had
in bed; so graphic that, hours later, she's still trembling.

But he doesn't call. It's Sunday evening, and he still
hasn't called. Of course, it's really only been two days. No,
one day, really—Saturday.

And yet there's only Monday to go. Well, Monday, and
Monday night. And Tuesday, of course—Tuesday during
the day . . . before Elizabeth returns. At least during the
day after Lupe leaves.

"Think you might eat something ever again?" Jamie
says, on a visit to the apartment. "Just as a favor to your
fans? Or are you intending to spend the rest of your life
in this room?"

Rosie rolls over in bed to face the wall.

He sighs. "Want to tell me what's the matter?"

"Nothing's the matter," she says. "Nothing. Just nothing."

After Jamie leaves, she gets herself into the tub, and stays, for hours, with her friend the duck bobbing blankly between patches of suds on the water's dirty surface. Her skin is tormented from thinner, but she scrubs away at it, crying.

Her friend the duck! She grabs it and hurls it into the corner, near the toilet. Could he have lost her number, possibly? Did he expect *her* to make the call? Well, but maybe he did, actually . . . What he'd said was he'd be at loose ends "until Tuesday evening." And, actually, he might not have put it that way, in fact, exactly, if he *wasn't* expecting her to make the call.

When after the fourth ring he picks up the phone, she can hear a little scrap of voices even before he says hello; obviously he's in the middle of dinner, or something. A conversation. Rosie uses her thumb to cut the connection, soundlessly. A jolly enough dinner, that's for sure—they were laughing, all of them, whoever they were. Well, not *all* of them, exactly—the *others* were laughing; Harris, the fact is . . . was *chewing*.

Three cheers for Mrs. Howell's Fiorinal. It's eradicated the time perfectly. And Rosie has finally, after all these months, got a truly decent sleep. Two dear little pills took care of Sunday night, then three eliminated Monday, and only five more, actually, were needed to roll Wednesday morning right up to Rosie's bedside.

For several hours now, Rosie has had to stand up and walk and talk—and she's been able to, though her hangover still makes an odd, gauzy curtain over everything in view. Just as well: the view has included Elizabeth; the great, rumpled bed, all its noisy turmoil exposed in the glare of Lupe's day off; and, of course, Harris. Who could not have been friendlier or more pleasant, to Rosie and Jamie as well as to Morgan.

The five of them have stood together, looking at the bedroom walls. There's no doubt that Morgan is satisfied, although, Rosie notes through her hangover, he's more muted—softer—than usual; it'll probably be some time till he runs into Jamie again. And Elizabeth is clearly pleased, in her surgical way. And, naturally, it's all just fine with Harris.

They're quiet for a minute or so, turned toward the glinting blue out the window as if a trance had fallen over them. Elizabeth speaks dreamily into the silence. "Let's get a boat next summer, darling. Let's get a boat and go sailing off, right into the sky . . ."

"We'll discuss this," Harris says.

Elizabeth laughs. "Sloth," she says affectionately. "You know you'll love it . . ."

They make their goodbyes. Morgan delivers his gracious little speech of thanks to Jamie, and, as Elizabeth begins her gracious little speech of thanks to Morgan, Harris takes Rosie's hands in both of his and looks at her. "The important thing," he says in a low, vibrant voice, "is to keep painting, Rosie . . . Trust your talent. Trust your future." And he gives her a special little smile—formal, final, but just for her. She'll see that smile more vividly, she knows, in the starkness of memory, when the curtain rises.

"It's been real," Jamie says to a wall, and turns to Rosie. "Ready?"

"Just a moment," Rosie says. "Let me wash my hands."

The slip glimmers as though it's been waiting for her; it tumbles into her arms as she touches it. A rescue? Oh, no, not at all. Rosie stuffs it violently into her backpack as she will later stuff it violently to the rear of Vincent's dusty shelves, and then, she assures herself, she'll never give these people another thought.

But what will *they* think, Elizabeth and Harris? Or, to put it more precisely, what will Elizabeth think, and what will Harris think? Because—Rosie removes a fleck of paint from the faucet—they'll be thinking about her, all right. They will. Yes, *let* them think about her . . .

Mermaids

"GOOD? NOT GOOD?" MR. LASKEY SAID. "WHAT
do you say, girls?"

"Kiss kiss," Alice said, making two spoons kiss, and
Janey was just staring rudely into space, so it fell to Kyla
(as it had all day) to make things all right. "It's perfect,"
she assured Mr. Laskey, and, true, the old-fashioned gleam
and clatter, the waitresses in their pastel uniforms, the
glass dishes with their ice-cream spheres, the other little
groups of wealthy tourists and even New Yorkers, all of
this would be exactly what her mother was back home
picturing.

Spring vacation had been hurtling down toward Kyla for
weeks and weeks, at first just a fleck troubling the margin
of her vision, then closer and larger and faster until it
smashed into place, obliterating everything that wasn't itself, and Kyla's mother was dropping her off at the Laskeys', where they were waiting for her, and Mrs. Laskey
was smoothing Janey's dress and giving little Alice a hug,
and for one fractured and repeating moment Kyla was saying goodbye to Richie Laskey, and then the car door shut
Kyla in with Alice and Janey and Mr. Laskey, and Mrs.
Laskey and Richie were waving goodbye, and Alice began

to cry at the top of her lungs, as though she were being snatched away by killers. "Oh, grow up, Alice," Janey said.

The airport was gray and shiny, like a hospital where Kyla was to be anesthetized and detached hygienically from home. A corridor of shiny gray time sucked her in along with Janey and Alice and Mr. Laskey, and then the crowd in which they were to be conveyed away compressed itself into the tube of the airplane.

"You get the window seat," Janey said to Kyla. "You're the guest."

Seven days, Kyla had thought; seven days before she could go home, seven days of being the guest, seven days of having to have a good time—even though she was with Janey Laskey. "That's okay," she said. "Take it if you want it."

"You take it," Janey said. "I've been on lots of planes before. I get to go on planes all the time."

Kyla looked around for Mr. Laskey, but he was already settled into the seat across the aisle from Alice, and one of the stewardesses was leaning over him, laughing and laughing, as he told a joke about a fox and a bunny rabbit. And Kyla would have taken the window seat then (because someone should show Janey she couldn't always get away with that sort of thing) but the thought of her mother's pleading look intervened, so she just shook her head and sat down, thunk, where she was.

Janey shrugged. "Okay," she'd said, squishing her porky rear end past, to the good seat, "I guess some people don't like it. Some people are scared to look out the window." She opened the big book she was carrying and squinted down at it, following the print with her finger; her thin hair, the color of cardboard, drooped forward; obviously she should be wearing glasses.

Poor Janey. "What's your book about?" Kyla asked.

Janey jumped slightly. "Oliver *Twist*?" she said, and looked at Kyla. "Is about orphans."

"*Sor*-ry," Kyla said.

Air whooshed through some little spouts above them, the lights flickered, and a heartless angel's voice instructed them to strap themselves in.

No, Kyla thought. No no no no no. She closed her eyes; the gravity of her will flowed around the seats and into the little compartments: *The plane was growing heavier and heavier*—it would sit, the plane, heavy with her will; darkness would come; someone would open the door, and they could all go home. But for one instant there was a flaw in her concentration—or was it in her sincerity? Her will was flicked aside like an insect and the plane rose, through a great roaring.

The stewardess returned to make a big fuss over Alice. "Kindergarten, *already?*" she sang out, amazed, to Alice, who confirmed this with a gracious nod. The stewardess straightened up, twirled a bit of stray hair around her finger and tucked it back into place, smiling brilliantly at Mr. Laskey. Janey stared at her with loathing and then turned to the window.

"Guess what you can see from up here," Janey turned back to say to Kyla. "You can see the bodies in the lagoons."

"There are no bodies in the lagoons," Kyla had said firmly, for Alice's benefit, but Alice was playing happily with the safety instruction card, like someone who has no troubles in the world.

"They look just like mermaids, except they're face up," Janey said. "Their hair floats, and their legs are green and slimy."

"*Don't,*" Kyla said.

"*Eleven-year-old Courtney Collier disappeared from the mall at ten o'clock this morning while her mother was buying a new tie for Mr. Collier,*" Janey said. " '*Courtney was a beautiful little girl,*' authorities said. '*We're totally positive it was a sex crime.*' "

Seven days; seven more days. Minus the three hours and fifteen minutes between getting from the Laskeys' house to wherever it was they were now. Minus this second. Minus this second. Kyla leaned across Janey to see: Naturally there were no dead girls. You couldn't even see the lagoons—all you could see were clouds.

Now most of that seven days was over with. Sunday night Kyla had settled into the room she was to share with Janey and Alice, with the blue carpet and the alien blue-flowered wallpaper, and she'd carefully put her clothing into a bureau drawer or hung it on the hotel's heavy wooden hangers—how strange it looked on those hangers in that big, dark closet that smelled like wood and furniture polish and very faintly of other people, though nobody in particular. Then she and Janey had to play Brides with Alice to calm her down and they had all gone to sleep.

"I want you girls in bed early," Mr. Laskey had said, "except on the nights we've got tickets. And there are going to be some serious naps around here. Agreed? The days will be pretty strenuous, and I don't want to arrive back home with three little zombies. Now. I'll be right next door, but I'm looking forward to a little stress-reduction myself, and you have an entire hotel staff downstairs at your disposal. Kindly take advantage of that unusual fact. If you need anything, Donald will be at the concierge's desk every afternoon and night."

And it *had* been . . . strenuous. On Monday evening they'd gone to a restaurant with waiters in tuxedos, where Kyla had worn the new party dress her mother had gotten her for the trip, and Tuesday night she'd worn the dress again, when Mr. Laskey let them stay up late and they'd gone to a show with poor people who were singing and dancing. And yesterday evening they had gone to another amazing restaurant, in Greenwich Village, where everyone—all the waitresses and all the customers—looked like models. And during the days they'd gone to the Empire State Building and the Planetarium and the Statue of Liberty and the Museum of Natural History and various other museums (which Janey claimed to enjoy) and they'd walked in the big, dirty, interesting park with the little fringe of silver buildings at the edges, and they'd gone in a horse-drawn carriage, and had taken a boat around the whole island, and along with all that there had been a revolving display of fascinating delis and coffee shops and people you couldn't believe had even been *born*, and long, sludgy naps in the sad blue room where it seemed Kyla had been living with Janey and Alice forever.

So now there was only tonight and then Friday and then Saturday, and on Sunday they'd get back in the plane, and on Monday morning Kyla would wake up in her own bed and all the big blank obstacles that at one time had been between her and home would have dissolved into a picture she could remember for her mother at breakfast.

Because at the time something was happening, of course, you didn't know what it was like. At the time a thing was happening, that thing was not, for instance, *New York*. *New York* was what her mother was at home picturing. The place where you actually *were* was a street corner with wads of paper in the gutter, or it was standing there, facing the worn muzzle of the horse that had pulled your carriage, or it was sitting in front of a little stain on the tablecloth. *It* really wasn't *like* anything—it was just whatever it was, and there was never a place in your mind of the right size and shape to put it. But afterwards, the thing fit exactly into your memory as if there had always been a place— just right, just waiting for it.

On Monday morning, she would be home. She would be telling her mother over breakfast all about *New York*. And Kyla would know—because she'd be remembering it—just what *New York* was *like*. But today was the biggest obstacle so far. She was so tired that her body kept forgetting to do things in its usual way—even to sit in its chair properly, and Alice was easily upset, as though the nightmares that had plagued her all night long were rustling and hissing at her feet. And Janey was behaving . . . *abominably*, so Kyla had to be extra careful about everything. "It's just perfect," she said.

"Yes, this, girls, is New York as it used to be," Mr. Laskey said. "Genteel, clean, gracious . . ." He sighed. *"Oh, where are the snows . . ."*

Janey rolled her eyes.

It was preferable, Kyla thought, when Janey just *said* whatever horrible thoughts were in her mind. Otherwise, they just leaked out and dripped all over *your* mind . . .

"Try to have a wonderful time, darling," Kyla's mother had said. "And make sure to remember everything for me." And she looked at Kyla so sadly and sweetly.

Her mother was far away now. And tiny, standing there and peering through a dark distance for Kyla. Oh, why did her mother look so sad? Why? *Kyla* knew: because of her, because she had made her mother feel bad. She had made her mother feel—and this was a fact—as though she had forced Kyla to go on this trip against her will. And now, there was her mother, tiny and fragile across the miles, straining anxiously, as if Kyla had become lost right in the field of brilliant stars that at home shone so sparsely and coldly and far away.

Mr. Laskey raised his hand in the air to summon a waitress. "We'll see if the ice cream is as good as it used to be," he said.

"When Grandfather Laskey used to bring you here," Janey intoned.

Mr. Laskey hesitated. "Yes, Jane . . ." he said seriously, as though Janey had brought up some interesting point (but soon, Kyla thought, and her insides felt odd and sparkly, Mr. Laskey was going to decide to get angry) ". . . when Grandfather Laskey used to bring me to New York—"

"—on business!" One of Alice's spoons said enthusiastically to the other.

Janey snickered.

"Put those spoons down, Alice," Mr. Laskey said. He signaled again for a waitress. "It's not nice."

Alice dropped her spoons on the table and put her hands over her face. "Aha," Mr. Laskey said as a waitress appeared. "There you are."

The waitress smiled unhappily around the table. "What pretty blue eyes," she said to Alice, who was peeking skeptically through her fingers.

The waitress turned to Kyla first. She would be supposing, Kyla thought, that Kyla was one of them—that she belonged to the handsome man who only had to raise his hand in the air to bring over a waitress. Kyla, and not Janey. Because no matter how much Mrs. Laskey paid for Janey's clothes (plenty, Kyla's mother said), Janey always looked as if she'd been dressed out of some old lady's trunk. Yes, the waitress was smiling in such a kind and unhappy way—she must be admiring Kyla's soft brown hair, the dainty little skirt and sweater her mother had chosen for her at Baskin's. The waitress herself was not pretty at all. Although that, of course, made no difference. Just, it was what Kyla could feel *Janey* was thinking. "I'm sorry," Kyla said. "I haven't decided."

"So what can I get you, doll face?" the waitress asked Alice.

"What will it be for Alice?" Mr. Laskey said.

"Ice cream for Alice," Alice confided huskily to the waitress.

"Yes?" Mr. Laskey said. He smiled at the waitress. "Are you sure? Or do you want cinnamon toast?"

Alice looked at Mr. Laskey uncertainly. "Cimona . . ." she began, and halted warily.

"Do you know, Alice," Mr. Laskey said, "that this is one of the few places on the planet, along with our hotel, that still has cinnamon toast on the menu?"

He looked at the waitress, who made a little giggle and then looked surprised at herself. "That's right," she said.

Mr. Laskey tugged a lock of Alice's soft hair. "She's been eating nothing but cinnamon toast since we got to New York," he said. "Haven't you, Alice?"

Alice appeared briefly puzzled, then nodded vigorously.

"Good old Alice—sucking up to everyone as usual," Janey remarked, in some neutral area between audible and not audible.

Mr. Laskey's expression wavered, then settled down. "And what's your pleasure, Kyla?" he said. "Decided yet?"

This was always a terrible moment, and it was one that occurred about three times every day. Her mother had told her to be especially careful not to order the most expensive thing on the menu, but it didn't seem that the price of something was what Mr. Laskey was particularly thinking about.

She shook her head, watching him.

"Well, I'm having a hot fudge sundae," he said. "Why not join me?"

She felt herself beginning to blush. "Okay," she said.

"Good girl," he said, and Kyla tossed her hair back.

"Alice . . . Alice . . ." Alice began.

"Chill out, Alice," Janey said.

"You want cinnamon toast, sweetheart," Mr. Laskey said.

"Oh," Alice agreed cheerfully.

"Janey?" Mr. Laskey said.

Janey turned to him with the look she could make that was as if she were gazing at something on the other side of a person.

"A promise is a promise," Mr. Laskey said. "Would you like a hot fudge sundae, too?"

Janey continued to stare at him as red waves came up into her face. "Fruit salad," she said.

Mr. Laskey looked down at the table as if it were an old, old enemy. "I'd like the fruit salad, *please*," he said.

A promise is a promise. And what it was that had been promised—Kyla had been there; she had heard it—was *anything we like.*

It was a night she'd had to sleep over at the Laskeys'.

"I hate going to the Laskeys'," she'd said.

"Well, where will we put you, sweetie?" her mother said. "Because you've had too many sleepovers at Ellen's lately."

Kyla hesitated. "Could we call Courtney?" she said.

"Oh, no, sweetie," her mother said. "I don't think so, do you?"

"Why not?" Kyla said.

"Well, we don't really know the Colliers very well, do we? We can't ask them for favors."

Favors, Kyla thought; was she a "favor"?

"Besides, we don't really know what kind of people they are."

Kyla looked at her mother. "They're nice," she said.

"I'm sure they are, sweetie," her mother said. "But, no."

"Why do I have to sleep over at anyone's?" Kyla said.

"Oh, because," her mother said. "I'm going out to dinner with a friend."

"But—" Kyla said. "So why can't I just stay home by myself? Until you've eaten dinner?"

"And what would you do for dinner?" her mother said.

"I could have something," Kyla said. "From the microwave. Just like I do when you work late."

Her mother stroked her hair. "Just *as* I do."

"Why not?" Kyla said.

"Well, darling—" Her mother smiled gently. "Because I need time to see my friends just as you need time to see your friends."

But the point was, Kyla thought, she didn't need time to see her friends. All she and her friends had was time—

time and time and time. Waiting through the long, dull afternoons, the whole funnel of Kyla's memory, playing upstairs with the dolls or games or trading cards they'd been given to play with, doing each other's hair, pretending Brides or Baby or Shopping just like Alice did now, pretending—there was nothing else to do—that they were pretending, until it was time to come back down for milk and cookies or for one of them to be taken home. Waiting to understand the point of the dolls or games they'd been presented with, waiting for the afternoon to turn into night or for Sunday to turn into Monday, or for August to turn into September, or for nine years old to turn into ten and ten to turn, heavily, into eleven. Waiting alone in front of the television for the long evenings to fall away. Staring at the screen as if they were staring through periscopes for land, and in the dim evening rooms, the world, the distant world—which was what they must be waiting for—approached, welled into the screens, and the evening fell away in half-hour pieces. And then, finally, there was bed, and another long day had been completed. "What friend do you need time to see?" Kyla said.

"Stand up straight, darling," her mother said. "You don't want to look like Margie Strayhorn, do you? Doctor Loeffler."

Dr. Loeffler—Kyla stared. Dr. Loeffler had come over the week before and filled up their pretty living room, which he was much too big for, and her mother had made Kyla sit there for no reason at all. And the whole time—while Kyla looked at the shiny black hairs on the backs of his hands—this Dr. Loeffler had had a little smile, as if something were funny, or ridiculous. "You were planning this!" Kyla said. "Why didn't you tell me before? You knew you were going to do this!"

"Darling," her mother said with a breathless little laugh. "What do you mean?"

A tear had squirted into each eye, and yet the thing that Kyla meant, which had been so clear the instant before, was gone—simply gone—as if a hand had materialized and closed around it. "I don't like Dr. Loeffler," she said.

"Sweetie," her mother said, and no trace of the laugh was left, "you mustn't be so severe—you only met him once. Dr. Loeffler's a very fine man—He's only forty-two years old, and he's the head of the entire division of internal medicine at Hillsdale."

"*Only* forty-two years old," Kyla said.

"Don't be such a *cross* old thing," her mother said happily. "Besides, maybe the Laskeys will give you spaghetti again."

The Laskeys had not, however. Instead, there had been some sort of meat with a strange dark sauce and a fancy name.

"How was everyone's day?" Mr. Laskey said—which was what he said first thing every time Kyla had ever had dinner at the Laskeys'. He looked around the table. "Richard?"

Richie raised his serious dark eyes and then lowered them again. "Fine," he said.

"Yes?" Mr. Laskey said. He waited, his fork in his hand.

Dinner had only begun. Soon Mrs. Laskey and Janey and Alice would be crying and shouting, and then there would be after dinner, when Kyla would have to play with Janey, and then there would be morning, when she'd have to play with Janey yet again, before her mother came for her.

"Biology was interesting," Richie said. "We're studying the wheat rust cycle."

"Very good," Mr. Laskey said. "And what about calculus? Didn't you have a test the other day? I never heard how that went."

"That's a third-year class," Mrs. Laskey said. "Isn't it enough that—"

"It went fine," Richie said. "I got an A."

Mr. Laskey nodded. "There you go," he said. "You see?"

Chew slowly, one of Kyla's teachers had said once. *Your stomach has no teeth.* But what she was chewing, she thought, was the body of an animal, with blood cooked into it.

"And track?" Mr. Laskey said.

"Okay," Richie said.

A silence rose separately from Richie and Mr. Laskey and consolidated.

Richie was so . . . dignified, really, was the word, Kyla thought. Everything about him was clean and dignified. Even the way he ate—as if food were clean, as if all the frantic things your own animal's body did with it, with even the body of other animals, was just clean and ordinary.

"*Alice*—" Mrs. Laskey said, and the block of silence over the table became porous and dissolved.

"I came in ahead of Nelson Howell today," Richie said.

"What did I tell you," Mr. Laskey said.

"—You don't have to kill it, Alice," Mrs. Laskey said. "It's already dead."

"I did my report on Native Americans today," Janey said loudly. "Miss Feldman said it was the best report."

Kyla glanced inadvertently at Richie.

"Mother," Richie said, "Jane's prevaricating again."

"I am not!" Janey said. "It was really interesting. In lots of tribes the girls—"

"Pre . . ." Alice began, scowling quizzically at Mr. Laskey. "What does—"

"Absolutely nothing, Alice," Mr. Laskey said. "In this case."

"In *lots* of *tribes* the girls bleed and they go out to little—"

"*Not* at the table, Jane," Mrs. Laskey said.

"Janey made it up?" Alice said.

"No," Mr. Laskey said. "Yes."

"They *do*," Janey said. "They—"

"You heard your mother," Mr. Laskey said. "Not at the

table." He turned to Kyla. "And what about you? Did you do a report today, too?"

"I did mine last week," Kyla said. And then, because it looked like Janey was about to erupt again, "It was about ballet dancers."

"Bal*let* dancers," Mr. Laskey said. He dipped his head as if he were tipping a hat.

"Bal*let* dancers," Janey said. "Yeah, wow, bal*let* dancers. Well, throw *you* a bone."

Mrs. Laskey snorted.

"Now," Mr. Laskey said. "Who wants more of this excellent . . . This . . . Kyla?"

"No, thank you," Kyla said.

"The child eats nothing," Mr. Laskey said admiringly. "She will vanish into thin air."

"More for Alice!" Alice shouted, flinging herself at the serving plate.

"Alice," Mrs. Laskey said, "kindly restrain yourself— look what you've done to your father's tie."

"Plus guess what, Alice," Janey said. "Your table manners make us all puke."

"Jane," Mrs. Laskey said warningly, "Alice—"

"Incidentally," Richie said. *Incidentally*, Kyla thought. "Scott Ryerson invited me to go skiing with him and his family over spring vacation."

"I want to go, too—" Janey said.

"Oh, were you invited as well, Jane?" Mr. Laskey said.

"Mother," Janey said. "Why does Richie always get to do everything?"

"Nobody said anything about—" Mr. Laskey said.

"But Alice and I never—" Jane said.

"Stop that this instant," Mrs. Laskey said. She turned to Alice, who was plucking at her. *"No,"* she said. "And I am not going to ask you one more time to behave."

Mrs. Laskey's fury was always like a gun pointing at the table; it made you tired, Kyla thought, waiting for it to go off. Her own mother never raised her voice, and she was always kind and patient. Everyone knew how patient she was. Lots of people said it was why (and the other people said it was because) she was such a good nurse. But that was frightening, too. No matter how angry Mrs. Laskey got, it was better than the look of disappointment her own mother got when Kyla did something wrong. Because when people got angry, they were angry and then they stopped being angry, and it was something that went from them to you. But when people were disappointed in you, it was something that went from you to them. You did something to them. It was as if you had made a hole in them, or had gotten a spot on them that could never be taken away.

"Where do Scott's people ski?" Mr. Laskey said.

"See, Mother?" Janey said. "Mother, don't you—"

"Jane," Mrs. Laskey said. "If I don't get—"

"All right," Mr. Laskey said, and everyone stopped talking. "Yes," he said, quietly. "Fair enough. Janey, your point is well taken. And has given me an excellent idea: Rich will go skiing over spring vacation, I will take you and Alice to New York, and your mother—your *mother* will have one entire week of peace, all to herself."

Mrs. Laskey put down her fork. "Excuse me?" she said.

Richie continued his pristine eating. "Correct me if I'm wrong," Mrs. Laskey said, slowly, "but weren't you just in New York?"

"On business," Mr. Laskey agreed pleasantly.

"And now you propose to go right back," Mrs. Laskey said.

"Not *right* back," Mr. Laskey said. "No."

"May I please be excused?" Richie said.

"You may," Mr. Laskey said. "In the future, please do not interrupt."

"I'm sorry," Richie said.

"Apologies accepted," Mr. Laskey said.

"And when did you become so enamored of New York?" Mrs. Laskey said. "The last time you and I were there together, *hellish sewer*, I believe, was what you . . . It's a filthy place, and you loathe it, and you are now proposing to go right back and expose the girls to it, for what reason I cannot—"

"*As* you know"—Mr. Laskey overrode her—"As you *know*, Carol, the events of my childhood upon which I look back with the greatest affection are those trips I took to New York with my father. As you know, I consider those excursions to be the single most meaningful experience of my childhood. It was during those trips that I felt closest to my father and learned to honor his values . . ."

Mrs. Laskey was staring at him incredulously. "His *values*," she said. She picked up her glass of water and drank until, to Kyla's amazement, the glass was empty. "I should go with you," she said. "That's what I should do."

A long, long look, arcing between Mr. and Mrs. Laskey, was pierced by a rising wail from Alice.

"Alice—" Mr. Laskey said. "What's the matter, sweetheart?"

Alice put her head on the table as though it was about to be chopped off. "It's all right, darling," Mrs. Laskey said. "You're just tired."

"Soon to bed," Mr. Laskey said. "But first, what's for dessert? What kind of ice cream do we have back there? Ice cream, Kyla?"

"No, thank you," Kyla said, because before you knew it you could turn into a clump, like Janey.

"Yes, please, chocolate," Janey said.

"There's some fruit for you," Mrs. Laskey said. "Remember those five pounds."

"Daddy—" Janey said.

Mr. Laskey glanced at Janey; his glance held and sharpened. "Your mother has spoken," he said.

"And *you* can take it easy, too," Mrs. Laskey said. "I don't want to get a phone call from New York telling me you've dropped dead in your hotel room."

"I don't want to go to New York," Janey said suddenly.

Mr. Laskey took Janey's wrist and Kyla heard her quick

intake of breath. "You cannot have it both ways, Jane," he said. "You cannot complain that Rich has privileges and then behave like a prima donna yourself. Of course you want to go to New York. We'll have a wonderful time, if you'll just stop this nonsense." He released her wrist and patted her hand. "We'll treat ourselves like royalty. We'll do anything we want and have ice cream whenever we want. A trip to New York City! Isn't that ideal? Ideal, girls? Ideal, Alice?"

Upstairs in her fancy bedroom Janey had more toys than anyone, a whole closet stacked with games and toys, and dolls, too. She was *spoiled*, Kyla thought, and that was a fact. But the only thing she ever wanted to do was play Scrabble or read one of her great, thick books. Or worse, talk.

"My Great-aunt Jane who I was named for," she said, "used to have a mansion in New York. She had a lot of famous paintings, that you see in books, and jewels. Unfortunately, she passed away, or I'd get to stay there when I go to New York."

"What happened to all her stuff?" Kyla said. Oh, why was she doing this? Encouraging a person who couldn't help lying was worse than *being* the person. "How come you don't have it?"

"Because unfortunately," Janey said, "her husband gambled it all away. At the . . . gaming table. So we'll have to stay at a hotel, like the Plaza, or the Carlyle. But places like that are all right."

"Do you stay at those places a lot?" Kyla said.

"Well, not just actually," Janey said. "But whenever my parents go anywhere, they always write me letters about it and bring me back . . . mementos. When they went to San Francisco this fall they brought me back a whole huge suitcase full of presents."

"That's nice," Kyla said. She stood up and stretched. "I don't feel like talking anymore."

"So what?" Janey said. "Neither do I. I want to read my book."

And then, in the morning, of course there was Scrabble. Kyla could see Richie out in the front yard with John Hammond and then, finally, her mother's car.

"My mother's here," she said. "I'm going down."

"Relax," Janey said. "She'll call up for you when she's ready. We've got time for one more game at least."

"You're cheating," Kyla said.

"Cheating!" Janey yelped.

" 'Sosing' is not a word," Kyla said.

"It is, too," Janey said. "It means to send an S.O.S. Besides, you have to say something when the person does it."

"I'm not playing anymore," Kyla said.

She wandered down to the living room, where her mother was talking to Mrs. Laskey.

"Good morning, sleepyhead," Mrs. Laskey said.

"Hello there," her mother said, as Kyla leaned on her arm. "Have a good time?"

Kyla nodded.

"We'll go in just a minute, sweetie," her mother said, "but first I want to talk to Carol a bit. Now, run on back upstairs, quick like a bunny."

Kyla freed herself from her mother's careless arm and wandered out to the hall, where she inspected Mrs. Laskey's collection of little crystal animals.

"I *saw* him get the idea," Mrs. Laskey was saying. "I saw it happen. And then he hauled in this load of horse shit about his father—his father's *values*—as vile an old swine as ever lived. What a genius Dick has for exploitation! He exploits his children, he exploits his poor old dead disgusting father . . ."

"Well, Carol," Kyla's mother said carefully, "you have been dying for a break. And this is the . . . And besides, he probably does want to spend some time with—"

"Dick?" Mrs. Laskey snorted. "That's very funny, Lorraine."

"Well, that's what I mean," Kyla's mother said, encouragingly. "After all, it's not something he does very often."

"And poor Janey," Mrs. Laskey said. "That poor kid is a born stooge. She was so *cute* when she was little. Of course, he simply adored her then. Now, there's nothing the poor child can do to—"

"She just needs friends," Kyla's mother said. "If she just spent more—"

Oh, no! Kyla thought.

But fortunately Mrs. Laskey had interrupted. "The worst thing," she was saying, "is you can see the man operating from a mile away."

"Well," Kyla's mother said, "of course this is a side of Dick I never—"

"*And* it's compulsive," Mrs. Laskey said. "He doesn't even know he's doing it. Do you know, I actually used to feel flattered by it?"

"Still," Kyla's mother said, "it is a wonderful opportunity for the girls. I only wish Kyla could—"

The little glass owl Kyla was examining almost slipped from her hand, but Mrs. Laskey had interrupted again.

"I used to feel flattered that he would expend so much energy just to manipulate me," she said. "That's how pathetic I was. That's where my self-esteem level was. But then I realized he was expending the same amount of effort manipulating everybody. He can't just *buy* a quart of milk, he has to get the store to *sell* it to him. But he's really got me over a—I'd just love to call him on this, but I don't dare give him a reason to—"

"No, no," Kyla's mother said. "At this point, I don't think you want to do anything to—"

"*New York*," Mrs. Laskey said. "All those filthy people from God only knows where . . . I just wonder how long this has been going on."

"Carol," Kyla's mother said. "I'm really serious. I really don't think it's prudent to jump to any . . . And besides, it's bound to be a wonderful learning opportunity for the girls. I only wish I could give Kyla an opportunity like this. And if anyone deserves a little time to herself, you know it's you."

Mrs. Laskey sighed loudly, and for a moment—since nothing else was happening—Kyla wondered if she could go back into the living room to get her mother. But then Mrs. Laskey laughed. "So, speaking of duplicitous sons-of-bitches," she said, "how was last night?"

"Why do you have to do it?" Ellen had said.

"I don't *have* to . . . ," Kyla said.

"You *want* to go on spring vacation with Janey Laskey?" Ellen said.

It was already the end of February. Snow from a recent storm still covered the ground and lay along the branches, and the sky was a glassy blue. But Kyla could feel spring marshaling strength right behind winter's fortifications.

"I feel sorry for her," Kyla said.

"I feel sorry for her, too," Courtney said.

"Well, I feel sorry for her, too," Ellen said. "When she's not around. But it's really hard to feel sorry for her when she is around."

"She's troubled," Kyla said.

"*Kyla*—" Ellen looked at her. " 'She's troubled.' "

"Besides," Kyla said. "I get to see New York."

"New York's great," Courtney said. "I used to get to go all the time. It's the worst thing about moving here."

"We'll probably stay at the Plaza or the Carlyle or some-place like that," Kyla said.

"I still don't see why your mother's making you do it," Ellen said.

"She *isn't*," Kyla said. She looked at Ellen in bewilderment. Oh. Of course. *Ellen was jealous.* "She just wants me to be able to go to all the museums and the ballet and that stuff. And Mrs. Laskey's her friend . . ."

"Kyla's mom is so sweet," Courtney said dreamily, and Kyla looked at her with gratitude; she was so pretty, sprawled out on Ellen's bed. The prettiest girl in school, and she was *their* friend—Kyla's and Ellen's. Her short blond hair fluffed out evenly, like a dandelion. Her blue eyes—lighter than the sky—reflected nothing.

"But why does your mom like Mrs. Laskey so much?" Ellen said.

"*Ellen,*" Kyla said.

"They have bags of money," Courtney said. "They have a big, huge money bin in their basement, my dad says."

"I think Mrs. Laskey's crazy," Ellen said. "My mother doesn't like her at all."

"My mother feels sorry for her," Kyla said. And then she said the thing she was never supposed to say, not about anyone, or was even supposed to know. "She used to be in the clinic where my mother works."

"I bet she takes pills," Courtney said. "You know the way she's all puffed up?" She studied her fingernails and frowned. "Mr. Laskey's handsome, but I'd hate to be married to him. They came to my parents' cocktail party last week, and Mr. Laskey and Peter Nussbaum's mother were flirting away like crazy."

"Really?" Ellen said.

"Mr. Laskey was flirting with everybody," Courtney said.

Kyla looked at her. Flirting. Flirting, actually, was when you . . . "What was he doing?" she asked.

"Just . . ." Courtney said. "Just nothing. He was flirting. He was flirting with my mother, too. I bet he flirts with your mother."

"No he doesn't," Kyla said, and her heart veered.

"Rich Laskey is nice, though," Ellen said.

"Rich Laskey?" Courtney said. "Rich Laskey is *gor-*

geous. But you know what? He looks exactly like Mr. Laskey, actually."

Ellen and Kyla looked at her. "Yikes," Ellen said. "That is so *strange* . . ."

Outside, the air was as clean as an apple, and the crystal branches were glittering. Kyla shut her eyes, to keep Mr. Laskey's face from Richie's, but the two merged unpleasantly. "I'm sick of sitting around," she said. "Let's go outside."

"It's cold," Courtney said. She shifted on the bed and sighed.

"What should we do?" Ellen said.

All around them were Ellen's toys and games. The television sat, opaque, in the next room. Dark, Kyla thought, but still seeing—still receiving everything that was happening. You could turn it off, but that only meant that *you* couldn't see, behind its darkness, what it was seeing. Sometimes at night, when you had to turn it off to go to sleep, you could feel the world seeping out from the blocked screen—the hot confusion of laughter, the footsteps pounding like a giant, besieged heart, the squealing tires, the eruptions of gunfire, and fearful pictures you couldn't help staring at before they vanished, and people at desks, smiling as though you'd imagined all the rest of it—rising up on all sides of you, staining the evening with the smells of blood and perfume and metal, staining the helpless moments before sleep, and your dreams, and the tattered edges where you broke through into morning.

"I know what we can do," Courtney said. She propped herself up lazily on an elbow. "One of us can pretend to be Richie Laskey."

How nice it would be to be at home, Kyla thought, in her own room. With soft darkness outside and her mother right downstairs . . .

Ellen was looking at Courtney strangely. "How do you mean?" she asked.

Then Kyla turned to Courtney, too, and her heart veered again.

"It's easy," Courtney said. "I'll show you."

"Okay," Ellen said.

The sounds of Ellen's mother moving around downstairs were fantastically loud in Kyla's ears.

"We'll take turns," Courtney said.

"Okay," Ellen said again.

Kyla heard Ellen speak, but she couldn't take her eyes off Courtney.

Courtney was watching her. "I'll be Richie," Courtney said. The clear blue silence of her eyes was like the silence of a clock. "Kyla first." She held out her hand. "Okay?"

"Why do I have to go to New York with the Laskeys?" Kyla said.

"You don't have to, darling. Of course." Kyla's mother looked surprised. "I didn't realize you were so upset about it. I was just so astonished when the Laskeys offered—it's extremely generous of them. Of course, I knew Carol would be so happy if Janey had a friend along, but I only accepted because it seemed like such a wonderful opportunity for you."

If her mother knew that Janey lied all the time and used words like *buns*, and *piss*, and even worse things, she might not think the Laskeys were so wonderful. And if she only understood how Janey really treated her when she came over to their house for dinner—that blank *yes, thank you, no, thank you*—You could feel exactly what Janey was thinking, that Janey was thinking about Kyla's mother as if she were the maid.

"I know Janey isn't your favorite person," her mother said.

"I hate Janey," Kyla said.

Her mother waited for a moment. "I know Janey isn't your favorite person," she said again. "But your kindness to her means so much. I'm very grateful, and I know her mother and father are, too."

"I feel sorry for Mrs. Laskey," Kyla said.

"For Carol?" Kyla's mother looked at her with amusement. "Carol's one of the most fortunate women I know. She's just as capable as anything—you don't remember that house when the Fosses owned it. *And* she has the means to enjoy her life, which is very important, darling, as I think you'll find one of these days, though, of course, there are other things that are more important, aren't there. And she's so *attractive*. I happen to know she hasn't done a thing to her face. You're very unusual, darling— most little girls would want to be just like her."

"I'd hate to be married to Mr. Laskey," Kyla said.

"Would you, darling?" Her mother laughed a little. "Well, fortunately, that's nothing you have to worry about. But it could be worse, you know. Dick is demanding, I suppose, and you could say he's a selfish man—or self-involved—but he's cultured and he's broad-minded and he's attractive and he's energetic and he can be loads of fun. And he's certainly a good provider. All in all, he's what I'd call a good catch."

Kyla looked around at the pretty living room. Didn't her mother even like it? It was so much sweeter than the Laskeys' big white glassy house, with all its ugly paintings and statues—*sculptures*. "Wasn't my father a good catch?" Kyla said.

Kyla's mother stroked Kyla's hair. "Your father's a very fine man," she said. "He has a kind and generous heart, like you. He just . . . lacks ambition. I suppose it's a good quality to be content with things as they are, but not when you're the father of a young child. It used to—" She stopped, and laughed a regretful little laugh. "The fact is, your father and I just never really belonged together. Although"—she smiled at Kyla—"if we hadn't been together, I wouldn't have you, would I, darling? And speaking of you, what do you want to do this afternoon?"

"Stay here," Kyla said.

"Oh, darling. It's Saturday. You can't just stay in and mope around all day. Isn't there any special thing you want to do? Don't you want to call Ellen?"

"No," Kyla said.

"Or Courtney?"

Kyla shook her head.

"Don't you like your friends anymore?" her mother said. "You haven't seen Ellen or Courtney in so long."

Kyla leaned against her mother's coolness.

"Don't *cling*, darling," her mother said. "You're getting much too big."

Kyla jumped away. What if her mother were to see what she herself had seen only this morning, in the mirror, for the first time? She was getting big. It was possible, after all, that she would get those legs that bulged out. Or the horrible little stomach that Judy Winner's sister got when she went into high school. Little things seemed to be happening to her face, too. In the mirror that morning, it had looked as if someone else climbed into her face during the night and was stretching it out into their own. And where was *her* face going? The face that her mother loved? She turned away.

"All right, darling. Please don't sulk." Her mother sighed. "You don't have to go to New York. I just want more in the way of advantages for you than I ever had— I want you to have an exciting life."

"But your life *is* exciting," Kyla said. She stared at her mother. "Isn't it, Mother? Isn't it? Your life isn't boring. Isn't your life exciting?"

"My darling," her mother said, and Kyla saw that there were things happening to her face, too. "My good, kind little girl."

"Janey," Mr. Laskey said, "just eat that nicely, please, like an adult. If you didn't want fruit salad you shouldn't have ordered it."

"Want fruit *salad*," Janey said. "I didn't want to come on this *trip*."

"That's not how I happen to remember it," Mr. Laskey said.

"I *wanted* to go skiing with Richie," Janey said.

"When, like Rich, you are fourteen," Mr. Laskey said, "and when, like Rich, you have a friend whose parents own a condo in Vail, then, like Rich, you may go skiing."

"When, like Rich, I am a boy," Janey said.

The waitress loomed hopefully. "How is everything?" she said, looking at Mr. Laskey.

"Just fine," Mr. Laskey said irritably. Then he seemed to remember who she was, and smiled. "Everything just as good as it used to be." He nodded commendingly.

"Well, that's nice," the waitress said. She appeared to be waiting for him to say something more.

Janey cast a small, contemptuous smile at her fruit salad, but Alice burst into tears.

"What's the matter now, Alice?" Mr. Laskey said.

"Anything we want," Alice announced belligerently.

"You have what you want," Mr. Laskey said, looking bewildered.

"What do you want, Alice?" Janey said. "Just calm down and tell me."

"You said you wanted cinnamon toast," Mr. Laskey said.

"No!" Alice roared. She pointed at Kyla's sundae. *"That."*

Mr. Laskey sucked in his cheeks and stared at his own sundae. "Miss? Miss?" he called. "One more hot fudge sundae, please. For the young lady."

Alice's noisy tears were absorbed into the general cheerful clatter of the restaurant. But it was amazing, Kyla thought, how loud the voices of little children were. Whether it was joy or sorrow or terror, you could hear them screeching blocks away. Not just Alice, though she did seem prodigious, but all little children. It was nature, probably; it was nature that made Alice loud and it was nature that made Alice cute. Nature made little children helpless, but nature protected them, too, with loudness and cuteness. Kyla herself had probably once been able to produce sounds just like Alice's, and she'd never even noticed! And now, no matter how much she might want to let out a howl that would bring the whole neighborhood running, there wasn't a chance of it. Because the minute people struggled to get a bit free of nature, and could begin to take care of themselves, the point was, they stopped being loud, and they stopped being cute.

"All right, now," Mr. Laskey said as the waitress put an enormous hot fudge sundae in front of Alice. "Does everybody have what he or she wishes? Is everybody happy?"

"You bet, pal," Janey said.

"Jane," Mr. Laskey said. "Are we having some kind of problem today?"

Janey held his gaze for a moment and then looked away. "No," she said.

"You're sure," Mr. Laskey said.

"Yes," Janey said.

"Because," Mr. Laskey said, "if there is a problem, maybe you'd like to tell me what it is so we can clear it up right now."

"There isn't," Janey said.

"Isn't what?" Mr. Laskey said.

"Isn't a problem," Janey said.

"What was that?" Mr. Laskey said. "I didn't hear you."

For a moment Janey didn't speak. "There isn't a problem," she said finally, in a low, dead voice.

"That's my girl," Mr. Laskey said. "All problems forgotten. Now—" He looked at his watch. "We'll go back to the hotel for a three o'clock nap, then we'll get up at five-thirty, and at six forty-five we'll have had our baths and be ready to go. Everybody with me?"

"I'm with you," Janey said. "You mean we have to have a two-and-a-half-hour nap."

"Aha," Mr. Laskey said. "Another mathematician in the family."

"A two-and-a-half-hour *nap*?" Janey said.

"No!" Alice said in alarm. "It's ideal!"

"You're confused, Alice," Janey said.

"On the contrary," Mr. Laskey said. "Do you know what an adult is? Jane? An adult is someone who's learned to delay gratification. We're going to the ballet tonight, and we're going to have a very late night. In short, this is non-negotiable. But the question is, we have time for one quick activity before our nap, so what do we all want to do?"

"We all want to go to the children's zoo," Alice said.

"We all want to go to the Museum of the American Indian," Janey said.

"Kyla?" Mr. Laskey said.

"Either's fine with me," Kyla said. *She* just wanted to go home.

"Well," Mr. Laskey said, "we were just at the Museum of the American Indian yesterday. Besides, it's very, very far away—I'm afraid it's impracticable."

"It's only one-thirty," Janey said. "We have time."

"Let me be the judge of that," Mr. Laskey said.

"But it's only one-*thirty*," Janey said.

"I think we all heard you," Mr. Laskey said. "And *I* said, let me be the judge of that."

"Children's *zoo*, children's *zoo*," Alice chanted.

Mr. Laskey peered at Alice. "Are those dark circles I see?" he said. "Didn't you sleep well last night?"

"No," Alice said nonchalantly.

Mr. Laskey looked at Janey. "What does she mean?" he said.

Janey and Kyla looked at each other. "She had nightmares," Janey said. "She kept me and Kyla awake all night."

"Is this true?" Mr. Laskey said.

"Janey wouldn't let me call mommy," Alice said.

"Did you want to wake mommy up?" Janey said fiercely. "Is that what you wanted, Alice?"

Alice hung her head, and large tears began to form in her eyes. "No," she said in a little voice. Though actually, Kyla thought, Janey was no mathematician at all—it wouldn't have been much past ten at home when Alice first woke them.

"What upset you, Alice?" Mr. Laskey said. "Was it the museum yesterday? Was it the Indians?"

"You weren't there," Alice said. Her shoulders were bowed and she stared at her melting sundae, tears sliding from her wide eyes. "The pond was there, and ice was on it, and it opened up, and you were thin air."

"I'm here, sweetheart. It was just a nightmare. I'm right here."

"That's what I told her," Janey said. "I told her it wasn't real."

"I was—" Mr. Laskey began. Then he looked at the wall, as if something had suddenly appeared there. "Jane," he said, "I'm proud of you. I'm gratified that you took responsibility and stayed calm."

Janey stared straight ahead; amazingly, it looked as if she was about to cry.

"And you know what?" Mr. Laskey said. "I have a thought. I think what we should do before our nap is to get Mommy a present. Isn't that a good idea?"

Janey and Alice nodded soberly.

"We'll get Mommy a present to show that we're thinking about her and to congratulate her for having two such good girls. Now, I'm just going to make a phone call, and when I come back Alice will have finished her sundae and we'll march along."

"We'll call Mommy?" Alice said, still furrowed and dubious.

"We'll call Mommy when we're all together," Mr. Laskey said.

"When . . ." Alice said, and shook her head slowly.

"When we can be all together at the phone in the hotel," Mr. Laskey said.

Well, it was true; Janey, of all people, had taken responsibility last night. There had been no alternative. When Alice awakened for the second time, rattling as if in the grip of a high fever, and could not be consoled, Kyla had said to Janey, "Should we get your father?"

"I don't know," Janey said. "Daddy said if we needed anything we should ask Donald."

Alice, in a damp heap, continued to sob. "But what do we need?" Kyla said.

"Hmm," Janey said. She and Kyla looked at each other. "True . . ."

"Daddy Daddy Daddy Daddy," Alice screamed.

"Be quiet, Alice, *please,*" Janey said. "You're going to wake up everyone in the hotel."

"Daddy—" Alice screamed again, at an increased volume.

"All *right,*" Janey said. "I'll get him."

But she was not able to rouse him either by knocking on his door or—when Kyla located a plastic card that told you how to call the other rooms—by telephone.

Kyla could hear her own heart pounding, or maybe it was Janey's, as they both snuggled against Alice on the little cot. What if Mr. Laskey had actually had a heart attack? What if he was lying there dead in the next room?

"Hey, Alice, let go," Janey said. "I'm going downstairs to get you a cup of hot milk, and then you're going to sleep."

Janey put her coat over her nightie and went out the big wooden door of their room, and Kyla remembered that there were many other people, in many other rooms, all around them. Beyond the sad blue flowers on the wallpaper, in fact, millions of people, who couldn't help them at all, slumbered on in the twinkling city. At least Alice was still cute, lucky for her; Kyla thought of the new plainness spreading like an illness through her own face. *Don't cling*, her mother had said. "Do you want to play something, Alice?" Kyla said, when Alice grew quieter. "Do you want to play Baby?"

Alice hiccuped. "No!" she shrieked.

And then Janey had returned, with, in fact, a big mug of hot milk. "Here, Alice," she said.

Alice accepted the mug and held it out to Kyla. "Baby drink," she said, and hiccuped again.

"Stop that, Alice," Janey said. "You drink that yourself. Pronto. Donald made them put honey in it for you, wasn't that nice? So I want you to say thank you to him the very next time you see him."

Janey sat down stiffly and looked out the window while Alice drained her milk with gulps and sighs and, finally, a little belch.

"Donald said nothing can wake him up when he's asleep," Janey said. "He said once there was a burglar in his apartment and his roommate screamed and called the police and the police came and he slept through it all."

Kyla nodded, though Janey was still looking out the window.

"Lucky Richie," Janey said.

"For sure," Kyla said. And then it was as if Janey had lifted a curtain, and what was there—and had been there all along—was Richie. But Richie blending back and forth with Mr. Laskey—blending with Mr. Laskey helplessly because she had done something to him. She had done something to him, with Ellen and Courtney; she had let something happen to Richie.

The next morning when they got up and got dressed, Janey was still frozen slow and pale. But then there was Mr. Laskey, reading his newspaper at the breakfast table, just as always. "Daddy's here!" Alice observed superfluously. Janey paused; Alice scampered ahead to the table, and Janey went right into the cross mood that had lasted her all day.

"There," Mr. Laskey said when the bracelet they had all—including Kyla—chosen for Mrs. Laskey was put into its beautiful little velvet box. "I think Mommy's going to be very happy with that."

And no wonder, Kyla thought—delicate strips of gold, flashing with stars. It wasn't fair—it would look so much prettier on her own mother. And her mother deserved it, which Mrs. Laskey did not, and her mother would have been so much more grateful to have it. Kyla could just see her mother's face, radiant with surprise and love, if Kyla could present her with just such a little velvet box.

Mr. Laskey raised his hand in the air again, and this time what appeared was a taxi. They all climbed into the back seat quickly enough—Kyla landed a bit sideways between Janey and the door—but when Mr. Laskey gave the address of their hotel, the driver shook his head in disgust. "You'd be better off walking," he shouted over the loud fuzz of his radio. "The whole East Side is a nightmare."

"Thank you for your concern, sir," Mr. Laskey said. "But we'll keep the taxi. It's a good fifteen blocks, and the little girls are tired."

"You're absolutely positive," the driver said. He turned down his radio. "In three more blocks we're not going to budge."

Mr. Laskey smiled. "I understand, sir," he said. "But what do you suggest? We're too tired to walk, and our hotel's on the East Side."

"What I suggest, sir," the driver said, "in that case is, you move to the West Side."

"Ha, ha, ha," Janey said.

"Because furthermore," the driver said, "once I get into this shit I'm not going to be able to get out."

"I'll bear your difficulties in mind, sir," Mr. Laskey said.

"It does me good to hear you say this," the driver said, "because in a situation like today I starve."

The cab, which had been hurtling from side to side, causing Alice to turn a delicate green, was indeed slowing down almost to a standstill. "It costs me more to hire the fucking car on a day like this than I can make."

"I will, as I've said, sir, bear that in mind," Mr. Laskey said. "Jane, human beings do not lead difficult lives for your personal amusement. Our driver is understandably anxious, but once we get past the bridge traffic everything will be fine."

But within one more block they had entered a solid mass of honking horns in which Kyla's fatigue seemed to entrap her like amber. And after a time Mr. Laskey leaned forward. "What's the problem, driver?" he said. "We haven't moved for twenty minutes."

"What's the problem?" the driver said. "The problem is we aren't moving. Or, wait—you mean to ask what's *causing* the problem."

"That was my intention," Mr. Laskey said. A pulse had begun to throb in his forehead. "Yes."

The driver turned around and stared at Mr. Laskey. "Oh, hey—" he said, and struck the side of his head with his palm "—I get it! From which, ah . . . *planet* do you folks hail?"

"Perhaps you'll be so kind . . ." Mr. Laskey said.

"With pleasure," the driver said. He turned the radio up savagely, but it was almost impossible for Kyla to hear through the static and the honking what it was saying. There was an apartment building, somewhere near their hotel, and there were policemen—

"Who?" Janey was yelling over all the noise. *"What did he do?"*

" 'Who?' " the driver yelled back. " 'What?' Incredible. Every radio station in the city. Every television network in the universe. More blood per cubic foot than the siege of

Stalingrad. Where are you from, folks, seriously now—
New Jersey?"

"Tell me, tell me, tell me!" Janey was shouting.

"This is not important, Jane," Mr. Laskey said.

"Not important," the driver said. "Right. Not important.
Well, of course it's not important. You types really stick
together, don't you? Sure, if the guy's rich enough, if the
guy's handsome enough, if the guy remembers what kind
of mineral water each of his patients drinks, it's just not
important if he bludgeons his wife to death with a floor
lamp, is it. It's not *important* that he pulverized her."

"I don't think this is strictly—" Mr. Laskey began.

"Oh, pardon," the driver said. "I have the honor of ad-
dressing a gentleman of the law, I'll wager. It's been *alleged* that this guy liquefied his wife; it's been *alleged* that
the neighbors waded in through body parts; it's been *alleged* that he fled, dragging his poor little child with him,
to his girlfriend's apartment where the cops later found a
sweater, all gunked up with hair and blood that allegedly
matches his wife's; and now it's being alleged that he's up
on the roof with this kid and he's—"

"Sir, I do not think—" Mr. Laskey said, and Alice began
to cry.

"Nothing's going to happen to you, Alice," Janey said.
"No one cares about *you*."

"That's right, Alice," Mr. Laskey said. "Nothing's going
to happen to any of us."

"Oh, hey—" The driver turned around. He looked into
Alice's eyes and took her hand. "Hey, I'm sorry, darlin'.
It's going off, right now." He turned the radio off. "Click,
right? No more depressing stories."

"Sir," Alice said, and rubbed her cheek against his
hand.

Mr. Laskey sighed. "Alice, sweetheart," he said, "let the
man drive."

"Why did he do it?" Janey said. "Daddy?"

"We'll never know, Jane," Mr. Laskey said. "Normal people can never penetrate the mind of a sick individual." He rolled down his window and thrust his head out.

"The wife was trash," the driver said. "What do you want to bet? A slut. A nag. A gold-digger. All the same, he should've just divorced her."

"Girls—" Mr. Laskey looked at his watch. "I'm afraid it would be a great deal faster to walk at this point."

"Hey, listen to this guy, kids!" the driver said. "The original rocket scientist. *It would be faster to walk!* When do you think Mr. Wizard got a chance to perform the calculations? Say"—he turned around with raised eyebrows —"how's *right here* for you folks?"

"Do we get to pat the goaties?" Alice said as Mr. Laskey opened the door.

"Alice," Janey said, "you're confused again."

Mr. Laskey handed the driver a bill. "Here you are, sir. I sincerely hope this will recompense you for your time."

"And I, sir"—the driver dropped the bill into the gutter—"sincerely hope *this* will encourage *you* to reinsert your patronizing shit back up your butt, where it came from."

"The second we get inside," Mr. Laskey said as they straggled up the steps to the hotel, "I want you to get yourselves upstairs—It's way past three. Way, *way* past three," he added, shaking his head ominously. "And I want you to wash those hands. Alice's especially."

"Her hands are clean," Alice said loftily. "She washed them after lunch."

"That was after lunch," Mr. Laskey said. "You've touched God knows what since."

As they stepped inside the hotel, five or six young men in uniforms—bellboys and desk clerks—swiveled away from a small television on the front desk. Their eyes, brilliant with excitement, dimmed immediately into courteous greeting. "Hello, Mr. Laskey," one of them said. "Horrifying, this business, isn't it?"

"Horrifying," Mr. Laskey said, glancing at his watch irritably. "Come *along*, girls."

"Oh, Mr. Laskey—" Donald disengaged himself from the group and hurried over.

"What's that?" Mr. Laskey frowned back at Donald.

Donald hesitated.

"Yes?" Mr. Laskey said. He paused, looking at his watch again, and Alice bumped into his leg.

"That is," Donald said, "Miss Shawcross was here for you. I'm afraid she just left."

"Didn't she get my message?" Mr. Laskey said.

"I don't know, sir," Donald said.

"My mother's on the phone?" Alice said.

"Shut up, Alice," Janey said.

Alice tugged Mr. Laskey's sleeve. "Janey said, 'Shut up, Alice,'" she reported.

"Be quiet, Alice," Mr. Laskey said. "But I left her a message at her office. Didn't she get it?"

"I don't know, sir. She didn't say."

Alice sat down suddenly on the carpet.

"Your dress, Alice!" Janey exclaimed. "Get off your butt. Mother would kill you!"

"My mother would kill *you*," Alice said, but she scrambled to her feet, swatting at her rear end.

"How are my girls?" Donald said. "Imaginations cooler in the light of day?" He winked at Janey, who gazed serenely at a point on the other side of his head.

Mr. Laskey appeared to wake from a trance. "Don't we say hello to people who say hello to us?" he said.

"Ah, Stan—" Donald said, and one of the uniformed men wrenched himself away from the TV screen to open the door for a man with a briefcase, and the blaring of horns entered the lobby.

"This is the damnedest business," Mr. Laskey said. "God damn it."

"Horrible, sir," Donald said. His eyes flicked eagerly toward the TV. "Incredible what a human being can do, isn't it?"

"You can play with your toys, Alice," Janey said. "You don't have to just lie there."

"Yes, I do," Alice said. "It's nap time." A large tear trickled from each eye.

"What's the matter?" Janey said. "Are you afraid to fall asleep? Are you afraid of having another nightmare?"

"I want to go home," Alice said. "I want to see Mommy. I want Billy and the big rope."

"Is she all right?" Kyla said. "What does she mean?"

"Oh, nothing," Janey said. "She gets Billy Jacobs to tie her up."

"I don't feel well," Alice said. She rolled over into her pillow.

Kyla looked at Janey. "Should we get your father?" she said.

"No," Janey said. "She's playing. Are you playing, Alice?"

"Yes," Alice said mournfully. "I'm playing Disease."

"Nurse—" Janey said. "The patient in bed number one has a horrible disease. She needs a sleeping potion."

"Right away, Doctor," Kyla said, and poured a glass of water in the bathroom.

Alice fell asleep before she even finished her water, and Janey picked up the big book she'd brought along, but Kyla looked at the dark TV screen. "Don't you want to see what's happening?" she said.

"No," Janey said. "I'm reading."

Kyla stood up and looked out the window. But of course there was nothing to see except tall apartment buildings, where everyone would be watching television to see what was happening. And below, nothing but stalled traffic stretching on and on, lines of cars like strands of colored beads. Lots of blue and green and black, more yellow, not so many red . . . If there were fewer than fifteen red, it wouldn't happen. If there were more than fifteen . . . The steely hand on the child's shoulder, the caress of metal against soft hair, the entire universe exploding in her skull, vanishing into thin air. The entire universe exploding—the universe—how many times was Kyla going to have to see it? To hear it? *"Please* let's turn it on," Kyla said. "Just for a second."

"No," Janey said. "I don't want Alice to wake up. I don't want Alice to freak out again. My father said we should rest, because we're going to the ballet tonight. My father's the one who's paying for this hotel. My father's the one who paid to bring you along."

"I know," Kyla said.

"Stuff like this happens all the time," Janey said. "Even at home. There was this person at home, in fact, who was a famous judge, but his wife was a secret drug addict, and he was afraid someone would find out. So one day he said, 'Goodbye, dear, kiss kiss, I'm going away on a trip to get lots of presents to bring home to you, and I'll be back in a few days.' So he drove his car down the street and waved to all the neighbors and he put a plastic bag over his clothes so he wouldn't get blood on his tie, and he snuck back. Lucky for him, it was the coldest winter in a hundred years, and there were icicles hanging from all the trees and houses. So he opened the door and dragged his wife outside and snapped off the biggest icicle he could reach and he stabbed it into her stomach stab stab, and there was splash splash blood all over the place and his wife tried to scream but she was dead. And then the judge snuck back to his car and drove to the airport and flew away. And the next day the sun came out and all the blood and the murder weapon melted into the ground."

"So how did they catch him?" Kyla said.

"How should I know?" Janey said, and turned back to her book. "Nobody, ick, talks about it, obviously."

From down below the soft tumult rose gently, like the

sounds of a beach, Kyla thought, when your eyes are closed. What was going on out there? What was happening? Everybody else could see. Donald was watching, and the taxi driver and the waitress would be somewhere by now watching, and all the people in all the other rooms of the hotel and in the little buildings out the window, and Miss Shawcross, and far away, in the mountains, Richie was watching—Richie was watching helplessly—and across the body-choked lagoons, Mrs. Laskey and Ellen and Courtney were watching, and her mother and Dr. Loeffler, twisting together on the sofa, were watching, their blood pounding and their eyes shining—

No—her mother was alone, pale, sitting bolt upright and trembling for the poor little child, *not* with Dr. Loeffler, that was what *Janey* thought; Kyla sprang up and turned on the television. ". . . to de-lethalize the situation—" a voice was saying. Janey reached the dial before the picture even came on, but Alice was awake already, and crying. "Thanks, Kyla," Janey said. "Thanks a lot, old buddy."

"I'm sorry—" Kyla said.

"Where's Daddy?" Alice roared. "Where's my daddy?"

"Hush, Alice," Janey said, curling up beside her on the cot. "Daddy's asleep in the next room."

But Alice had begun to scream. "Should we get your father?" Kyla whispered. "Do you think we should go get your father?"

"Our father's asleep," Janey said. "Our father's resting. Our father's asleep in the next room, and he doesn't want to be bothered, and plus, she's going to get over it."

All Around Atlantis

WHEN DO I THINK ABOUT YOU? NEVER, THESE days—almost never. When I was what, about twenty, I suppose, I finally got around to reading the little book you'd written about Sándor. It only took an afternoon, and when I finished, I put the book away, along with various old, disorderly feelings, and just left the whole clutter for about thirty years' worth of dust to settle over.

Well, except for once, when Neil (a person who used to be my husband) returned from a business trip to somewhere and mentioned that he'd happened to catch a glimpse, on some highbrow TV talk show, of a man— perhaps the man I'd mentioned at some time—who seemed possibly to have been something of an authority on my uncle, or my mother's uncle, or whatever it was Sándor had been to me. Naturally, that sort of called you up for a bit, and then you sank back out of my thoughts again.

But you know what, Peter? Yesterday at the service, I turned around at exactly the moment you showed up and slipped into the back row. So what do you think of that?

After the service, I walked through the park. It was raining and the sky was a kindly color, soft and gray. The fountains were steaming in the cold. I was glad for the mournful, commiserating weather—the gentle, chilly rain and the vaporous air. I'll bet you were annoyed, though. You were probably scrambling for a taxi, running home for a hot shower and a nice, relaxing something or other before cocktails or a dinner. Or maybe you ducked in someplace to brood over a cup of coffee. Or not to brood.

In the park we were all bundled up. Everyone was wearing big, dark coats and silly, serviceable winter hats. I'd grabbed that beautiful old challis scarf of Lili's—remember it?—from her closet to wrap around my head because I left my own particular silly, serviceable winter hat on the plane, in some fit of pure hysterical disorganization.

The children were covertly testing their galoshes in the puddles, and the adults were all soldiering on with big, black umbrellas. And then something happened. The rain got gentler and gentler, and then even gentler. And then it simply stayed where it was, hanging in the air like a beaded curtain. Everything halted; the world was between breaths—no motion, no sound . . .

And when the world started up again, what was falling was snow—large, airy clumps of it, like blossoms tumbling silently from a bucket.

In a moment everything was covered with big, white blossoms—us, the trees, the ground . . . The umbrellas looked like parasols. Everything was silent. Everything was muffled and remote, as though it were a picture. A distant brightness and the scent of flowers swelled into the air, and my heart fluttered as though I'd awakened in a picture of something that had existed briefly a long time ago—a memory.

But whose memory was it? Not mine, exactly; it wasn't a memory of mine.

Did you look for me yesterday? Well, of course, you might not have recognized me. I wish I hadn't been so timid! But *did* you look for me—did you have some thought like, *Yes, Anna must be here* . . . ?

Imagine, talking about Lili all these years later! What

would you have said, I wonder. For that matter, what would I have said, myself?

Because now, of course, we're the same age, you and I, but the gap between us used to be so large! Especially when you first appeared—my eleven or twelve to your eighteen or nineteen. And naturally I developed a habit of thinking of you as the given—immutable, an adult; and I, a child, as open to scrutiny, correction, evaluation . . . So it didn't even strike me until last night, hours after catching that glimpse of you (and then it struck me forcibly), that you probably didn't even notice, back then, the things that felt, from the inside, like *me*—what constituted *me*.

Did you ever hear that once when Lili cut her finger I fainted? The fact is, I've been waiting my whole life for her death. When I was little, years before you arrived, I used to watch her so intently . . . making breakfast, getting dressed for work . . . as though it was only my vigilance that would prevent her from vanishing off the face of the earth.

Even years after I left home, I knew when she was sick, I knew when she was frightened, I knew when something had happened to cause her pain. When the phone rang, I knew if it was Lili who was calling. And I thought surely that when she died a jagged line would streak through my heart, cracking it in two.

Well, as it happened, not at all. When the time came, as it happened, I was out in the desert, working quite serenely on some old bits of a pot, trying to grasp what they had to say about a group of people who seem to have once lived in that area, in vast pueblos. The sky was just *shining*, Peter—shining and blue—but all day long, messages were flying around right over my head.

And when I got back to Albuquerque, my answering machine was choked with frantic calls—Lionel's, from Brooklyn, my son, Eric's, from L.A. . . .

But how did *you* hear, I wonder. I doubt your heart cracked in two. Did you learn from a colleague at whatever university you're adorning these days? Or maybe one of those old men who sit all curled over on the park benches like fallen leaves spotted you and beckoned you over. Or maybe you saw the tiny notice in the *Times*; I imagine you've begun to check the obits these days, yourself.

A jolt, yes? Sándor, Lili, the apartment, even the sullen, dark-haired child who was me, shoved out onto the stage in front of you. I can just imagine your face: Human feelings! Right there for anyone to see—irritation, smugness, mortal panic, regret . . . I'm sure you cleaned it all up immediately, but it must have hurt, really, didn't it? I'd love to know that it hurt.

Oh—the synagogue, I hasten to add, was Lionel's doing, not mine, obviously. It was all arranged by the time Lionel got ahold of me. It was what your mother wanted, he said, preemptively. I'd absolutely sworn myself to niceness, Peter, but I'm afraid I let a long silence speak for me.

She'd have been appalled, yes? Or—what do you think?—maybe she'd just have gotten a big laugh out of the whole thing. Or is it possible that *was* what Lili wanted? Vaguely, I suppose. Who knows what sort of thing people simply suppress for decades. Or maybe she was hedging her bets there at the end. But, still—a synagogue? I doubt she'd set foot in one more than half a dozen times in her life—and as a tourist, at that. Certainly we were no more religious—she and Sándor and I—than potatoes! Not to doubt Lionel's word, of course. He's as honest as someone can be who can't distinguish what he'd like to be true from the evidence in front of his face.

It's pretty startling to see Lionel (of all people!) coming out of Lili's old room in his bathrobe, that's for sure. But I have to say he was good to her, after his fashion. He outwaited all the others, and eventually she was ready to be taken a little care of. She was pretty tired by then. You would have been surprised. Really, Peter—surprised.

A saint, is what Lionel says, missing the point, as usual.

And what I say is, all right, make people into saints if that's what you want; there are worse things to do, I suppose. But I can't help thinking that what Lili really died of was boredom.

Actually . . . I wonder now; I'll bet you don't even remember Lionel. That is, I think there wasn't ever a time in my conscious life before Lionel was around, but he wasn't around all that *much* till fairly recently. (Well, "recently." You know what I mean—the last couple of decades.) But even when Lionel was around, I doubt you noticed.

Sorry. I exaggerate. I do you an injustice—you and Lionel both. I'm sure you noticed. I'm sure you noticed something taking up the best chair. Let me remind you— Lionel: Lionel drank his tea; he praised the pastry (even when he brought it himself); he'd suddenly speak up and drop onto the conversation some weighty, worthy, immovable subject that left everyone speechless; he actually seemed *delighted* when Mrs. Spiegel dropped in from across the hall ("for just a little moment," as she always put it) . . .

But the fact is, Lionel sort of actually came into his own on those occasions when Lili disappeared into her room; at some point during those episodes, Lionel used, without fail, to show up, hesitating in the hallway, whispering, clearing his throat, clutching a basically useless offering of soup or coffee cake to be left at the door of Lili's room.

During the period you were around, I know it didn't happen so often—that Lili would just *vanish*, into the darkness behind her door. Oh, there were a couple of episodes, yes—and you, like everyone else, faded away, to leave us in "peace"—but when I was little, before you sat yourself down in our life, it was a pretty frequent occurrence.

Could you have known what that was like for me? I always, I think, simply assumed you did. But, really—how would you have?

That silence! I could cry, of course, but Lili was falling through darkness, down to a world where I couldn't be heard or seen.

The whole apartment was silent when Lili was in her room. No visitors, obviously. There would only be Sándor, working in his room, or taking me back and forth to kindergarten or grade school, trying to entertain me with cards or alphabet games, and to make our small meals cheerful. Did I want to go out and play? No.

Go out? Go out and play, when Lili might just dematerialize forever in my absence? So you can imagine the state I'd be in, back in the days I was small, when Lili would reemerge from her room, as affectionate as ever, utterly tranquil, as though there'd been no break in continuity whatsoever.

I was in sole possession of that terrible silence then, and our apartment was full of conversation again, and laughter.

Constant visitors! All those men! Where could Lili have found them? There sure aren't any around *these* days. Not that I much mind, Peter. But every country in Europe must have been represented, serially, on our sofa, wouldn't you say? And then there were those big, rectangular Americans, too! But maybe you never noticed *any* of Lili's admirers, come to think of it—even the handsome, boastful ones. To you, I'm sure, all of them would have been . . . just . . . *old*. And really, it was Sándor you were there for, wasn't it.

Actually, of all those far-ranging types of men, there was only one that Lili had no use for: Lionel's—that worried, deliberate, "cultured" type. She liked men who were fun —who drank whiskey, who would take her out dancing or to hear jazz, out into the world.

It never occurred to me until much, much later, of course, to marvel at the way she kept moving. She *worked* so hard, too. I think she'd cut back a lot by the time you showed up, but when I was very small she put in outrageous days at Dr. Weissbard's office. Doing, I believe, the most tedious possible chores—the files, the phones, the bills, the checks, the appointments . . . Sándor would take me to school and pick me up, and sometimes one of Lili's admirers would be drafted to take me to the park or the skating rink, but Lili managed to make me breakfast and dinner, she read to me before bed . . . It wasn't until I had Eric and was working myself that I had any idea how much energy it all must have taken.

I never heard her complain. And I'd be very surprised if you did, Peter. I remember once trotting along behind her when she went into the kitchen for something to put a bunch of flowers in. She looked at the flowers as if to solicit their views on the matter, shrugged, and dropped them into a vase; I think no matter where she'd found herself, she would have experienced her life as a faintly comic, wholly inexplicable spectacle that was being rolled out in front of her.

Did it charm you? Did it irritate you? Did you find it childish? *You*, of course, were an adult. Oh, and here's something else I remember, as if it were holy—Lili stretched out, frowning studiously at her fashion magazine, absently reaching out an arm for me to tuck myself under while I waited for the verdict: *No, this is not elegant . . .*

Well, she was so young; she was scarcely nineteen, I think, when I was born. But one could hardly consider that frivolity of hers an adjunct of youth, could one? I, personally, at least, consider it to have been an act of courage and gallantry—a radical choice.

Fairly early on in my marriage (when it seemed worth it to me, I suppose, to bid for Neil's sympathy regardless of the cost) I confided in him what I'd never tried to confide in anyone else: the sheer terror of those days when Lili would retreat into her room. The moment the door closed, I told Neil, I knew perfectly well Lili was somewhere I simply did not yet exist; anything might happen to her, and there I was, on the other side of the wall, being absorbed into that obliterating silence.

So, what was Neil's response? Naturally enough, he seized the opportunity to point out that I had "personal problems." "And no wonder," he said. Yes, yes, any question would kill her, she was going to disappear into her bedroom one day and just die there, of suffering. No wonder I had nightmares! No wonder I had migraines! "Because she never once just sat you down," he said, "to have a normal conversation about her past situation. She just simply allowed that whole thing to develop instead—that atmosphere of violence and danger."

Oh, Neil had a point or two, I suppose; I've had my share of "personal problems." But what other kind of problem can a person have? And a lot of those problems simply faded away, along with the vestigial nightmares and migraines, after he and I got ourselves together to file for divorce.

It's strange to think my dreams wouldn't have been visible to you at a glance. I was still having them at the time you showed up, after all—almost every night. As soon as I closed my eyes, the dark pools behind them deepened; I floated, was caught, and down I went—toward the scream of the train. The bolt rang shut across the door like the report of a pistol; my shattered vision recomposed into silence and the small white disk of the sun. Through the slats, the silent figures in the fields; the small white disk of the moon, light beating down like nails on the silent insects that scurried, slowed, stopped . . .

How many mornings did I stand at the kitchen door when I was little, trailing a blanket, throbbing with nausea and cold, as the silence of my dreams—a silence like a chloroformed rag—thawed slowly, until I could hear the spoon against the table, the juice pouring into the glass . . . Sándor poured a bright arc of juice from the beaker; Lili's long, restless hands spread the toast with delicious unsalted butter. Was that really Sándor? Was that really Lili?

The night's dense net was lying slack and invisible around us in the sunlight.

Lili could always feel me looking, and she'd turn anxiously.

I approached, hesitated, and leaned myself abjectly against her. *Bad dreams?* she said.

She was made out of glass, my mother, wasn't she? Out of pale silk. I straightened myself up and shook my head: no.

But Lili turned to the window that looked out onto nothing—onto the brick of the airshaft. Her fingers were pressed at the corners of her closed eyes.

Yes, I had nightmares—children do. After all, it takes some time to get used to being alive. And how else, except in the clarity of dreams, are you supposed to see the world all around you that's hidden by the light of day?

But I also had dreams that were just like heaven: A little lake with leaf-shaped boats . . . a tiny theatre with amazing, living puppets—yes, the most marvelous park, elegant in the snow, against the gray sky, like a deserted palace, or twinklingly awake again in spring, the trees all in flower . . . blossoms scattering on the surface as I broke back up through the reflections.

And there were other dreams, too, those dreams that just *twist*, you know—a sunny meadow, the black shadow . . .

I sometimes watched you. Did you ever know that? When you began sacking out on our sofa now and then. Tossing about, emitting your little sleep-smothered bleats of terror. I stood watching you, breathing stealthily, afraid to break into those dreams of yours; who knew what would come pouring out?

Sleep was a serious business in that household! You probably heard Lili or Sándor, every once in a while, murmuring breathlessly, pleading . . . Even Walden Tócska, poor thing—flopping and twitching, whimpering in his little bed and sending up smelly eddies of hair . . .

Sweet dreams! Get some rest! Sándor and Lili and I going our separate ways, the dark pools opening, the whisper of the trawling nets. And then mornings, watching, walking forward to join Sándor and Lili behind the thin screen of daylight, sitting all together in the kitchen, buttering the toast . . . *More juice? Yes, thanks. And the jam, please.*

Those mornings were like a seam, joining two worlds, one invisible by night, one invisible by day.

Now, how's this for a thought: Suppose you and I had spoken yesterday, after all. And suppose we'd wandered out together, talking. Suppose we'd strolled over, you and I, to this coffee shop where I've imagined you ducking in out of the rain.

I can see you—some version of you—looking at me with incredulity: But what could have been in my brain at that time, you might have asked me; how did I account for my existence? Did I think I was descended from . . . pilgrims? From a distinguished line of, what—cowboys?

Well, now, it's true that none of those people who hung around our little apartment talking, talked much about their "past situations," as Neil put it. That prohibition relaxed, of course, as time went by, but when I was little, no adult I encountered ever spoke in any personal way about the years of the war or the decade or so preceding it. And you can be sure that none of the others inquired!

It seemed perfectly natural to me, when I was a little girl, that English was the language of choice for our visitors—most of whom were not madly comfortable in it, to say the least; of *course* they spoke English—that was what people *spoke*. And perhaps you simply took it for granted in your own way, when you eventually showed up; for you, I suppose, English was just one more language to explore and then inhabit.

But for those others, obviously, it was altogether a different matter, wouldn't you say? A language so new, so clean, so devoid of association and overtone as to be mercifully almost unlike, I'd suppose, human speech.

But new and clean as it was, and new and clean as I was myself, I could detect—trembling there in the depths of those accents—clues and evidence; it was as if iron vaults, sunk to the bottom of the sea, couldn't prevent the radioactive waste buried in them from transmitting its toxic, shining signals.

The child should be out in the fresh air, Mrs. Spiegel would lament from time to time. *It's not healthy to be all the time indoors!* But Lili would only smile, as if she hadn't quite heard, and put an arm around me. And I curled up closer, to listen.

But, you know, Peter, despite what people say about children (their unerring ear for truth, their piercing vision—all those platitudes), children can't pluck actual specifics out of thin air.

Where did I come from? Frankly, children are philosophers and theoreticians and seers only by default; they're so ignorant they *have* to be philosophers and theoreticians and seers. It's not that children disdain hard data, it's not that they're too lofty for it—on the contrary, they're dealing with as much hard data as they can! Think how much hard data is entailed in just getting the applesauce to stay on the spoon!

Where did I come from? "Europe," all right? That's what I was told, and that was plenty. Mrs. Spiegel might have been happy to share with me her exhaustive knowledge about who in the neighborhood purported to be from Vienna or Budapest or Berlin though they were actually from some miserable shtetl near Lwow, but frankly, Peter, when I was four or five or six, I had other things to worry about! "Europe." That was plenty. "Hungary." *Plenty.*

My first words were Hungarian. Naturally; I was almost one and a half when we left. By the time I was seven, I didn't speak *any* Hungarian. By the time I was twelve, I couldn't—as you may or may not have noticed—understand it!

Isn't it strange? If we can remember, why can't we remember everything? Why can't we remember where we once were? The words we once understood? Little snippets of conversation we heard? If I, for example, can remember back forty-seven or so long years, why can't I remember back forty-nine? Just a few little years more? Why can I not remember my father? I spent almost a year of my life in his presence "over there" until he "developed problems" and evidently blasted himself into literal fragments of despair. So why is it that what I have with me now, instead of a memory, is a solid space that nothing—no memory—can occupy?

I'll tell you what I think. I think we can't remember all the way back because God (to speak metaphorically) arranged it that way. And God arranged it that way, in my opinion, so we can be deceived.

These highly compressed, enigmatic, and largely private lyrics, anticipatory, even premonitory, in their elegiac tone and obsessive cataloguing of a world which was not yet lost, reflect, inevitably, their broad cultural contexts. Certain theoretical orientations, therefore, may be comfortably invoked with a view to illuminate . . . (etc., etc.).
—From *Atlantis: The Poetry of Sándor Szabados*, by Péter
(orthographical-marks-fetched-up-from-the-murk-and-pasted-back-on-for-credibility) Kövi

The cover's faded now, you know; the paper has discolored. No matter—I'm sure the book stays modestly in print.

And how did I feel about it, how did it seem, your little book, when I took a look at it again last night after all these years? That is, aside from the embarrassingness of the prose? Well, you can count on me, Peter, of course, not to be able to identify a lot of the distortions and inaccuracies a book like that is sure to be rotten with. And it's hardly original, I know, to observe that biography is bound to be at least as much about the author as it is about the subject. Yes, that's *not* an original observation, I know. And, all right, your book isn't biography, anyway—it's a translation, plus a "critical appreciation" (or some such slithery disclaimer), which "inevitably" entails "illumination" of the subject himself. Well, I know, Peter.

Oh! But how did I *feel* about it! Hm. All right, yes—how did I feel . . .

Well, I'd have to say . . . I felt . . . *ambivalent.*

Were you aware, Peter, how Sándor responded to Mrs. Spiegel's admiration? Were you aware how completely insane it drove him? "The genius," as she sometimes referred to him. He could detect her footfall with absolute accuracy, as if the two of them were in the forest, and he'd fade instantly into his room for hours, to write, or to read his Thoreau or Dickens or Auden or Stevens, while Mrs. Spiegel chattered on emptily with Lili in the kitchen, stalling. "Did I hear something?" she'd say, glancing over her shoulder. "No."

Oh, Peter. How he hated to hear her go on about his "brilliance," his "originality," his "place in European letters"! Even when his work was available in German, I once heard him say to Lili, could Mrs. Spiegel have—in any meaningful sense of the word—"read" any? The woman's brain, unfortunately, was a Möbius strip of clichés; things went in, he assumed, in working order, but emulsified there, through a continuous, twisting process of Mrs. Spiegelization. Besides, *what* place in European letters? No Europe, no letters, no place. He had no place anywhere but in our apartment, thank you, he added to me. And that was the only place he wanted.

I remember the way Lili patted his arm, and smiled the lazy, inscrutable smile that kept all those men prisoner on our sofa or tamed them to the yoke of irksome tasks and errands, like picking up groceries or fixing the lamp or taking me to the playground.

When you first met us, were you flabbergasted that Lili never became irritable with Mrs. Spiegel? That Lili always had time for Mrs. Spiegel? Did you realize that Lili actually chided me for mimicking the irresistibly mimicable Mrs. Spiegel? Did you marvel how the two of them used to sit at the kitchen table over interminable tea and cookies?

When I was little I used to sit there at Lili's side, supplied with cookies, myself, and a teacup filled with milk. It made me truly sick, Peter, it made me furious, to look at Mrs. Spiegel's arm, just lying there casually on the table—her sleeve riding up over the blue brand that looked so similar to the numbers stamped on the meat at the grocery store: Did Mrs. Spiegel want to be a human being, or did she prefer to be a slab of meat? The truth is, it was as though that dark number of hers could activate Lili's, even under the "decent" (as I felt) cover of her clothing or bracelets.

They never spoke about the past, really, either, those two. At least when I was around, they never, to use Neil's formula, had "a normal conversation" about their "past situation."

And what do you suppose he *meant* by that, Peter? *A normal conversation about her past situation*—It seems to be one of those things words can construct independently of meaning, doesn't it? Because how could there have been such a thing?

In fact, I don't remember anything that sounded particularly like "a normal conversation" about *anything*! Mr. Korda's arthritis, what the hairdresser said about her son's girlfriend—no subject was sufficiently mundane as to resist a septic influence.

I submit to you, Peter, this example: The day Lili found Walden Tócska in the street and brought him home. Well, as you would imagine, Mrs. Spiegel was simply horrified. "But, darling!" she said. "The beast is filthy!"

Not so, Lili said. That very morning, we'd gone to the vet, where Tócska had received numerous shots and his leg was bound up; we'd bathed and deflead him all afternoon.

But there was no telling where an animal like that had been! What habits it had acquired, or what secret diseases, clever enough to evade the vet's medications, it might be harboring, to spread among us at any instant!

Absurd, Lili said; not scientific. Besides, every child should have a pet, and clearly—she shot a guilty look at me—Anna already adored this dog.

Adored, Mrs. Spiegel protested—though I'd steeled myself to pat, illustratively, the great, snoring, quivering heap of hair—it was completely obvious that, on the contrary, the child was terrified!

Lili inhaled deeply, and put her palms down on the table in front of her. "Lise, are you saying that poor dog should be . . ."

No, but of course not! Mein Gott! (And both women, Peter, had gone absolutely white.) Mrs. Spiegel hadn't *meant* . . . She had only meant . . . She had meant only . . .

And then, Peter, there was just a long, long silence, which Lili brought to a close with a sigh, and that was that.

I mean, *Lili* allowed something terrible to develop? It was *Lili* who created an atmosphere of violence and danger? *Lili* was responsible for an atmosphere of violence and danger?

If the silences around our household were vivid and eloquent, was that Lili's fault? Look, I said to Neil, we were all careful back then. And wouldn't you have been, in my place? It was as if Lili were sleepwalking over the abyss of her own life. What if she were to wake? What if I were to wake her?

What about us, I asked him—Did he think he and I were starting Eric out on some perfect, pure, unpopulated, white-sand beach? Did he actually believe Eric was not going to bear some indelible, if illegible inscription?

Neil looked at me steadily, wagged a finger, and lowered one eyelid. I'll get back to you on that, he said.

I wonder what impression I made on you at first. Oh, I know, Peter, none. But I mean, by the time you showed up, I suppose I wouldn't have been all that worrisome; I'm sure I resembled a child: I was taking piano lessons, I had my friend Paige . . .

Of course, I had no friends *but* Paige. I sometimes imagined my schoolmates rising up unblinkingly to tear my arms and legs from the sockets with a juicy pop and stuff my slippery remains under the bulgy asphalt of the playground. I was even afraid of our poor, raddled dog. You were forced to notice eventually, of course, that, for someone so scowling and skinny and unwholesome, I was an amazingly poor student; that I couldn't fix my attention on anything, that I seemed actually impervious to information; that all facts, the whole world, disassembled into identical meaningless units and slid off my brain into a heap of smoking rubble. That my sole talent—and it wasn't pronounced!—was for satirizing my mother's suitors.

So, did you ever happen to observe how surprising it was that such a child had become interested in playing the piano? Especially in view of how little ability, I'm sure, I demonstrated.

Well, in fact, I had not been interested in playing the piano. There was a sound, however—partially embedded in a piece of chamber music that I overheard one day on a neighbor's radio—by which I was utterly bewitched. The other voice, speaking to me from just beyond articulation . . . my unknown twin . . .

I hung around our school orchestra a bit, traced the

sound, and announced at home that I wanted lessons. Music lessons? All right, good, Lili said. But why the viola? Why not the piano? On the piano one could accompany oneself. Pianists were always in demand. The repertoire was splendid and inexhaustible. We might even manage to find a small piano, second-hand, for ourselves . . .

Ourselves . . . "Did you ever play the piano?" I asked, beadily.

Lili, of course, went instantly vague. Oh, she said, not well. But how did you learn? Mmm, we all played a bit. We? Oh, you know, just . . . girls . . . of our class . . .

I stared around at the boxy furniture, the threadbare rug, the pad of scratch paper lying on the table that said, Dr. Martin Weissbard, Optometrist, and Lili drifted off toward her room.

She wants to play the viola? was what Mrs. Spiegel had to say. No, darling! She wants to play the violin!

Lili shrugged. She says she wants to play the viola.

Impossible! Mrs. Spiegel turned to me: The viola was for girls who wanted to play the violin but weren't gifted. Surely I was gifted! Therefore—she turned back triumphantly to Lili and Sándor—I wanted to play the violin!

Such a word, Sándor said. Gifted. Not to be used in front of a child.

And besides, Lili said. She wants to play the viola.

I was just sitting there, Peter, watching the three of them as they debated, and I had an extremely strange sensation. It was as if it had been given to me to see them in the vast, unruly time before I was alive, weighing and meting out, like beings in an old story, a fairy tale, the destiny of a child, soon to be born—the destiny with which that child was to be equipped against the time when they themselves have become weak, have become mere human beings.

No, I said, and the three of them stared as if I'd dropped in by parachute. I want, I announced into the silence, to play the piano.

Lili and I looked at one another for a long moment. Well, she said comfortably to Mrs. Spiegel, so there we are.

And that's how I met Paige. You didn't imagine I'd met Paige at my school, did you? There *were* no girls like Paige at my school. I met her at music school. And if she and I hadn't become friends, Peter, you would have come into a very different situation, I can tell you—at least in regard to me.

What Paige was doing taking up the violin, I couldn't say. No—what I couldn't say is how she would have *heard* of a violin, in that family of hers. But I don't think she had any more interest in music, per se, than I did. I suppose she was just determined, however briefly (and in whatever manner was available to a ten-year-old who would have been slaughtered if she hadn't behaved "nicely"), to be a mutant.

I don't think you ever met her mother; you weren't around yet the time Mrs. Chandler came for tea. A ritual inspection, I have to presume, which, I have to presume, we failed. Mrs. Chandler was wearing a suit of a kind I'd never seen outside Lili's magazines; the driver was parked downstairs, waiting between a row of garbage cans and a game of stickball. That incredibly courtly old man had just dropped by—Mr. Kecskeméti—and Mrs. Chandler couldn't understand one word out of his mouth. At first she kept saying, Pardon me? Pardon me? And then she gave up and simply carried on her side of the conversation as an improvisational solo. Mr. Kecskeméti was totally bewildered, Lili proceeded to forget her English, Sándor basically left the planet, and Paige and I were clutching each other with merriment.

In Paige's family, there wasn't a loose end in sight. Everything was hermetically sealed; her parents had encased themselves in a veneer of propriety so effective you could have lain right down on their floor, screaming in agony, and never have been heard by a living soul.

I, of course, was a walking loose end. And Paige spotted me immediately: something at last to unravel! And not to be vain, but I must have looked worth unraveling—I suppose it was the very weaseliness of my demeanor that was so promising. And once Paige had set her sights on me, she went about me the way she went about everything— calmly, inexorably, sure of success: Why can't you come over and practice with me? Won't your mother and father let you? Well, next week, then. Or the week after that. So, if it's too far, I'll come to your house. My mother won't mind—she'll have the driver bring me.

So, there was Paige—sitting right in our living room. And needless to say, I was numb with embarrassment. But on whose behalf? On behalf of everyone who'd ever been born, I suppose. Though to my astonishment, all parties other than myself appeared to find everything perfectly natural.

Lili was delighted, of course, that I'd found a friend— so well-mannered and self-possessed a friend at that. Sándor was fascinated by the black velvet headband in Paige's glossy, American hair, her perfect impenetrability, her sudden (calculated, I was quick to inform him) dimplings. Mrs. Spiegel adjudged her gifted—not unbecomingly gifted, but gifted. And Tócska! Poor Walden Tócska, who flattened himself against the wall whenever I appeared, heaped his great bulk across Paige the moment she sat down on the sofa, and wheezed with love as she crooned to him and ran her fingers through his nasty fur.

Paige herself was aglow. I guess she'd had something rather concrete in mind for us ("exotic" or even "colorful," I'm afraid, is how she might have characterized us in later years) and we must have accorded satisfactorily to her specifications—the accents, Sándor's marvelous white hair and elegant posture, my blond, stunning, soigné mother, the mere functionality of the furniture, the noisiness of the street outside, the casually shifting landscape of visitors, the—the-what-was-that-thing-called, Paige asked Lili, the delicious thing with the apples? And how ever could Lili have *made* it!

Oh, one learned, Lili said absently; she'd often watched the cook . . .

Paige and I practiced our duets, and then Lili would give us a snack. Paige would be all smiles and dimples, while I watched Lili tremulously, hoarding the sight of her as she took the glasses for our milk down from the cupboard . . . the plates . . . It was as if Lili were about to undergo, unknowingly and at my hands, an operation which would either save her life or kill her.

Because as soon as Paige and I were alone in my room, Paige would get right down to business: *What* cook? Well, then, what was my mother talking about? Where were she and Sándor from? Who had taught her to play the piano? So why *didn't* I ask? Why had she stopped playing? Well, so why did her whole education stop? Then why did she have to go away? But didn't she have to go to school there? So why did her mother and father let her go? But anyone could get off a train—they must have come with a car! What had she done wrong? But that was impossible—she couldn't be! Didn't I know what they looked like? Like Kathy Frankel, or like that girl with the bassoon, Risa Loeb. Well, we didn't eat funny food, did we? Anyhow, what did that have to do with it? So what did their friends do then? Their neighbors? The cook?

And where was Sándor when she was away? Did he go with her? But no one could really live in someone's closet —how would you go to the bathroom? And where were all the others? The *others*—like Lili's mother and father; I had grandparents, didn't I? Or aunts and uncles—didn't Lili at least have a brother or a sister?

Paige and I stared at each other, and then I exclaimed: *No*, breathless, as though running at top speed I'd smacked right into an invisible wall.

Of course not, I said. Obviously Lili had no brother or sister.

Paige frowned. But anyhow, she said, what happened to the piano?

It was very much a common enterprise that Paige and I pursued on those afternoons. It was Paige who could lower me down into the world I couldn't reach by myself, and Paige who could haul me back up, to tell what I had seen. But she couldn't go down there herself. And she couldn't see it—not even at second hand, as a nightmare, the way I could, or even as a migraine. It was up to me to tell her what was there; Paige couldn't see that world at all.

We'd stare at one another, concentrating, going over and over it, straining to fit fragments together—straining to look all around, to see its landscapes, its weathers, its populations . . . Sometimes both of us fell asleep, quite suddenly, like travelers. Often we found ourselves at a cul de sac and had to discard a question or an answer in order to proceed.

But slowly, slowly, from the shadows of overheard conversations, as I felt my way around the shapes of skirted subjects, pictures began to distinguish themselves from the welter of my dreams, refining and embellishing themselves; Paige and I watched, as though we were watching a photograph immersed in a solution developing details from a blur.

What did it look like, Paige asked, staring at me.

I lay across the bed and closed my eyes.

Suppose I'd been able, Peter—by bending my entire self to it—to imagine adequately some tiny element. Just, let's say . . . oh, one barb of the wire fence. Its taper, its point, its torque, its dull gleam altering with the play of the searchlights, the small rag of flesh, the faint, high, venomous raging of the current . . .

Fix it in your mind, I'd instruct myself; focus in on it

. . . Can you see it—really see it? Yes? And now—*Step back!*

I don't know, I said, though by then I could hear the boots in the courtyard, smell the dank, urgent anxiety of the dogs, see the beautiful boy . . . Did he sense me through the layers of time, struggling back for him? No, it was something quite different he was waiting for, his eyes huge and blank, growing dull, but still stormy blue, like the ocean. Like Lili's.

Oh, I just fry with shame, Peter, when I think of it. Of course, I felt plenty of shame at the time—Lili's shame, probably, the shame of the body; the shame of the disgusting things that can be done to your body—the disgusting ways your body can be made to fail—by someone whose body is itself intact.

But eventually (unclearly, of course, at first—as an uneasiness or unhappiness) a different shame began to emerge from behind that one: the shame of what Paige and I had been doing. Was I exposing Lili needlessly? Was Paige's interest trivial or merely morbid? Was mine? Had I been using Paige, and to do something that I was too weak or too cowardly to do myself or that I had no business doing in the first place?

I discussed it with you, actually. Constantly, in fact, for some years—in imaginary conversation. And what it seemed to me you had to say on the subject, was, basically, that we all live in one world; that everyone is exactly the same distance from the core of the earth. That it was, therefore, if for no other reason, very much my business. And that Paige—even after her nerve gave out and she buckled down to being a socialite—was no less involved than I was in everything that had ever happened.

Well, I still fry with shame, Peter, as I say. But this notion of yours (that I feel almost certain would be yours) does provide some consolation; and actually I think you've got a point.

One time, just one time, I went to dinner at Paige's house. House, yes! Right in the middle of the city! With great, tomb-like beige-and-gold rooms, old, gold-framed —*ancestors*, Paige said, spying down from every wall, massive, closed, oak doors . . .

There was the desolate sound of the dinner bell, and then the maid brought the serving platters around to the five of us—Paige, her older sister Pamela, their parents, and me—docking, departing, docking . . . we might have been towns on the shore of a huge lake. And just as the platter of steak completed its stately voyage, Mr. Chandler's head lifted slightly, as though he had caught a scent. Very unusual, my name—what sort of name was it?

I looked frantically at Paige. "He wants to know where you're from," she said, coolly. "Anna's parents come from Hungary, Daddy."

Mr. Chandler's fork hesitated in the air; his head rotated toward me like a planet. Were my people in Budapest? There was a family friend in Budapest—a prominent person, an elderly, highly respected woman— If my people were there, perhaps they knew her . . .

His stare was cold and flat, a dull blade . . . What *had* happened to my mother's piano? Because Lili had nothing, not even a locket . . .

"Mummy," Pamela said, "I don't think Anna eats meat. Do you eat meat, Anna?"

A ring was collecting around the bloody lump on my plate, soaking the potatoes red. "Oh, dear," Mrs. Chandler said.

"No, I do," I said. Paige was watching carefully, consideringly, as I sank my ornate silver fork into the steak. "Really . . ."

You might not have taken much notice of Paige, Peter, but Paige took plenty of notice of you. It was as if she'd been waiting to see what we really added up to—and *voilà*, yes? It was you.

She insisted to me you were beautiful. No, I said, you were—and this was the very word—creepy. The most beautiful person in the world, Paige said. Next to Sándor, of course, but Sándor was too old for her.

I didn't see why, I said. In only one more year we'd be in high school and her parents would let her go on a date, and Sándor would only be sixty-two. Though naturally by then Mrs. Spiegel might have nabbed him.

Paige's sigh fluttered like a long silk scarf. She said: I have nothing but pity for mean-spirited people.

Well, how would you have felt if I showed up from nowhere at *your* home the way you did at mine? The fact is, you just slid right in there, and then *I* was the stranger.

I was asleep; I woke up suddenly, the way children do when something is wrong. My room was unfamiliar in the dark. I listened, but there was only the usual slightly eerie lullaby of voices and laughter from the living room.

I reached for my clothes, which I'd slung over the chair, and I crept down the hall, blinking in the light.

Oh, my, Peter—how unfed and pretty you were! So different from the sleek, the . . . oh, let's say "personage" I got a glimpse of yesterday. You were like a weedy little flower poking its way through a crack in the pavement. Even your clothing, your dark little jacket, your trousers, your shirt, were as thin as ragged petals.

But what on earth was happening in that room? It was as if my ears were scrambling what they picked up—just ever so slightly—before passing it on to me! Was I, in fact, still asleep? Ah—no, you and Sándor and Lili were speaking Hungarian . . .

I remember your small, pointed chin and huge, sleepy, skeptical eyes. You looked as though you might bite if someone tried to pet you. I remember your hair falling around your face in black squiggles, and your white, white skin. As white as mine, but bad—a catalogue of privations.

The faintest ray of daylight would have scorched you lifeless.

You lifted your eyes to me; you seemed entirely unsurprised to see me there, peeking out from the entranceway. Sándor was speaking—I heard a cataract of water as you and I gazed at one another.

I wonder what it was you were seeing. In my jeans and plaid shirt perhaps I looked like a boy, myself—a delicate little boy; perhaps you were gazing at yourself, younger, in some vision of alternate possibilities. It certainly seemed to me, as I stood there—the happiness of your conversation deafeningly amplified by the unrecalled language—that the three of you were together in a vivid, hardy, enclosed past, and that I was looking on longingly, dissolving into the shadow of an unsatisfactory and insubstantial future.

What did you want from us? You'd arrived in the country, I gathered, some two years earlier, equipped with that most powerful item—a slip of paper, on which were a few names and addresses. Your formidable gift for languages provided you with sparkling English in no time. You'd distinguished yourself at college and had already catapulted, at your tender age, well into graduate school. In short, you had plenty. So couldn't you leave us alone?

No, Lili said. What was the matter with me? It was a marvel, a blessing that you'd come to find Sándor, that you'd tracked him down. That you intended to bring his work into English; it was the most precious gift possible that Sándor (according to you) once again represented something to young people back home.

"Home," Sándor said mildly. And just what was it he was said to represent, he mused, wandering back into his room.

But why did I think, Paige asked me, when we first discussed you, that every single person who was in this country had "escaped" from some place? "Maybe he just *left*, you know, Anna."

In school I learned simple facts: *such and such a country is rich in natural resources; a railroad was built between this place and that; the area was contested*—"simple facts," staggering volumes of blood.

Paige was too polite to say it in so many words, but I'm sure it had occurred to her, nearly as often as it had occurred to me, that everything I said in my room was a lie. Actually, I don't think it was until I was in high school that the particular tragedy which Paige and I had struggled to fathom on those afternoons cooled down into Facts, which people spoke of publicly, as if what my mother experienced in her room were a matter of dates and numbers, a distant aberration.

Your own, much more modest, catastrophe was quite a different thing. Now, there was a disaster one could *speak* of; the sort of disaster that might be experienced by human beings like ourselves; victims we could all—including Mr. and Mrs. Chandler—endorse! I must have been right, Paige told me excitedly, only a few days after her Doubts, you probably escaped—there'd been *Communists* swarming all over Budapest!

How gratified you would have been to hear Paige's conjectural account of your escape, lined as it was with monuments to you—You Scrambling Over Tanks in the Streets, You Dodging Bullets, You in Hand-to-Hand Combat with Soldiers . . .

"Peter?" was what I said. "I'll bet Peter was hiding under the bed."

You, of course, having brought it with you, were unable to appreciate the new atmosphere of industry and purpose that permeated our apartment. Which seemed to be twice as full of people as it had been, though in fact the only newcomers were you and some intermittent girlfriends of yours.

And, oh, what a dilemma you posed for Mrs. Spiegel— Too bad you never got to hear her fretting to Lili in the kitchen! On the one hand, she was elated: Finally they'd come to rescue Sándor from anonymity! On the other hand, *they*, she'd remember, was *you*. Disorder saddened her and made her fearful, and the truth is, Peter, even if you hadn't been a mere student, you were a little raffish for her taste, really. A little oblique.

But Lili! Seriously, Peter, no sooner had you arrived, it seemed to me, than there was a rapid diminution in her sensitivity to the idiotic. *Time to stop practicing, girls—* Do you remember the way she'd say that? *Peter and Sándor have work to do.* Do you remember the way she enumerated our accomplishments to her bored and irritated beaux—Sándor's accomplishments, your accomplishments, even my accomplishments. And I can promise you, Peter, those guys were every bit as impressed that you'd read Herzen, Gombrowicz, and Freud in the original as they were that I could play *To a Wild Rose* on the piano!

Sándor himself never would have demanded silence. Sándor wasn't a show-off. Don't you agree? Peter? But Lili was suddenly never without an ornamental book. Oh, all right, without a book, I mean. And do you remember those funny, unconvincing horn-rims she brought home one day from the office?

Once I came upon you reading to her. In Hungarian, naturally. That day it was she who was stretched out across the sofa, and you were sitting in an awkward, straight-backed chair next to her. Neither of you even noticed me come in! And I was simply stunned, I have to say, by Lili's dreamy, unformed expression, as though she were still only a girl, to whom anything might yet happen.

Oh, look. Do you think I grudged my poor mother pleasure? Well, I didn't! And obviously it was a tremendous relief to me that there were so few of those episodes, during that time, in her room. But how deeply, deeply unfair it all was. There you were, conducting Sándor and Lili back and forth between me and the world that had more than *wished* them dead so long before. And how eager they were to see that world; how much you had to show them! What everyone had been doing, what everyone had been saying, in the years since they'd left. So many questions, so much talk! *Europe.* Who cared? I didn't even *exist* there. We'd been going along so happily where we all actually did live—America; I had welcomed Lili into America—that was what I'd been born to *do.*

I was the *American* on the premises! That was my position and it was an exalted one. But the moment *you* come sauntering along, my position and I get a demotion! What's that all about, please?

Sándor, at least, didn't think you were so very wonderful. Sándor didn't just jump up from his desk and throw open his door every time you came over. Sándor wasn't looking to you for some muzzy little miracle. Sándor hadn't lost his sense of humor.

Oh, yes, I know he sat with you in his room . . . "working" (as I thought of it) hour after hour. But it was clear to *me*, at least, that he was indulging you. That he lent himself to your purposes out of sheer respect for the surrealism of . . . reality. It's true, Peter— He shook his head: *No good will come of this*, he said—as though he had no power over the matter at all, as though it were all a fait accompli. He seemed to be standing on a bridge, watching himself be carried along on the currents below.

I shook my own head in sympathy; things had been thus far ideal for him, I felt—sitting outside on the benches with the other declassé Europeans, gossiping, reminiscing, playing chess . . . coming back in to write, for a few hours, in a language that few around him could even read, or to read in a language that he would never speak with complete ease . . . What more could anyone ask, Sándor and I agreed on one of our walks—he had a very good life.

I happen to remember, Peter—do you?—the occasion on which it seemed to occur to Lili that you, like her suitors, could be put to practical purpose. It was an afternoon when you were still draped over the sofa, following several hours of "work." Yes, Lili proposed, she and Sándor, if you would consent to stay and look after me, could go out simultaneously.

I can still see your momentary look of astonishment! And recall my own little frenzy. But of course they could both go out, I objected; I was virtually fourteen! I was actually starting *high* school and I certainly didn't need looking after!

Imagine how I felt when Lili's gaze rested absently on me for only an instant, and she said, "No, you don't mind, Peter? A few hours only?"

You closed your eyes, haughtily. I longed to clamp my teeth around your ankle. Lili riffled your hair; you opened your eyes, sniffed, and closed them again.

I remember you and Tócska on that evening, and subsequent ones, padding around after Lili and Sándor had left, humiliated and sorrowful. I generously offered to entertain you by turning on the TV, and was rewarded by a blank look that sent me flouncing off. You, I'm sure, remember none of it (your nubby little sweater, the way you lay on the sofa, reading, with your feet up rudely on the arm, some coffee with hot milk you made once and shared with me—its profound, mysterious taste) . . . but I, Peter, remember it all, with a special, ringing clarity. I was—I admit it—that happy.

Perhaps your own demotion—from severe scholar, or from spoiled princeling—to domesticated animal, gave you some feeling of solidarity with me. I couldn't say, of course, but I certainly remember the moment you abruptly put down some journal you'd been reading and looked at me narrowly, as though I were a specimen that had just been brought to your attention.

"Why are you such a barbarian?" you said. "Why are you having trouble with your math? It's impossible that you're an actual imbecile, but look at you—you're always staring as though you've been lobotomized!"

" 'Lobotomized'?" I scoffed.

"And your vocabulary." You invited me to marvel with you. "Your vocabulary is a disaster."

You demanded to see my math text. I can see you this instant, plucking it disdainfully from the pile of schoolbooks on my bedroom floor and thumbing through it, frowning. What page was I on, you wanted to know.

Why? Were you so great at math?

You were great at everything, you said, squinting at the book as you settled yourself on my bed. Or hadn't I noticed? No! Off! Who was I to sit next to the great You? I was to grovel respectfully in the little chair over there.

So how was I supposed to see the book, please?

Hmm, you conceded. A plausible argument; evidently the situation wasn't hopeless.

"Anna's doing so well at school," Lili boasted to Mrs. Spiegel. "Thanks to Peter."

You and I looked up at one another from whatever we were reading, and glowered. Mrs. Spiegel drew back. "So sweet," I can remember Lili saying, imperturbably. "Aren't these two? So dear."

When I cried with frustration, alone with you in my room, and hurled my book onto the floor, you waited, you retrieved the book, and you explained again. Don't be so frightened, you told me. Don't be so impatient. Don't fight so hard against it; if you want to know something you don't already know, you have to let yourself change.

It was quite natural, don't you think? That we began to speak of Lili and Sándor. How, in fact, could we have avoided it?

Were you surprised to find how little I knew? That I knew virtually nothing at all about either Lili or Sándor? I wonder at what point it dawned on you that I was only then learning—and from *you*—how Sándor had been smuggled out of Berlin after his brief stint in hiding, with the best fake papers money could buy; how, at the end of the war, Sándor haunted the agencies, going daily to study documents, sign papers, scour the records for anyone who might be left. How, when Sándor went to meet the stranger who was to arrive on the boat, it was Lili who appeared, wearing a little navy-blue coat presented to her by some organization or another, carrying a small suitcase and a one-and-a-half-year-old child.

Her cousin's uncle? I said.

Anna, you said. I could see my own shock in your face as I stared at you, measuring the great, blank space that lay between Sándor and Lili.

And what could have gone through your mind when I asked if you knew whether I might have cousins somewhere, myself: when you realized that the only person there to answer was you; to inform me that (as you'd gathered from Sándor) my father's large family had been eradicated, and that in Lili's there had been only the one other child.

Another child? "Oh—" I remember saying. "Her brother . . ."

It collected in the room as we lay there, stretched out—the pink and silver city; the river, reflecting the pink and silver sky, the sleepy stone lions guarding the tunnel through the mountain, the lights twinkling on in the dusk below the castle, the twinkling bridges, the stone, the tile, the arches, the marble, Europe and Asia washing over each other, converging and diverging, the park, glorious with its drapery of snow or blossoms, the cafés, the Gypsies, despised and magical, playing music in the streets, the crowds strolling, laughing, drinking, dancing . . . or at least that's how it must have been, you said, while Lili was growing up.

It was over, of course—all changed by the time you

yourself were growing up—gutted, buried. A gray city now, the ghost of itself.

Lying there, side by side, you and I explored the rainy park, the broad, silent avenues, searching for the big house with the piano and the cook, searching through the ghost city for the missing—you searching for the living city, I for traces of Lili. We were ghosts in the ghost of Lili's city, just as she and Sándor were ghosts in mine.

And you were the stranger, then, everywhere . . . Where was your home, Peter? Were you frightened? I envisioned my own fear rising from my body, encased in a luminous globe—you accepting it into yourself as though it were precious; it left a rift in me like a wound. I remember the springy feel of your hair against my cheek; once in a while I dared to reach out one hand and touch my fingertips to yours. Were you aware of my hand? Whose did you think it was—a girlfriend's? My ghostly mother's? The missing boy's? Mine?

How often did we talk like that? Every afternoon for a while? Every few weeks? Maybe, in fact, it was only once.

Because at a certain point you were just *there*; at a certain point, as long as I could imagine you alive in the world, going about your business, I no longer required for our conversation—which was so necessary to me—your physical presence.

You know, Peter, Paige was much more grown up around that time than I was. I'd go so far as to say she was actually infatuated. She was getting rather dignified, in her way, and she'd all but stopped talking to me about you.

I could at least point out to her, I felt, that you were vain, *not* pleasant, and that you had a different girl tagging along behind you all the time.

Yes? she said, in an idle manner. And what kind of girls did you especially like?

Oh, who could tell, I said. You probably didn't notice

what any of them were like. And you dropped them all, anyhow. Or maybe they just got sick of you bragging.

In fact, though, you liked a very distinct type of girl at the time, didn't you. I wonder if you still do. Of course, we don't really produce that type any longer; probably even Europe doesn't—at least, not in quantity. Fragile, restless, sloe-eyed, ill-tempered, *very* squeamish, in their little striped T-shirts, as if someone had just handed them a sickeningly poor translation of Sartre . . .

Those girls! Did you get around to marrying one of them? Maybe you married a whole bunch of them. Or maybe you never bothered yourself about getting married at all. Maybe you married that girl you brought to the party someone gave when your book about Sándor finally came out. Did you, I wonder. That girl had her hand on your sleeve every second.

That afternoon with Voitek, which changed a lot of things for you—it changed some things for me, too, you know.

Didn't you always think, when you were young, that real time starts the year you're born? You're born, and then time begins to move—forward. Didn't you think that there's sort of an ocean of space that separates you—but *completely*—from the big lump of everything that went on before?

Were you particularly aware of Voitek? I wasn't, as far as I remember. I don't think Lili had been seeing him long. And she didn't seem all that interested in him, really— maybe she just felt a little sorry for him. Or, anyway, he was just . . . there. Thinking about it now, I can see that he was very good-looking, but at the time he just seemed to me like a large—like a large apparatus of some sort, humming with silence . . . Like, in retrospect, an atomic reactor.

It started with Tarot cards, that day—isn't that right? I think Paige had seen a deck of them somewhere, and was sort of going on . . . to impress you, it seems fair to say: *Didn't we believe there were cultures that were special? Didn't we believe that there were people who had learned how to*—oh, I don't know—*to harness invisible currents, to see something, the future, in cards, in your hand . . . ?*

I don't really remember what all she was saying, but I remember it seemed so persuasive to me, *fascinating . . .*

And the first thing I do remember clearly is the way Lili simply cut Paige off—how shocking that was: *This is not interesting, a movie would be interesting. Voitek? A movie?*

Paige was simply stunned, and I remember looking at Sándor, for help, because he really did like Paige, you know, and always listened so seriously to all those ideas and opinions of hers—but instead he just made that little bow and said something to the effect that he himself could see clearly into his future, by looking at his hand or by not looking at his hand, that it was the past that was opaque, it was the past that only special insight could reveal, and as for what was going to happen tomorrow, I think he said, *that* was something anyone at all could see if he would only consult his memory of what had happened yesterday, and now, if we would excuse him . . .

Of course by then I could feel it on my skin, in my body. But Paige was simply *lost*. Everything was happening so fast, and she was talking and talking, something, something about the Gypsies, *didn't you adore them? didn't you love to see them, at least, and talk to them?*

And obviously it was to pacify her that you grabbed her hand and looked at her palm and said—goodness knows what you said, yourself—that yes, you'd known some, you'd learned all sorts of this or that: *I see a concert hall . . .* I remember you saying, and then Voitek saying, *This guy sees a concert hall; I see a two-car garage in Bronxville . . .*

Of course he'd intended no more than a flippant little end to the business, I'm sure, but instead of sealing something shut, it tore something open, and where was Voitek then?

Where were we all? And how many people were in that room? Millions, yes? Literally millions of people had been there all that time, just waiting to be recognized.

And who, in particular, was Voitek seeing, I wonder, in the white stillness of your face, when he started to scream, *yes you adored them, "adored" them, shit, shit, opportunist, coward,* or whatever it was, exactly, until it became really impossible to make it out because it was all in Polish, I guess, except for a word here and there of German.

Thank heavens for Lili, yes, Peter? Because you didn't even have the presence of mind to duck. And thank heavens, too, that evidently Voitek had some dim awareness it was Lili, out of all that vast crowd, who'd touched his arm. Otherwise, he would have killed her, I'm sure, within moments.

Was it I who went to the door? Usually that's how I remember it, but sometimes in my memory it was you. Actually, I suppose, it could have been any of us, but usually I remember myself, threading my way toward the pounding on the door through the whirlwind of debris that had just been our possessions, and the curiously weightless way it was flying around, as though our apartment had only been waiting for one touch to send it wheeling, in splinters, through the air.

But the thing I always remember in exactly the same way is how Mrs. Spiegel just stood there in the doorway as those guys tore in and tackled Voitek. I'm sure neither Lili nor Sándor ever forgot it, either—the uniforms, the truncheons, the sound of Voitek's head as it hit the wall; the utter absence of expression on Mrs. Spiegel's face . . .

And what was I thinking as I watched Paige cry? I was thinking about the way she looked, crying. I wouldn't have imagined that something so extreme, so complete, could happen to someone's face from the inside. Paige's pretty face—where was it?

I wonder if she ever noted that she got her date with Sándor. Because I gathered, eventually, that after he called her mother, Sándor took Paige to the coffee shop to wait for the driver, and the two of them had a soda.

He certainly did his best to get me out of the wreckage, too. And if you hadn't offered to stay with me, I would have had to leave. But how could I have left? I knew Lili would go to her room. I knew she would, and she did, and then there I was, evaporating, and she was on the other side of the wall, unreachable, spiraling back down . . .

I guess I never really had a chance to thank you. But obviously you understood how serious I was when I asked you to leave me alone and go check on Lili. I know it took courage, Peter, to open that door and go in.

And once you had—do you know?—I calmed right down. I stopped shaking, and that blinding silence dimmed. I raised my head and opened my eyes. There was the world, all around me—the sky, the earth, a bird, a voice . . .

Did it ever occur to you to wonder what happened when Sándor came back? Well, he looked around mildly for a moment, and he asked how I was. I realized I was holding a book you'd stuck in my hands when you'd gone in to see Lili. I was fine, I said. And Lili? What about Lili? And Lili was fine, too.

Sándor glanced at Lili's door. "She's all right," I said. "Really. She's fine."

"Yes?" he said, and hesitated. "Well. So, what would you say to a movie?"

Lili was perfectly serene when I came in for breakfast the next morning—as serene as you found her when you eventually joined us yourself, looking disheveled and mightily confused. I hope I didn't snicker, Peter, when she said she was glad you'd stuck around, that there was a lot of cleaning up to do.

You, though! You were really insufferable, there, for a while, were you aware of that? I don't know who you thought you were—my brother? my father?

I suppose you were just panicked, really. These days no one bothers even to remark on a very young man and an older woman, but it certainly was a novelty back then.

With all due respect, Peter, I have to say that I don't really attribute Lili's happiness in those days to any individual qualities of yours; no doubt any pretentious twenty-one-year-old Hungarian would have done as well.

But I very much doubt that anyone else at all could have parlayed, as you eventually did, some translations and what amounted to a small essay into so much celebrity for Sándor (and celebrity, consequently, my point is, for . . . well, you get my point, I'm sure).

Of course it was just one of those moments, wasn't it, when attention was on such things, when even writing as rarified as Sándor's was likely to be hijacked—and by just about anyone. Absolutely every poor shnook seemed to be out there scrounging up some piece of art with which to beat up some ideological adversary or intellectual competitor, something that could be said to validate some thesis, or buttress some argument, or represent some something or other—an indictment of totalitarianism, or an indictment of repressive capitalism, or these particular currents of psychoanalytic thought, or those particular currents of Marxist thought, or an esthetic of the elite, or an esthetic of the people, or currents of Jewish mysticism, or an expression of Christian acceptance, or an expression of Buddhist acceptance . . .

Now, of course, no one wants art for any purpose

whatsoever—let alone for its own. But that was the moment, wasn't it? And you seemed to have a perfect understanding of just how to exploit it, how to take it all as far as possible. Something so very exactly what Sándor never wanted.

Hypocrite, you say; ingrate—*Gon*eril couldn't have put it better. What do I think you should have done? Surely I can't mean to vilify you for having had a few *thoughts* about work to which you were so devoted! And don't I think a readership deserves something useful in return for its admiration? Besides, anyone whose stance (like Sándor's) is fastidious high-mindedness is simply demanding that others be exploitative on his behalf. Also, who am I to say that you *were* in any way exploitative? Were you not, in fact, entirely sincere in your efforts to bring Sándor's work to a wider and more receptive audience?

Did it mean nothing to Sándor to make contact with the living? Or that his lyric, glimmering salvagings from a lost world were received with deep gratitude? Did it mean nothing to Lili that her life, too, was in some measure reclaimed? What did I wish for them—that they be eternally voiceless, adrift? Plus, where did I think my tuition came from, and how did I think I would have gotten into college in the first place, the way I'd been going on without you?

All right, I give up, you win, thanks. But *Sándor*? A *bastion* against *Communism*? Oh, please, Peter. For shame.

A paradox, as Sándor once said; a conundrum. If no one was listening, at least no one misheard you. If what you made was of no value to anyone, no one stole it and went running off; no one bothered to colonize it and set up little flags. It was his home, he said, his work, and all *I'm* saying is that it seems very hard, that a man who was exiled so many times over was harried again, and in his most intimate refuge.

I'm not going so far as to say it killed him, Peter. Of

course not! It merely exasperated him; obviously it was his *life* that killed him.

Some months, I suppose, after you'd more or less dropped out of sight, I was just sitting idly, in our apartment, gazing out the window at the dark sky and dreary rain, and I saw the reflection of Lili's face overlap mine as Lili came and sat down next to me. "Poor Anna," she said. "Do you miss Peter?"

I shook my head.

"No," she said, and in the window I watched drops of rain trickle unevenly over our reflections as Lili stroked my hair. "Good. Well, I don't miss him, either."

Naturally, no liaison between you and Lili could have lasted forever. That was understood. You were very young—Sándor and Lili were careful to impress this notion on me; your life was moving very fast.

But still, you might have come around a little more often, Peter. Lili would have liked to see you, you know. After all, you were family.

Enjoyable, and even appropriate as it is, to mock Lionel, I do have to say that in a way I'm not horrified through and *through* that he arranged yesterday's service the way he did. I certainly wouldn't have done it, myself, but I wasn't entirely sorry, I must admit, to see that dark, strange, creaky, stained-glass spaceship swoop down through the millennia to reclaim Lili. Though it was impossible, of course, to say anything of the sort to Lionel when I got up this morning, and there he was, first thing, in the kitchen.

Fortunately, he didn't want to see me any more than I wanted to see him. To Lionel, obviously, every presence is a presence that isn't Lili. He fussed around making a breakfast, and both of us pretended to eat it, and then Eric called, to see how we were doing, and to say again how sorry he was he couldn't be here with us.

"I hope he knows," Lionel said, after we hung up, "how many people loved his grandmother."

It *is* a beautiful day, isn't it? Lionel was right. Not warm, certainly, but just so bright! The benches along the avenue are filling up with old men and old women, sitting out in the sun—do you remember?—just the way they used to all those years ago.

When I visit Eric in Los Angeles, he takes me driving way out, to those elastic, self-generating peripheries, where the most recent immigrants are hoping to establish a life for themselves, and I marvel at everything, as though we were coasting down into the future.

Ma, Eric says, not every manicurist or waiter here used to be the most promising poet or physicist in Nigeria or Guatemala or Korea, you know.

Well, yes. I do know. But a few of them must have been something of the sort. And then, the point is, what about the others?

These old men and women have probably been coming out in the spring for half a century to sit on the very same benches. They're probably the very same people I used to see around here in my childhood. And let me tell you, Peter, they looked every bit as old to me then as they do now!

They're like little birds, perched on a phone wire, cheeping away from time to time in a sheer exercise of being alive, blinking in the indifferent American sun. They sit in the sun, they buy their few groceries, they play chess, they gossip. A few of them must get themselves to an occasional chamber-music concert. I suppose they still read their newspapers in Yiddish, in Polish, in Hungarian, in Czech . . . This spring, the next spring, maybe one more . . .

The elevated train still clatters by in the distance, and the old people gaze out through the traffic and fumes as if they were gazing across the Atlantic. If the great empires of Europe exist anywhere now, I guess it's right here, on these benches.

He seems to be a nice man, Eric, and I think things are working out pretty well for him. Neil was a very good father, I have to say, for what it's worth. Neil, in fact, is not such a bad human being—he and I just have various complementary horrible qualities. I, obviously, am possessive, jealous, resentful, dependent, quick to censure, slow to forgive . . . and there's not all that much I've been able to do about it, I'm afraid, other than keep my distance. On my own, in fact, I'm perfectly all right.

I *am* grateful, Peter (and if we'd had that cup of coffee yesterday, I hope I would have told you so) for the few sentences in your book that pertain to Lili. Because her mother's jewelry, the silver, the piano, the house—all that stuff must have belonged to the neighbors for a long time now. Or, actually, I suppose, to their children. Except what's just floating through Europe these days, from one antique dealer to another.

So, aside from those few sentences of yours, what's left? The challis scarf, a few strings of beads, some inexpensive furniture, bought on Lili's small salary or given to her by those admirers of hers, or organized by some relocation agency or charity . . . That's pretty much it.

Yes, so obviously I'm grateful. Well, I'm sure you know that.

I hope you'd be glad to know that I'm well—that I'm fortunate in my work, that I'm happy enough . . .

The time Neil told me he'd seen the talk show where there was someone who might have been the person he thought I'd mentioned, I asked him so many questions! *What did he look like? What was he saying? Did he say where he was living?* And I must have sounded frantic, because Neil stopped answering and just looked at me. He didn't know, he said slowly; he hadn't been paying attention. He'd simply *happened* to turn the show on while he was rummaging around in his suitcase for a presentable shirt, and he couldn't remember one single thing about whoever it was he'd happened to see.

Oh, I said, after a moment. Well. And I turned away to escape Neil's stare. There was really no need to have seen you myself; I knew it was you, and at least I knew you were safe.